A Muse Gone Rogue

by

Kacey Mark

Dark Muse, Book 1

A Muse Gone Rogue

Cover Art by *The Wild Rose Press, Inc.*

The Wild Rose Press, Inc.
PO Box 708
Adams Basin, NY 14410-0708
Visit us at www.thewildrosepress.com

Publishing History:
Previously published by Evernight Publishing, 2011
First Black Rose Edition, 2020
Trade Paperback ISBN 978-1-5092-3130-0
Digital ISBN 978-1-5092-3131-7

Dark Muse, Book 1
Published in the United States of America

Heat threaded through her veins at the thought of being in his room, knowing at any moment he could return to find her. Her impish thoughts cheered her on. Fueled by flames of excitement, they danced around in her mind as if coaxing him to materialize out of thin air.

She ran her shaking fingertips along the surface of his nightstand until she came in contact with the worn edge of a leather-bound book.

Good enough for now, she thought and tucked it under her arm.

Nearly home free.

She spun to the door, but her breath caught in a gasp. Quenton's massive silhouette slipped in front of her, and Marie braced herself against the doorjamb to keep from running into him.

He seized her wrist before she could pull away. Not a painful squeeze, just catching her and holding her in place. He stood as a solid, unreadable blockade of darkness. But the heat in his touch filtered into her skin, causing a rash of goosebumps to race up her arm and across her chest.

"Let me guess…learning disability?" he asked.

She banked the fear that gripped her and pulled her wrist free. She crossed both arms over the book. "I—"

"I told you to stay out."

"I want to talk to you about Heather."

He stepped forward, backing her into the room. "First things first. Why've you come to my bed?"

Fast. Think fast. "Not your bed. Your room. I was looking for…for the book." She rushed to explain.

"This isn't the library, sweet thing."

Chapter 1

Quenton Blake wiped the vehicle clean of any prints then pried the aged book from the corpse's hands. He left the pale body twisted over the steering wheel and stepped into the war-torn alley, where two pairs of headlights continued to face off. His words were concise, just loud enough to carry to the microphone hidden in his collar. "We're done here."

He removed the prints from his own car and rounded the corner away from the idling vehicles and one less documented threat to his kind.

Every Muse had their book, and when their spirit tore free without an heir, it was up to their guild to recover it. He glanced down at the cracked leather binding. So, this was it. Myrna, the last known fertile Muse of the western guild, had become a Shade.

That's what happened when an incomplete soul split free. As a Shade, it would spend an eternity making an enemy of the very guild that reared it. Always hunting for the missing bits and pieces to make itself whole.

He kept his head down and attention on his surroundings as he angled through the streaming crowd of tourists and night worshipers. Exhaust rose from the asphalt, screening high-rise spectators from the lewd acts going down on the street.

But as luck would have it, even the spectators came

out to play tonight.

He wove through the mass of pedestrians traveling every which way, like a restless hill of ants. Hot tension engorged his shoulders. The commotion served as a great cover, but as a Muse, the hoard of impressionable youth posed another problem. An irresistible urge to inspire.

He jumped aside to avoid a mini skirt vomiting on the sidewalk and continued without breaking stride, passing neon lit doorways that spilled pulsing music into the street.

Barros's voice buzzed low in his left ear. "We've got heat. Cops at eleven o'clock. Six-hundred yards and closing."

Quenton took a sharp left into a fire-blackened side street and moved on. His ears primed for his second-in-command to speak again.

"All clear. Mission complete," Barros said.

Quenton cringed when the twang of a second voice made his earpiece emit a metallic shriek.

"Hot damn! Did you see that body? The crime scene unit will have a field day," Artino said.

True. Myrna ceased to be one of them, but as a Shade, her soul needed to hunt. And to do that, it needed a body. When she invaded another corpse, she stretched it beyond recognition. The one twisted over the steering wheel wouldn't be the last. Cops would get used to seeing her leftovers pretty quick, because Myrna was not about to stop.

She would keep ravaging the dead until colder weather drove her south to warmer bodies. That's how it worked, and after all these centuries, the Shades outnumbered the Muse guild ten to one. On a good day.

"Blake, you buying tonight?" Barros asked.

Quenton's reply cut short when he approached a group of cackling women in cropped pants and heels. On instinct, his line of sight flicked up and met a pair of caramel-colored eyes. He compressed the empty spasm growing to life inside his chest and quickened his pace. His soul lifted with awareness and reached out from the pliable barrier of his subconscious.

"Oh, hells yes!" Artino cried, sending Quenton's eardrum ringing. "Blake's starting the party early."

Quenton winced.

The warm caramels winked back.

The magnetic pulse in his chest grew with every step in her direction, but he forced his legs to keep moving, ripping his gaze to the steaming concrete ahead. With a steady breath, he compacted the forward thrust of his spirit.

"What?... Oh, come on! You're letting her go?" Artino asked.

Quenton spared no glance to his men bleeding into the crowd a hundred yards back. His hand moved only a fraction, curling over his sleeve to press the hidden talk button. "Can it, ladies. This isn't talk radio. Get back to your stations. We ship out at 0800."

"Sure thing, boss, but when we get home, you owe double," Artino said.

A man with a pronounced swagger and a lewd smile crossed Quenton's path.

He felt the spasm again.

"Uh-oh," Barros said, his voice heavy with amusement.

Quenton's breath rushed hot in a silent growl. He tore his gaze free. Time to get off the street.

"Back to base, boys. Don't make me say it again."

Two blocks later, the crowd thinned to only a few civilians ambling under the streetlights of the business district.

Quenton shrugged out of his leather jacket and slung it over his shoulder as he marched through the lobby of the Gold Plaza Hotel. The glow of a hundred recessed lights reflected in the glassy marble at his feet.

When he stepped into the elevator, he pulled out the ear bud. By the time he reached the penthouse, his tie was long gone. After swiping his key card, he headed straight to the bar and a cold 961 Stout, one of the many things he took a liking to here. Shame he had to leave so soon.

He popped a couple of aspirin and took a long pull on the bottle. The sweet malt ran down his throat until his lungs burned for air. On the way to the bathroom, he gave the woman in his bed a quick once over.

She lay on her back, with gray eyes open and unblinking. Her choppy hair streaked with blue. In her cocoon-like state, she looked every bit a mindless doll and not a thing like the self-assured artist she pretended to be.

Seek them out and sap them dry, that's how it had to be—nothing personal, more of a symbiotic relationship, really. They got their inspiration. He got to top-off the aching cavern in his soul.

Quenton pressed the chilled bottle to her temple, but she didn't flinch.

Out cold. Probably would be for a few more hours.

He pressed her lids closed and covered her bare chest with the crisp cotton sheet. Not much of a conversationalist but at least with her energy depletion, he could still maintain control of his own craving.

As he rounded the bed, his attention snagged on the cell phone that buzzed face down on the nightstand. Only two people knew his number, and Barros wasn't dumb enough to call so soon after a mission.

He tapped on the incoming call.

"If it's about that witch again, tell her she won't get another cent until I see my daughter."

His brother, Tobin, chuckled. "Easy Quentie, you're about to regret those words."

He passed the neatly packed suitcase and kicked the flap closed. "Talk. And this better be good."

"Well, it's good for me…Where are you?"

"Beirut. Why?"

"Figured it's about time for a nice little family reunion."

He took another pull on the bottle and waited for a bomb to drop through the fuzzy static.

"You need to come get your girl," Tobin said.

The sober tone of his brother's voice drained the annoyance stewing in his veins, leaving only caution behind. "Why? What happened?"

"It's Christie. Your wife—"

"Ex-wife."

"Whatever…was killed in a car crash."

The warmth drained from his face. Images flashed through his mind of the feisty blonde who gifted him with a whole summer of her life. And nine months later, an anchor to mortality that she guarded like a mama grizzly. For all the years he'd been meticulous at using protection, Christy undercut him, then refused to allow him a life with his child. For good reason. She knew what he was. He couldn't ask for a better mother for his child, but he wouldn't wish that woman on his worst enemy.

He swallowed hard. "And her body?"

Tobin's voice lost all emotion. "They got her to the hospital but there was nothing they could do."

"Where's the body, Tobin?" He tightened his grip on the phone.

"Taken," Tobin said.

"And Anna?"

"Injured but alive."

He closed his eyes.

He told that stupid woman over a dozen times it wasn't safe to stay there. With all those dense forests, winding roads, and damn open space. While he stood, on the other side of the world with no way to get to her.

"I'll be there soon as I can. Stay with Anna," he said.

Tobin's voice distanced from the phone. "I'll call her daycare chick. That's what they're paid for."

"Not good enough," Quenton said.

There was an anxious shuffle through the crackle of static. "Look, kids don't like me. And she isn't going anywhere. She's in a coma."

The word "coma" caused a dark anger to ooze into his veins. His heart propelled the rush of fluid, harder, louder. He stepped to the balcony, braced himself on the rail, and stared beyond the blinking lights to the dark abyss of the Mediterranean.

"We're hunting them down, Tobin. Every last one of them."

"I hoped you'd say that."

****

Marie stopped short at the bold letters indicating

6

St. David's ICU. She tapped the desk's polished wood surface with the pad of her fingers—a soundless chant for someone, anyone, to notice of her.

When a young, curvy woman with a coral painted smile approached, Marie's shoulders set back with purpose. "I'm here to see Anna Blake."

"Are you family?" she asked.

Marie stretched her grin to capacity, as she performed a mental scavenger hunt for the winning answer. How ironic. About the same age. Only yesterday the two of them could have taught each other to tie their shoelaces, and now this woman had complete authority over her.

Oh, laces…she looked down. Hers were still untied. The phone call from Tobin came so unexpected after her run; she hadn't bothered to retie them.

She studied the name tag pinned to the girl's scrubs. "Well, Heather, I'm not *exactly* family." She knelt over one shoe and franticly manipulated the strings.

Heather's glossy ponytail cascaded over her shoulder with the sympathetic tilt of her head. "We don't allow visitors on the floor unless they're related to the patient."

She switched to the other shoe, as she grasped for random excuses floating through her brain. Her shoulders slumped. Where stress abounded, Marie's inspiration fell flat. Unless she wanted to make matters worse, she better go with honesty this time.

"I'm actually her daycare provider but I was called here by the family, and since I watch over her on a regular basis, surely you can make an exception."

Heather paused. Frowned. "I'll get the charge

nurse. Could you hold on a sec?"

Marie straightened as Heather twisted to retrieve her phone, feeling as though a giant "ACCESS DENIED" stamp just plunked onto her forehead.

Heather spun back to her but came to an immediate halt with the receiver poised midway to her ear.

Marie blinked then little by little, rotated her head to the figure standing next to her, and the source for what seemed to hold the girl as fixated as a department store mannequin.

She jerked back when she recognized Tobin, wearing a rumpled version of last night's tuxedo and the same sensual smile that promised to honor every hint of his mischievous reputation.

Little snake, he must've slid up to the counter during her loop, swoop, and pull lesson. His lean frame draped casually over the desk as he lured in his next unsuspecting victim.

A crime against nature, the way his gaze pulled people in. A glance by itself should never hold that much power, and yet somehow he acquired it. As if he'd bartered with the devil for the ultimate skeleton key. Whenever he turned those eyes her way, her hair stood on end. Every fiber in her body charged with apprehension.

Rumors in the small town labeled him the most influential talent scout in the world, with a list of clients a mile long, and a scope of practice that knew no bounds.

Based on his womanizing reputation, she had a pretty good feeling the talent he sought from Heather had nothing to do with her acting ability. And Heather's reaction was far from cautious.

Tobin lifted the phone from Heather's hand and set it back in its cradle. His eyes glittered beneath a fringe of dark lashes. "No need for the charge nurse. Marie's got a direct line to heaven, so I figure that's good enough."

Marie's fists anchored on her hips. "Already told you, Sacred Heart's a *daycare center*. Not a convent."

She fought the urge to cringe when Tobin cut his gaze to her. "Now you mention it, you do look rather sleazy for a nun today."

She looked to her form-fitting, black running shorts, and bright pink jacket, partially unzipped to reveal the matching sports bra, and her ever-present silver chain of segmented pearls tucked safely between her breasts.

She jerked the zipper to her chin. When the news hit, she hadn't wasted time on a shower, let alone a clean change of clothes.

She opened her mouth to fire a stinging retort, but snapped it closed when he turned to address the oh-so-helpful mannequin.

"Listen sugar, you think you could conjure me up some coffee?"

With only a few words and a bat of his lashes, Tobin rendered Heather speechless. On the positive side, she managed a slight head bob before scurrying off like a child seeking change for the ice cream truck.

Marie rolled her eyes as he stared after her. Apparently, any opportunity, however great or small, seemed a good one for him to chase a little tail.

As soon as Heather disappeared around a corner, he turned to face Marie. The grim set of his mouth and shadows beneath his eyes spoke volumes. A load of guilt dumped over her for the critical thoughts that slithered through her mind.

His tone was flat. "Anna's in surgery. She suffered some kind of head injury during the accident. It'll be a while before she comes out."

"I'm really sorry, Tobin," she whispered.

His offered a faint nod and gestured for her to follow him to the waiting room.

****

An hour later, Marie toyed with the ends of her cinnamon colored curls, scissoring the strands between her fingers. She stared at the six-month-old cover of *Vogue* that jiggled on her bouncing knees. It felt better to stand, but after several passes along the designated worry line formed in the carpet, Tobin's glares were enough to ground her.

When the double doors to the OR opened, the surgeon approached Tobin with a warm smile and took a seat in the chair across from him. Tobin leaned back, crossing his thick arms over his chest, and bringing one ankle to rest on his knee. Marie wasted no time, jumping up from several chairs down to take the seat next to the surgeon.

The doctor raised his brows.

She flashed a cheek-aching smile. "I'm Anna's daycare provider."

Tobin gave her a look. "Dr. Scott, this is Marie."

"It's a pleasure to meet you—"

"Shall we get down to business?" Tobin asked.

Dr. Scott nodded and fixed his eyes on Tobin. "Anna's doing great. Surprisingly well, in fact."

Tobin's shoulders seemed to relax a bit, but he remained silent. His stare followed the doctor's every movement, caught every expression. Not looking at him; *into* him, and the hum of energy it created made her sweat just sitting next to the poor man.

Dr. Scott, on the other hand, appeared perfectly at ease and more talkative than any white coat professional she'd ever met. As if Tobin had reached behind him and pulled an invisible cord, prompting him to babble non-stop.

The doctor sounded even and unrushed, never breaking contact with Tobin.

"You'll notice a small section of hair has been shaved off, and she'll have some stitches. Those will come out soon. We won't know the full extent of her neurologic damage for a few weeks. Her recovery will take time. And she'll need all of the help she can get."

Tobin nodded.

Scott bowed his head and a solemn timbre smoothed over his voice. "I understand the loss of Anna's mother puts a heavy burden on you, but I hope you'll find some comfort knowing that your sister didn't suffer."

Tobin glanced away. "Thanks for your kindness Doctor, but I'm not the kind of man you should feed that line to."

The physician eased forward onto his feet and stretched with his hands at the small of his back. "Well, if there's anything I can do, please don't hesitate. I'll be popping in on Anna every day or so."

"Thanks, Dr. Scott," Marie said.

"You're welcome." He turned to leave but paused. Then turned back to her adding, "And don't worry, these little ones are more resilient than they seem."

Heather returned and lowered a cup of coffee into

Tobin's hand. "She's in the second room on the left."

Tobin spared Marie a careless head jerk before fixing his eyes on Heather. "Go ahead, Mary."

"Marie."

"Yeah…I'll be there in a minute."

Marie stared at him for a moment. "Sure, see you in minute, *Turban*." She hoped she'd get some kind of a reaction, but the slam was lost on him. Too busy trying to burn a hole in Heather's retinas.

****

Marie's first glance of Anna's swollen face caused a sickening current to run through her. Anna's eye sockets were blotted with purple smudges—a startling contrast to the thick, white gauze bandage that capped nearly all of her golden hair. *How much did they have to shave off?*

The adult-length bed swallowed Anna's two-year-old body. Countless tubes and wires were strung between her and the supporting machines. The room felt suspended in an inhuman silence. No talking, no laughter, just the periodic whoosh of the ventilator and an occasional beep from the monitors.

How could this happen? Everything was fine last night at the Governor's ball when Anna's ballet class performed. She could still picture the smile etched into Anna's dimpled cheeks as she totted through her routine. Her face glowed brighter every time she caught her mother's gaze.

Marie wasn't obligated to attend, but she wouldn't have missed it. The daycare's blog spotlighted a new child each week, and the Governor's performance made perfect timing.

But it all melted away only a few hours later.

Her chin trembled as she covered Anna's still hand with her own. Her little friend was in there somewhere but seemed nothing more than a lifeless shell.

The thought of leaving Anna in the sole care of her uncle made her heart sicken. Dr. Scott was right. Anna needed all the help she could get. Tobin could raise a little Cain, but there was no way he could raise this little girl by himself. She pressed her fingertips to her temple.

Her friendship with Anna grew to life under months of bouncing balls and storybooks. Those kinds of bonds don't easily detach. They tear a gaping hole.

She'd received frequent offers for a permanent nanny position, but on each occasion, she'd declined. She liked her life in town, set apart from those expansive homes. She preferred the open predictability of her life. The term "Nanny" seemed like such a matronly title. It hinted at more trust and reliance than what her twenty-five years could offer.

"Guess it's time to take a leap of faith eh, Princess?" She wrinkled her nose. "Time for Miss Marie to become the Nan-word."

She paused, and then cocked her head to the side. "What no argument?"

Silence.

"You know what this means, don't you? I'll have superhuman power over both story time *and* bedtime. I'd be your worst nightmare."

Again silence.

"Okay then, it's settled. Now where'd I put that cape?"

Being the most happening nanny on the block did have some appeal. She could learn to crochet an awesome beanie, and the homegrown silver highlights could be a thankful ease on her tab at the salon. The only difficult part was Tobin.

The clatter of keys on the pressed wood table made her jerk to attention.

Tobin turned away and draped his jacket across the large rocking chair.

Her pulse picked up speed, but she refused to move from the edge of Anna's bed.

She watched over his shoulder as he scrolled through messages on his phone with an agitated flick of his finger.

"What are your plans after Anna's recovery?" she asked.

"She won't be going back to the nunnery if that's what you mean."

She rotated the strand of pearls around her neck in attempt to occupy her shaking hands "How do you plan to care for her?"

His narrowed eyes churned from aqua-blue to deep cobalt—a dangerous mix that seemed there one moment and gone the next. "Why would that be any of your business?"

She swallowed. Perhaps this would have gone over better if he had a few drinks in him first. Or maybe a tranquilizer dart.

"I'm sure you're perfectly capable. It just seems like you could use some help," she said.

He tipped his head to the speckled ceiling tiles. "Ah. And you think Anna needs *you*?"

She set her jaw, half-pleading and half-demanding that she would still have a place in Anna's life. "You called me to watch over her, remember?"

"For tonight."

"Anna's still going to be here tomorrow, and you need me whether you like it or not. She needs to be looked after while you're not around. Christie would've wanted me to."

Her nerve endings buzzed with warning as he turned that penetrating gaze on her. His sarcastic expression eclipsed to a surprised grin, like a mountain lion in a deep yawn, discovering he just sucked up a canary.

She didn't feel the kind of pull toward him she witnessed from Heather or Dr. Scott. Instead, it felt politely distant, as if he were simply making an observation—a very deep, very intimidating observation. One that left her wondering if she still had time to run away screaming.

Nope, too late for that. Anna took precedence. Her face heated with frustration, but she braced her legs, determined to stay put. "I've taken care of Anna since she was a baby. She knows me, and you won't find anyone more qualified to—"

He held his hand up. "Enough said. You don't need to get all emotional on me." He looked back to the phone cradled in his palm.

She fought the urge not to lob a bedpan at the back of his head. "So, that's it then?"

"She needs a nanny. You're it. There's an extra room at the family estate where you'll stay. You're required to care for her at all times."

Marie couldn't have looked less shocked if he'd backhanded her. "Oh-ho, wait just a second. I never mentioned room and board. That's completely unnecessary."

He pinned her with an icy glare. "I'm sorry. Am I talking too fast for you?"

She figured enduring Tobin-fueled frustration would only be a nine-to-five obligation. Not a padded cell. The mere thought of living under his roof made her skin crawl. She'd only lived in her own condo for a few years. She finally felt settled. She didn't want to move for anyone.

"Anna could stay at my place while you're away," she began.

"Anna is family. She'll be cared for under my terms."

She dug her nails into her palms to ride out the anger that threatened to erupt. She pushed out a breath. "Fine. Have it your way."

"Great. See you tomorrow," he said.

She froze. "But…I just got here!"

"And now you're leaving. Come back when you're more level-headed."

"Wha—"

"Out."

Her jaw clamped shut. She considered sticking around to spite him 'course doing so would only get her in trouble. She managed to reign in her mouth so far, but any minute, she would explode.

She rounded Anna's bed, and in a fury, she snatched her coat and purse. She marched out, waiting to unleash the string of curses until she rounded the corner from Anna's room.

****

Tobin slouched in the wooden rocking chair, elbows propped on his knees, trying to tune out the occasional rumble of medical carts and muffled intercom projections. His mind reeled over the conversation with Marie.

Christie would have wanted me to….

Christie's wants were no longer relevant, but the gears set in motion before her death continued to churn. An ember of resentment glowed to life inside him. He smothered it. He had no place to criticize his sister-in-law. Although misguided, her actions were carried out with only good intentions.

A light tap on the door caught his attention.

"Hey, handsome."

His eyes scanned over the brunette with a candy-pink smile and full delectable breasts that bounced with each step. He forced a smile. "Heather."

She paused mid-stride at the brisk inflection of her name. "Is a…is everything okay?"

He looked down at his clasped hands. He knew what she came back for, but fun and games would have to wait until he figured out the whole nanny thing.

"I'm good. Just need some time. Maybe I'll see you later tonight. You can wear the white uniform you told me about. And don't forget the sponge," he said.

Her smile deflated, and she shot a guilty look at the open door. "Oh. Okay. Well, if you need anything until then…."

"Yeah, I'll let you know."

He listened to the reluctant shuffle of her footsteps down the hall before returning to his thoughts.

Marie was easy on the eyes, but feisty chicks made him itchy. Why waste time trying to coax any inhibitions from that spiny little shell when the willing and able ones were all lined up?

Unfortunately today, the desperation flooding

Marie's bright green eyes had snagged his interest, and he'd learned that dismissing her had been a grave mistake.

For a Muse with his skill, it only took one glance to catch those tiny flecks of light in her eyes, exposing the brand of her soul. When the picture completed, his mind plowed through her dense collection of memories. The ones that lay hidden before the life she currently occupied. It pulled back an identity...pretty damn astounding.

His mouth watered. His control shook with the sensation of his spirit pounding against the wall of its physical barrier, demanding to be set free. The only thought powerful enough to restrain him, was the knowledge of who she belonged to. To consume even a small amount of her would create deadly repercussions from the most powerful being of his kind. His brother.

Shit!

Her presence here was more than an unfathomable twist of fate. Someone else had a hand in this, someone more skilled than his meddling sister-in-law.

Tobin's gaze swept over Anna in quiet amazement. She seemed like a typical child on the outside, but unbeknownst to all of them, this little prodigy already tempted fate. Somehow Anna had sensed Marie's connection to the fam and formed a bond with the one woman who could turn their lives upside down.

Tobin squeezed his eyes shut and pinched the bridge of his nose. No. He could fix this.

If it weren't for his brother, he could use Marie up and toss her away without a second thought. But with Quenton returning to claim Anna, those plans would never come to fruition.

Marie's strong will and attachment to Anna blew away any prospect of quietly slipping her out of the picture. Like it or not, his brother would find out about this.

His thoughts shifted to Quentie. He couldn't contain the grin. When it came to control, the nanny would put up quite a fight. Even with Quenton's lethal charm, he might come up empty handed with this one. If he pulled back a hand at all. And how great would that be? Waiting centuries to obtain his mate, only to watch her slip through his fingers. The justice would taste *so* sweet.

Quenton enjoyed a good challenge, and from what he could recall, his brother didn't exactly fight fair. Perhaps he could find a solution to this little problem with a few black cards shoved up Quentie's sleeve—the kind that might tip the odds against him.

It would take some time to plan, but in the meantime, damage control. Stay on his brother's good side and continue to earn his trust. To do that, he couldn't put off Marie's introduction any longer.

Chapter 2

Tension from the twenty-two-hour flight still pulsed through Quenton's skull. He scowled at the two women standing ahead of him in the elevator. Their colorful scrubs seemed as fitting for a midnight slumber party as their pointed glances and snickers. It didn't take a genius to know who they were talking about but playful wasn't in his vocabulary.

The elevator chimed to signal his floor. When the doors opened, the women stepped out—three floors ahead of the button they'd pushed. They didn't stray far beyond his line of sight, waiting for him to get off. He hit the close button instead and rode the elevator another three floors down. He'd backtrack.

His blood frothed with irritation for coming here so early in the evening. With physicians and nurses probably tying up last minute details and visitors saying long goodbyes, the hospital teemed with people.

The short staff working graveyard shifts would have offered more space and less distraction from impressionable mortals. And after a few words, even the impressionable ones would leave him alone. Thankfully, the woman he'd collected on in Lebanon had a strong enough soul to keep him sated for a while. Plenty of time to collect Anna and get the hell out, except for one problem, Anna wasn't talking.

He'd already been in to visit her once and reaching

through Anna's coma felt like trying to pierce a basketball with a swizzle stick. Not so different from most children in that respect. The young ones were always sealed up tight, protected from the full weight of influence until they met their teen years.

But shouldn't he be able to form a connection with his own daughter? What if there was something more to it? What if she deliberately sealed herself away, both mentally and physically from the entire world? Powers that strong could only mean one thing. His daughter was a Muse.

The elevator doors pinged opened again, and he headed for the stairwell. Why didn't he think of that in the first place? Too busy trying to get here, that's why. Tobin called the house nearly an hour ago, saying something about meeting to discuss Anna's care.

Was she better? Or worse? Tobin didn't elaborate, just said he needed to show up early tomorrow. Screw that. If something changed, he wasn't going to wait around to find out. He rounded the corner to Anna's room and slipped inside. His back pressed to the wall and his gaze pinned on her. Relief eased the weight pressing down on his shoulders.

She looked…better. He'd kept up on her progress by way of the daycare blog. She'd become the center of attention after the accident. Updates were posted by the hour until about mid-afternoon, and then dropped off until the next day. He knew she'd been improving but seeing her now made all the difference. The purple smudges under her eyes had faded to a yellow stain, and the swelling in her face had receded. Healing fast. A little too fast for a mere mortal.

A scuff of footsteps sounded through the doorway,

and his shoulders stiffened.

"I thought we agreed to meet outside." The woman snapped her mouth shut when Quenton turned his head. The periwinkle scrubs were the same, but he didn't recognize this nurse from the graveyard shift. From the surprise knitted in her brow, she didn't know him either.

"Oh, I'm sorry. I thought you were someone else," she said.

The tension cranked down in Quenton's jaw. No doubt who that someone might be. Tobin should know better than to go feeding off women in his own backyard, especially around Anna. "You see Tobin today? He said there was someone I should meet," he said.

"You mean Anna?"

He shook his head. "Already know her. She's mine...my daughter." Like a giant metronome, his guilt kept perfect time as it slugged him in the stomach. Although the last bit was true, Anna was his, he didn't really know her at all.

"Well, I'm Heather. Anna's nurse. Until shift change anyway."

The only reason Tobin would force an introduction with this woman, would be to gloat. But Heather didn't have any effect on him. He could tell even from here, she wasn't hungry for inspiration in any form. Completely satisfied with her life. No. There must be someone else.

Heather's voice jarred his thoughts. "You must be so proud. She's a really cute kid, and she's progressing so well. I know it must be hard to see her like this."

Yes, it was. Each time he saw her in that bed his

heart ripped open a fresh wound. He hadn't been much help in her healthy moments. Learning to walk, and talk—those simple things. How the hell would he help her through something like this?

"Come on over. I have something to show you," Heather prompted.

He frowned. He never liked it when a woman told him what to do. Especially curvy ones that tooled their good looks. The curves were fine, but her assumption of power was all jacked up.

She took Anna's hand and leaned in close. "Hey, Princess. You have a visitor."

Wonder cooled his irritation as Anna's head turned to seek out Heather's voice. The nurse waved him over. Replacing her hand with his, Quenton felt unexpected warmth. Anna seemed so pale and lifeless before but holding her tiny hand in his palm clued him to the life that pulsed inside her. She was strong. Alive.

"She likes to hear people talk. You should try it. She'll probably recognize your voice."

He stared at Heather's thick-soled shoes. "She doesn't know my voice."

Heather tipped of her head. A frown pulled across her brow. "What better time than now to get acquainted then?" She pushed the large rocking chair up to Anna's bed and gave it a pat. "She's a great listener."

He nodded but his feet didn't move.

"My shift ends soon…if you need anything just push the call button," she said.

He stared down at the tiny hand long after Heather disappeared. What could he say? "*I'm the deadbeat, come to steal you away from your life*?" Pretty sure she wouldn't like to hear that. Christie had been right to

23

keep him away. His lifestyle wasn't good for a little girl, least of all a mortal.

How would he answer all the questions? He could keep his work hidden, but he couldn't hide his immortality. If she were human, she would grow up, get older, and he would always remain the same. One day she'd look older than him. Good hell, he'd even have to bury her someday. The threat of losing her life now, at such a tender age, broke something in him.

He made a mistake when he left the first time, and he knew it. He should've been here to protect her. Watch her grow, even if that meant watching her grow old.

But would she? Looking at her in this suspended state he wasn't so sure.

A firm weight settled on his shoulder. "Outwitted by a kid." Tobin chuckled. "Never thought I'd see the day."

"Shut up, you ass," Quenton muttered.

When Anna's head rolled toward him with her eyes tightly sealed, Quenton wanted to suck those words back into his mouth and choke on them. With all the wonders of the world he could teach her, he decided to start with vulgarity. Perfect.

"I know what you're thinking," Tobin prompted. "But the only way to find out for sure is to tear into her mind. You really prepared for that?"

He shook his head. "Not doing it."

"You want me to?"

Tobin's voice trailed with reluctance. He knew his brother didn't like the thought of it either, but he could count on Tobin to do what needed to be done. He turned Anna's hand over, sliding his thumb beneath her curled fingers. "There's no point," he murmured. Whatever the end result, he had to man up this time. He wouldn't leave her again.

After a long pause, Tobin gave his shoulder a squeeze then pulled free altogether. "Well, I'm headed out. Got people to do." His voice faded under clipped footsteps. "And don't forget about tomorrow."

Tomorrow, right. Another one of Tobin's surprises. So far they had meant nothing but bad news, and he doubted this one would be any different.

****

The next morning, Marie marched into the hospital with her head up, shoulders back, and a pair of four-inch high, don't-mess-with-me boots. She'd spent the last two hours packing for the inevitable trip to Tobin's house of X-rated horrors. It wasn't a chore she looked forward to. She still planned to stave off moving until absolutely necessary, but at least this way it wouldn't be so easy to back out.

Tobin had left a message on her voicemail callously restricting her visits to only a few hours in the evening while he tied up the loose ends of Christie's death.

"Payback no doubt, for standing up to him about the whole 'Nan' word thing." There was still no love lost on that word.

"How am I supposed to take care of Anna if I'm not allowed anywhere near her? And what am I expected to do with all this spare time?" she muttered.

All the good stores in town were closed on Sundays, so shopping was out of the question.

If she had to spend any more time inside the blank walls of her condo, she'd lose her mind.

25

She stepped around the front desk.

"Your daycare blog's developing quite a fan base around here," Dr. Scott called out. "The night shift had a pretty good laugh at my expense when Anna knighted me with an enormous scalpel. Thanks by the way, for not lopping off any of my favorite appendages."

She grinned. "Yeah, I thought about that, but I wanted to keep things clean for the kids at school."

Because of the hospital's great internet connectivity, she spent most of Anna's sleeping hours on the daycare's blog, taking pictures of departments in the hospital, and cropping in a cartoon version of Anna. The little girl held court with the nursing staff, and flew down the hallway in a winged wheelchair, all without leaving the discomfort of her stark hospital bed.

She tipped her head to Anna's room. "How's our girl?"

Dr. Scott looked to the door with a deep sigh. "She's good. She's really good. Reacting like a normal kid, which is unusual." He frowned. "This might be the fastest recovery I've ever witnessed."

She opened her mouth to ask why such a miracle would leave him troubled, but a light rap on the countertop stole her words.

"I'm not bugging, am I?" Heather asked.

"Nope. You're right on time," Marie said.

Heather always made a point to drop in thirty minutes before Tobin arrived, and moon over him long after Marie's escape. She didn't mind the company. She'd actually grown to like the saucy little airhead.

In the short time she spent visiting the hospital, she discovered nurses like Heather were a godsend. St. David's was a small-scale children's hospital often short on staff. Some of the workers became burned-out and detached. Heather, on the other hand, caused people to gravitate to her, and she pulled Marie into orbit along with everyone else. Marie had stumbled into an unexpected friendship.

"And what sort of grand e-venture do we have planned today?"

Marie offered a sly grin. "Oh, just a little more fun with our mysterious visitor of the blog."

A digital chirp came from Heather's hip, and she glanced down. "You mean Frozen Knight? That one?"

Marie shot a quick glance to Heather's hip. "Yup. He keeps logging on but refuses to identify himself. He's overdue for some friendly encouragement."

Heather pulled the hem of her shirt aside and slapped the device with the palm of her hand. "Damn."

"Some kind of emergency?" Marie asked.

"No. It's my insulin pump acting up again. It's says it's running low, but I just filled it…"

"I didn't know you were diabetic."

"Yeah, sorry, I know how jumpy you get when alarms go off."

Now that Heather pointed it out, the correlation between the sound and her anxiety couldn't be plainer. For good reason too. Her father held high rank with special ops. They moved around a lot—sometimes from necessity for the job. Other times, threat and paranoia. When she started school as a child, her father made her wear a beeper disguised as a Snoopy watch.

He instructed her to head straight to the school playground the moment it went off. Her parents would then pick her up and leave town, sometimes with nothing more than the clothes on their backs. She grew to hate that stupid watch, and when she moved out on her own, she took a hammer to it.

On the same principle, she rarely carried a phone or any other electronic leash, but being in the hospital day after day, she couldn't escape it.

"So, what are we going to do with the blog guy?" Heather asked.

Dr. Scott turned his attention to Anna's electronic chart as he spoke, keeping his voice even. "There you go again provoking innocent strangers."

Marie's palm lifted in casual disclosure. "If he'd identify himself, he wouldn't *be* a stranger, now would he? The blog's for parents only." She tipped her head. "And the hospital staff in Anna's case."

"What if it's her father?" Heather's eyes grew wide. "What if its Tobin's handle, and he's posing as a reader to keep tabs on you?"

She shook her head. "Not possible. The father is absentee. Tobin already knows about the blog and hasn't shown the slightest interest. This has to be someone else."

"All right, good enough for me. What do you need?" Heather asked.

Marie tapped her chin. "How about a shot of the cafeteria? I'll bet if he wanders into a pool of green Jell-O, it could swallow him up to the neck like quicksand. We could leave him stranded there for a few days until Anna finds him."

She raised her brows at Dr. Scott. "See? Perfectly harmless."

He snorted. "Yeah. That's how it starts. But before you know it, he'll fall off his steed into the dirty linen shoot not to be found until midway through the wash cycle. Shrinking all his clothes and forcing him into a backless hospital gown."

She blinked. "Wow. Just…wow."

Heather clapped. "Awesome. Let's do that one next."

Dr. Scott made a tamping down motion with his hands. "Now hang on. Don't get too wound up with your dastardly plans. This vibe's going to kill my surprise."

Marie and Heather turned.

Dr. Scott gestured to Anna's room with a broad sweep of his hand. "Little Anna is awake."

Marie's smile felt like it stretched from one ear to the other, and she swallowed back the tears that constricted her throat. "Tobin must be so happy."

"Oh, he doesn't know yet." The dense frustration in his voice caused her happiness to falter.

"What? He left her alone?"

Scott frowned. "We haven't seen him all day."

Her face heated with anger. "Why would he keep me away from visiting Anna when he didn't plan to stick around?"

His mouth fell open. A mix of discomfort and confusion dimmed his brown eyes.

"Sorry, rhetorical question," she muttered. "I'll let you know if I find him."

Her gait picked up speed and determination again until she reached for Anna's door and yanked it open. When she met the heavy curtain that circled Anna's bed, she closed her eyes and forced in a deep breath.

Anna shouldn't see her as a tightly wound ball of fury. She'd save that little present for the next time she saw Tobin. And when she did, he'd wish she really was a nun, because all hell was going to break lose.

She waltzed in, with her grin stretched tight. She caught a glimpse of Anna from the corner of her eye, well aware she'd acquired a captive audience.

She slung her purse into the corner chair, whipped away her coat, and kicked off her high-heeled boots to play up her enthusiasm. "I hope you're ready for one wild trip, Anna. Because I've had a whole glass of Kool-Aid, and I'm ready to rock!"

A smile of utter delight played on Anna's face. In part, because of the mockery she was making, but even better, she'd done it in front of the majestic figure of a man sitting next to the bed.

She blinked.

She could see the family resemblance in the seductive curve of his lips, but this man wasn't Tobin. His hair was darker, almost black, in waves that tumbled over his forehead. His face wasn't as elegant either. It was thoroughly masculine; all hard planes and angles with a dusting of stubble that lined his jaw. Bigger than Tobin in every direction, including his unsettling gaze that pulled at her, even from across the room.

"And who are you?" he asked.

The gravelly depth of his voice made her cheeks burn, and her Kool-Aid high melted. "Um…I'm Anna's nanny." She turned away to shield her embarrassment, setting her car keys on the table. "We have a play date scheduled, and I am a bit early. I didn't mean to interrupt."

"A nanny." He spoke slow and deliberate, as if tasting the word. "Must be my lucky day."

Her spine went rigid. "Doubt it."

She wasn't sure how the idea of a nanny and getting lucky fit together in his book, but if he was anything like his brother, whatever fantasy he conjured wasn't something she cared to entertain.

So this was *him*, the political advisor who gallivanted around the world offering oh-so-valuable advice. The man who abandoned his child. Well, she had a few choice words of her own but given that Anna sat wide-eyed and stone silent only a few feet away, she would hold on to those gems for a later date.

His dark lashes swooped low then back up again, as if taking full assessment of her with imperceptible speed. "So I finally meet the woman behind the curtain. Your entries on Anna's blog have become more sporadic. I was beginning to wonder what happened to me."

Her eyes grew wide. "You? You're the Knightsicle?"

His eyes held a glint of irritation as he stalked toward her. "Frozen Knight…and yes. The man, the myth, and the victim of a misconceived centerfold shoot with X-ray. That was one of my favorites."

She inched back a step as he closed the distance between them, feeling her stomach twist into a nervous knot, as his unrelenting gaze yanked on her panic lever.

Her hip bumped into the side table, catching her off balance. She clamped down on the table's edge with one hand. Her phone skittered across the table from where she set it and fell to the floor. She bent down to retrieve it, but he swiped it away.

He glanced down at the phone's face, where she'd spilled nail polish a week ago. "I think you drew blood."

"Serves it right. All those prank calls from my back pocket." She motioned to retrieve the phone.

He offered his hand instead. "Most people call me Quenton. I'll be taking care of Anna from here on out, so it's good we finally meet."

A cloud of confusion swirled in Marie's brain and her eyes cast to the pebble gray linoleum. Anna living with *him?* The guy she'd been trashing online for days. And now she had to work for him? The whole situation left her feeling like a sheered sheep at the county fair.

Not just embarrassed, completely exposed, and downright pissed!

She offered him a half-hearted smile. "I'm Marie."

His nostrils flared, and his hand contracted, gripping hers tighter. Their handshake seemed to last for an awkward length of time.

With brows raised, she looked down at their clasped hands, then to his face again, wondering if he'd forgotten how long the simple custom ordinarily takes.

Her pulse quickened as she searched through what had to be the most engaging pair of eyes she'd ever seen. They were a soft, emerald green. Not unlike a color she'd found in countless others, in fact, they were almost a mirror image of her own shade. But if it wasn't the color that captivated her, what was it? She wasn't sure how to even define the dangerous magnetism that pulled her into their depths.

Tobin couldn't match this kind of power. Unlike his cold and empty gaze, Quenton's felt warm and inviting. It stirred a powerful longing from deep in her chest, one that fought her logic for dominance in an effort to pull herself closer.

He remained silent and motionless.

Wait. Not just him, the whole room seemed to grow still.

He searched through her eyes with a mixture of wonder and disbelief. It felt invasive and unsettling to the coherent part of her brain, and the alarm it set off began to escalate.

She attempted to retract her hand, but her own muscles wouldn't respond. What was wrong with her?

His hand radiated warmth, and the thick calluses felt oddly protective. The opposing team to her logic latched on to that, not willing to let go, as if they were bobbing their heads in time to that pulsing alarm, fired up at the prospect of a hormonal uprising.

He didn't seem to take notice of anything out of the ordinary, and his focus on her never wavered. The voice inside her head grew from a note of caution to an all-out scream.

What are you doing? You are not falling for this stupid ploy. Let go, you idiot!

In a spike of panic, she overpowered the naughty hormonal pep rally and jerked free. The faded flush of her cheeks returned in full strength.

For a fleeting moment, dark determination flared in his eyes but then it was gone. He took a step backward, forcing an apologetic smile. "Sorry if I scared you. Guess I got lost for a moment there."

Lost? She wondered. *Maybe. Have you been to this planet before, or are you only stopping to ask directions? And getting lost in my eyes? That's got to be the worst pickup line ever invented.*

"Ah, so I see you've finally met my good friend, Marie."

She recognized Tobin's sardonic voice before she

turned to address him. He leaned against the doorway, arms folded, and head angled, as if taking in the entire exchange and enjoying every moment of it.

Friends, what friends? She shot him a look. That pig wouldn't even fly over Facebook.

He strolled across the room and draped his arm over her shoulder. An act she was certain he carried out strictly to provoke his brother. Quenton's brows drew together, and he pinned Tobin with a ferocious glare. "You sought her out?"

"Not me." Tobin tipped his head in Anna's direction.

Before she could blink, Quenton snatched Tobin by his shirtfront and the two men were nose-to-nose. "How long have you known about her?" he asked.

She half-shoved, half-stumbled away from Tobin's arm. "Hello? Still in the room, remember?"

They continued to face off. A smug twitch pulled at Tobin's lips, and he leaned away from his brother. "I've been working with her for some time regarding Anna's new living arrangement. I take it you're pleased to meet her?"

She clenched her teeth. Why would he deliberately keep her and Quenton in the dark?

Quenton gave a clipped response as he released his hold, dropping his brother back onto his heels. "The matter's closed. Anna's leaving the state."

"What?" she shouted.

He gave her a dismissive glance. "Marie, you'll be going as well."

"Oh-ho, no I'm not," she sang out.

Her sassy retort dropped off her tongue and went splat when Quenton squared his shoulders at her. No match for his six-two frame or his paternal job description.

"If you still want to care for Anna, and I assume you do, you'll go where I say."

She gasped. "But you can't do that. This is her home and everything she knows. To tear her away from what's left of her life would make matters so much worse. She's been through enough already."

She wasn't sure if she was speaking for Anna or herself, and her argument sounded unconvincing even to her own ears. Panic twisted her stomach into some grotesque balloon animal.

She turned to Tobin, searching for any support he might offer her cause, but his attention never fell on her. Instead, he folded his arms and splayed a broad grin. As if pleased that from one kick of the domino, a delusional masterpiece came tumbling down.

With one quick move she could ram her elbow into his side…

No, bad idea. Any sudden burst of aggression wouldn't help her case. Not when it came to being a loving and attentive caregiver for Anna. She could do little more than glare at him until he finally spoke.

"You'll have to forgive Quentie. He's not used to working outside his own motives. I think a smooth transition would be best for everyone involved. Marie and Anna should stay here for a few weeks. Give them time to adjust. Then you can take them abroad."

She raised one brow. "And if they don't adjust?"

Quenton glowered over her. He pulled out each word slow and deliberate. "They. Go. Anyway."

She held up her index finger and replied in the same tone, her finger bowing at every word like a naked puppet. "You. Can't. Make me."

Okay, that didn't come out quite right. The little daycare tator tots had been rubbing off on her. The childish comeback wasn't exactly what she was going for, but at least it was a step in the right direction. She'd made her point, right?

The glow in Quenton's eyes ignited. "You want to bet?" He stepped forward to eat up the distance between them, and despite her erratic heartbeat, she met him head on.

She puffed up her chest. "Go ahead. Try it, big boy. I dare you."

Tobin's laugher filled the room, and he wiped an invisible tear from his eye. "Oh, this is turning out to be even more fun than I expected. Hey, Anna, you got any popcorn over there?"

All attention fell on the wide-eyed little girl, and Marie's anger fizzled under the guilt that poured over her. "Shut up, Tobin." She hissed under her breath.

He grinned and turned his attention to Quenton. "Marie talks big but underneath she's a pushover. Just give her some time."

Pushover my butt. She glared at him. *I'd like to open the window and push you right off the ledge.* She wanted to parrot the thought aloud too but held her tongue. She could tell Quenton was turning the matter over in his head as he frowned at Tobin, then to her, and back again.

"Fine. We'll stay for now, but this will go down under my rules."

"Sounds good to me." Tobin shot back with a mocking salute. "We'll be one big happy family."

Quenton didn't respond. Instead, he turned on his

heel and stormed out.

She tried to conceal her sigh of relief. Having one Blake male in the close proximity was unnerving enough, but two felt like intimidation overload.

Tobin and Quenton were vaguely similar with their dark features and even darker attitude, but the similarities ended there.

If shaking his younger brother like a baby rattle was any indication, Quenton proved himself the more dangerous of the two.

Like a modern-day Pied Piper, Quenton's magnetic gaze and charm could lead a girl anywhere. And if by some strange anomaly he couldn't lead a girl, she bet he had the muscle power to drag her kicking and screaming. And she had a bad feeling that's exactly what would happen to her.

She glanced down at Anna, whose tiny mouth remained slightly agape.

You and me both! she thought, as she wrapped her arm around Anna's shoulders.

"Now why didn't you tell me you had two knights? How about that? A shiny one and a slimy one."

She could feel the heat in Tobin's stare but refused to look up. She pulled Anna onto her lap and began rocking her from side to side, not sure which one of them she was trying to sooth more.

"It's easy to see where you get your good looks, but where on Earth did those beautiful blue eyes come from? Both of them have green eyes," she said.

"Like yours," Anna replied.

He waved away the conversation. "Try not to hurt yourself contemplating genetics. Let's get Anna packing. She's coming home."

"Wait. I didn't think you were leaving until next week," she said.

"It's all settled. I spoke to her doctor this morning. Said she's right as rain. Now let's get packing girls before Quentie comes back to throw another tantrum. He's not good at sharing his toys." He winked at her.

Toys? She could imagine herself as many things, but she was no possession or plaything.

She approached him and whispered through gritted teeth, careful not to let Anna overhear. "You're a real piece of work. I just got steamrollered by an absentee father I knew nothing about, and you didn't even bother to tell me Anna was going home today. If I arrived when you told me to, I would've missed her completely! How am I supposed to trust you when you act so underhanded?"

She fought the urge to shrink away when he drew close enough to whisper in her ear; his warm breath flowing over her cheek.

"Let's get one thing straight right now. You have no authority here, and no choice but to trust me. If you know what's good for you, you'll keep your head down and your mouth shut."

Yeah, like that's gonna happen.

Chapter 3

The hammer of Quenton's determined footsteps echoed off the concrete frame of the hospital's parking garage. Marching to Tobin's car, he hoped the autumn chill seeping into his skin would offer some relief.

It didn't.

Instead, the title wave of anger washed over him, spurring his transformation with inescapable force.

His vibrant green eye color was the first thing to go. He felt it drain away to the intense electric blue that always lay just below the surface, bleaching his vision in scorching halos of light. Pain seared through his body as every muscle swelled and expanded. Blood rushed through his head, pounding out an ancient battle drum that commanded him to answer.

Get a grip!

He squeezed his eyes shut and compacted the rage. Not since the early years of his transformation had anger flowed through his veins so freely.

As a long-limbed boy of sixteen with wild, dark hair and equally wild eyes, he fit the gawky teenager profile. The growing years were miserable for anyone, but try going through them with superhuman strength, a divine key to the human soul, and a hairdo that rivaled Einstein's.

The Muse gene handed itself down his family tree at random, but it never took long to figure out which members pulled the card. Those first few Muses that crept into ancient mythology were a frisky bunch. Before long, they had grafted throughout the continent, but somehow the gene always came with a fractured soul.

He could still recall the smell of sun baked earth and sweat of ancient Greece. How the dry wind brushed against his bare chest and gritted in his teeth. He sat under a small outcropping of acacia trees, with a rough six-foot long spear across his thighs.

His commander's voice droned on about the rigors of military life. His raspy voice muffled by the intermittent gusts of wind, and the papyrus held just inches from his nose. Beyond the sprawling circle of young men, the repetitive metal on metal clang of the blacksmith was the only sound that dared contend with him.

He stared out to the costal landscape beyond, his eyes sharp against the scorching sun. Arms crossed over his chest, and his fingertips drummed absently on his almost nonexistent bicep.

Without warning, an acute pang of nausea doubled him over, and his hands clamped to the rough wooden spear. The soft grunt that escaped him drew attention from the men sitting nearby, and they watched his internal battle with weary fascination.

He was taught from infancy to expect this change, but the knowledge held no reassurance against the blanket of dread that pulled over him. He could feel the curse approaching.

His heart pumped faster, more erratic, gaining in force until it felt it would explode from his chest.

A sharp pain lanced through his brain with such

brutality, his surroundings eclipsed into darkness.

The apprehension didn't end there. It only increased because he knew the worst was yet to come. He tried to brace himself against the wall of foreign memories that slammed into his mind, causing wave after wave of gut-wrenching remorse.

Memories of a life. No. Not much a life but an existence even before life became real enough for him to touch. Of all the experiences he could recall, the love he shared for one soul seemed the most prevalent. The one made to fill him completely.

He'd been told, a Muses' mate is fated long before their human form has a chance to screw things up. Their hearts pre-broken for their own good. To refine their insatiable hunger to inspire. His breaking time had come.

The anger and grief that came with the memory of her being torn from his arms felt so intense; his hands gripped down, and he thrust his knee up, snapping the spear in two.

The deafening crack of splintering wood drew the attention of every person in camp. The commander's face flashed from pallid surprise to anger. The boys stared in shock, and the girls, he was pleased to later hear, showed an intriguing mix of fear and excitement.

He buried the sorrow from that day deep inside. The pain so excruciating, he couldn't function. He didn't eat or sleep for days, and all his strength leached away under sweltering heat. He remembered how his mind seemed to float around inside his body, cocooned in the tunneled mesh of his subconscious.

The military of ancient Greece knew little about his kind, and left him alone to struggle through his infirmity, laid out in a stifling tent while others continued to train for battle. They expected him to die before sundown and be given a hero's funeral. Cremated and entombed with his armor and broken spear.

He could only imagine what extravagant tales his people would spin about the courageous and *devastatingly* handsome soldier who broke it in two while fighting off a hundred men.

"Quentie?" Tobin's childlike voice wove into his mind. It sounded lost and confused but far too distant to matter much to him. He let it slip away unanswered.

"Quentie, wake up." The voice came again with a faint prodding at his shoulder.

He frowned, wanting to swat Tobin like a fly, but lacking the strength to lift his arm.

"You're too empty. You need to feed," he had insisted.

The pesky fly of a brother was right. He knew coming of age meant answering the call to serve as a Muse to mankind. To ensure loyalty to this trade, he carried a curse. To suffer unquenchable pain and hunger without collecting on the souls of those he inspired. To refuse it would only prolong his agony. The pain would never end for him. Not until the day he found the only one who'd quench him completely.

In two days' time, if he didn't feed, they would cremate him. With his body broken and gone, he would become nothing more than a Shade, a ravenous demon who scavenged corpses, hunting for the lost piece of his soul.

Suddenly, soul collecting didn't sound like such a bad idea.

Tobin saved him that day. Forming a debt that would never be repaid. His brother mastered his appetite at a young age, but it never came easy for Quenton. Forcing his soul to partially emerge from his body and reach into a mortal was as difficult as it sounded. His inexperience and limited power often pulled back nothing more than empty space. Call it a premature accumulation of sorts. The kind that not even Dr. Oz had a solution for. It was beyond infuriating. Much like the fury he felt after leaving Marie.

The moment she had entered Anna's room he felt it. The same hunger for inspiration he'd detected in countless others. Oh, but she could return the favor better than anyone he'd encountered. The caliber of her soul could fill him to overflowing and offer the dream that every Muse lived for, completion and a mortal life.

This unplanned flight to Colorado brought him face-to-face with not only Christie's death and the injury of his only child but the woman he spent a lifetime searching for. Well, longer than a lifetime to be exact, but who was counting? And the timing couldn't be worse.

Christie's body got up and wandered away, which meant her accident wasn't an accident at all. It was murder. With his enemy growing in numbers, he couldn't afford to engage Marie. Not now. He had a job to do. Neutralize the Shades and get Anna the hell out of Colorado, preferably in that order.

There wasn't anything wrong with making Marie the cherry on top of his sundae. But his sweet tooth had a way of overriding all conscious thought, turning his motto from "savoring the spoils of victory" to "eating dessert first and asking questions later."

Unlike his brother, he outgrew the endless thirst for the female population. He still had a healthy craving for them but didn't make it his mission to screw every woman within arm's reach. He asked politely for them to come to him. And they always did.

Tobin's persuasive power was equally as great as his own, and he wouldn't put it past his brother to have already convinced Marie to share his bed. The memory of Tobin with his arm slung around her made his anger spark. He slammed his fist into Tobin's parked car. Then pulled away to reveal a large dent where his hand collided. His knuckles split, and blood oozed from the torn skin.

Whether she knew it or not, Marie belonged to him, and he wasn't about to let anyone stand in his way.

With one deliberate blink, his vision eclipsed back to emerald green. He turned in the direction of the hospital, but as he was about to charge, he caught sight of Tobin and Marie strolling toward him.

"You palmed my keys, Quentie," Tobin said.

He crossed his arms to hide his throbbing fist. "That's because your driving sucks. You can't keep your eyes on the road."

His attention shifted to Marie, as if applying his case in point. The thought of Tobin touching her still burned in his memory, and he found it difficult to hide the disdain from his voice. He took her in from head to toe, her image refining with every step.

Soft auburn curls kicked off tiny flecks of red in the sun and bounced merrily about her shoulders, keeping time with the subtle sway of her hips. It would have been nice to see what other assets came in that taunting rhythm, but Anna blocked his view.

Swathed in a giant, pink marshmallow blanket, she clung to Marie like a scared animal. Her white-blonde hair caught on the wind, flying in every direction.

When he leveled his glare on Marie, she stopped short. Fear seemed to grip her mid-step, and she staggered. She looked caught between heeding the instinct to run and knowing she'd never get away.

She glanced down at Anna.

Don't you run, he thought. *Don't you dare run.* The ball of his right foot planted on the ground, poised to sprint, as he waited for her to take even one more step back.

Anna buried her face against Marie's chest, but the abrupt halt caused her to pull back just far enough to look up. He couldn't see the expression on Anna face, or the brief exchange between them. Anna clutched her tighter and tucked her head back down. She seemed to urge Marie onward, confident she would comply.

He watched Marie mutter something into the folds of the blanket. Her shoulders set back with one deep breath before she rushed to him. "Quenton, will you please put this little one in the car while I go back for her things?"

She didn't wait for a response. She shrugged Anna off into his arms. Anna instantly latched onto his torso. A gasp caught in his throat. He wrapped both arms around his child, careful not to drop her or squeeze too hard. She had already broken once.

Marie continued her instructions, unfazed. "Just put her in the car seat and buckle her up. I'll be right back."

He watched as Marie turned back to the hospital lobby. Hair and hips keeping time again with the perky clip of those fuck-me boots.

He inclined his head to scan over the round curve of her ass. The combination of surprise and intrigue caused his ragged breathing to slow and the pounding in his head to quiet, calming the brute who threatened to erupt only moments ago. The swelling in his muscles began to recede. Well, except for one.

When she disappeared, he looked down again, and cleared his throat. "So, Anna, do you want to get in the car?"

She grunted and clutched him tighter.

He stared down at the featherweight child pressed to his chest. Her eyes closed, and her lips turned up in a faint smile as if savoring the sound of his heartbeat.

They were practically strangers, not having seen each other since the day she was born. Yet, she embraced him without hesitation.

His chest constricted with the thought that holding her should never have felt this foreign. A real man knows what it feels like to hold his daughter.

He dipped his head, savoring her warmth, and the lingering scent of what could only be Marie's perfume. He'd caught a hint of it earlier. The cream and honey concoction came as a welcome change from the antiseptic he'd been immersed in over the past few days.

He let the wild strands of Anna's hair catch the stubble on his chin and tickle his face. He held her until her arms slackened.

His own voice sounded strained and unfamiliar. Must be from the cold. "Okay, come on…let's get you in the car." He reached through the blanket and hooked his thumbs under her arms.

Anna squealed in protest and squeezed tighter around him.

He gave her a gentle tug, then another, but Anna held fast.

Strong for such a little thing. Must have gotten that from him. He threw his head back in frustration. Feeling like a grown man caught up a tree while rescuing his mother's cat. He *could* pull the frail and clingy girl away from him, forcing her into the car. But he didn't want to risk harming her.

He looked to the multi-colored car seat anchored in the center of the back seat, then to Tobin. Just how long had that shithead been planning all this?

Tobin smirked as he climbed into the passenger's seat. "I'm glad she likes you. You can change her diapers."

Quenton glared at Tobin and took a menacing step in his direction. Marie, however, hadn't taken long to retrieve the last of Anna's things and dashed around the corner before he could make Tobin's face match his paint job.

****

Marie smiled when she saw Quenton standing where she left him, both hands on his hips, and Anna fused to him like paper mâché. Peeking out from under the blanket, Marie detected a cunning grin on Anna's face.

"Is this little one house trained?" Quenton asked.

"Oh, she's completely potty trained." She tugged at Anna's waist, but the little girl held fast. "Well, except when you tickle her, she has a tendency to wet her pants."

She dropped the bags to the ground and wriggled

her fingers against Anna's ribs. On the first shriek of Anna's laughter, Quenton jerked her from his midsection and held her at arm's length.

She bit back a laugh when she took Anna away from him and hunched down to place Anna in the back seat. "Now be a good little monkey. Quenton isn't used to you yet, and we don't want to scare him."

Stepping back to close the door, his breath teased the back of her hair. The warm smell of brown sugar and winter curled around her senses. She allowed herself a slow savoring breath and felt the tension in her shoulders fall away. Her eyes closed in quick reprieve.

"Rough day?"

The husky sound of his voice pulled her back to reality. Her eyes popped open.

"What?"

She turned and another wave of his scent met her full in the face. He stood so close her chest almost touched his.

The weight of his palm settled on her shoulder. "You look overwhelmed."

Despite the heat of his hand causing her body to nearly melt beneath it, she shook her head. "No, no I'm good."

"Sure?" His palm turned to allow his thumb the barest caress over her collarbone. The gleam in his eye told her he wasn't quite as concerned as he was amused.

"Positive," she said, even as her pulse flickered with disagreement.

His lips twitched in arrogant skepticism.

Maybe she could convince him by introducing his toe to the heel of her boot.

"I want you settled as soon as possible. You need time to pack?" he asked.

Her spine went rigid, and she stepped back. "My bags are packed. I just need to stop and pick them up."

His expression blanked to an impenetrable mask as he pulled open the driver side door. His voice even. "Okay then. I'll follow you there then take you to Tobin's." He climbed into the car and jabbed a finger at his brother. "And we're gonna have a talk."

"Hope it has something to do with the fist that ran into my car," Tobin muttered.

Chapter 4

On the way to the Blake home, Marie glanced down every few minutes, using one hand to click through her playlist, while the other draped over the steering wheel. The picture of a Sunday drive. If only Quenton would let up on his little staring contest.

She watched him as they'd pulled onto the road, the car rolling into the glare of the afternoon sun. He winced just before sliding his silver framed sunglasses into place. The reaction seemed more exaggerated than she would expect of an ordinary person.

Of course, Quenton, as a whole, seemed far from ordinary. If his magnetic eyes pulled everything in as easily as it did her, she could understand why he'd want a filter.

But with his gaze boring into her from his rear-view mirror, she could use a pair of mirrored frames of her own. She forced her attention to the dial on her air conditioner and held her damp palms to the vent. She really needed to get this thing fixed but nervous system repair men weren't easy to come by.

The road wound through a deep canyon laced with pine trees and colossal mountains ranked on either side. She scanned the shoulder of the road for any sign that might indicate where they were headed. Her stomach grew more agitated with every mile she put behind her.

Her family never stayed in one place for more than

a few years, and with the constant change of pace, she acquired a loathing for travel in any form. Sleeping in strange places made her twitchy. She had seldom found enough time to secure a single friend, before her parents pushed on to the next adventure. And being led away again to some undisclosed location by two near strangers—warm fuzzy feelings were in short supply.

"Oh!" She looked up in time to see an oncoming car framed in her windshield. With a swift jerk of the steering wheel, she swerved from the vehicle's path to her own lane.

Her car tires shrieked as she veered to the right. The front tire met the shoulder, spitting gravel and tipping the vehicle away from the road.

She jerked again.

"Shit, shit, shit!" She fumbled with the wheel and tightened the vehicle's sharp, left-to-right weave until it recovered to a straight line. She pushed out a deep, shaky breath.

Her attention flashed to his rearview mirror again, and she gave him a shrug-and-grin combo. The dark sunglasses didn't move. Was he glaring at her?

Okay. Okay!

Her foot lifted off the accelerator, but her gaze didn't waver from his reflection. Why did she feel so drawn to him? Never before could any man hold her attention for long, and yet she rivaled obsession with this one.

From the moment their hands touched, she was reluctant to let go, and for some reason her mind still hadn't. It felt unnerving, embarrassing, and completely out of character. To survive under the same roof and convince him not to take Anna away she needed to get control over this situation.

She wasn't sure how long Quenton and Tobin's rivalry would last. After the confrontation at the hospital, she had her doubts about their ability to coexist. And if she didn't guard herself carefully, she'd become yet another pawn for Tobin to play, or perhaps a mindless drone led by Quenton's hypnotic power.

Then again, hypnosis didn't sound *so* bad. Maybe he could whip out his pocket watch and make his brother howl like a dog in heat. Admittedly, it wasn't much of a stretch but at least it would be entertaining.

She followed Tobin's vehicle off the main road and broke through the cover of lush evergreens to reveal an expansive home. A two-level rustic mountain style estate with enormous front-facing windows and an exterior composed of tumbled, gray brick and stone. It looked newly renovated but with the massive wooden beams framing the front entry, its layout still carried a hint of old-world charm.

She parked her car at the summit of a gravel drive. She reached for the door handle but Quenton was already there, opening it and offering his outstretched hand.

"That's all right. I can manage," she said, hoping she wouldn't have to repeat the day's earlier events. She felt rather fond of her hand and figured it'd be good to keep it around while she still had a use for it.

His hand fisted until his knuckles blanched white. Guess he wasn't used to being turned down, *poor baby.*

Tobin stepped out from the car and wasted no time lifting Anna into his arms. He rounded the car in Marie's direction with his focus set on the surrounding forest.

With a tense posture, he scanned the perimeter of the house not seeming at all like the predator she knew him to be. He looked more like prey. But what on earth could be hunting him, aside from the occasional scorned female? He seemed to fancy the stiletto type, he should be able to outrun them.

Anna raised her head from his shoulder, and her eyes grew wide.

Marie gave her a reassuring pat on the back. "Come, Anna, your castle awaits!"

"I'll show them to their rooms," Quenton interjected.

Tobin didn't protest but there was a sharp edge in his voice when he gestured to the front door with a tip of his head. "Shall we?"

Quenton marched down the main hallway, dictating as he went.

"I've put most my business plans on hold for this transition. I'll be working out of the study during the day, and those doors will remain closed." He gestured up a flight of stairs as he passed. "There's a seating room on the second floor, and the library is in the east wing. Basement has a full gym, pool, and hot tub that are all under construction. Most of the bedrooms here are being converted for other purposes.

"Anna will be staying here." He threw open two large double doors to reveal an imposing bed, adorned with blush pink linens. He paused for a second before continuing down the hall to the next set of doors.

"And this," he said with a measure of formality. "This will be yours."

He revealed a room of equal size and proportion to Anna's but lavishly dressed in white. Her feet sank down into the snowy carpet as she lingered in the doorway. The smell of lavender and new paint welcomed her into a space decorated with matching cherry wood furniture.

The gold-leafed mirror affixed to one wall was the only exception to its charm. Facing the bed and standing more than nine feet tall, the mirror towered over the other pieces in the room.

Tobin's name written all over it. Still, mirror aside, she could fit three or more of her old bedrooms in here.

"Will this work?" Quenton asked.

"Oh, it's beautiful."

"Good." He continued to storm farther down the hall as he called behind to her. "My room is down there just off the study, but you don't need to see that. Dinner is at five-thirty p.m. Lights out at seven. No exceptions."

He turned one last time. "For the little one, anyway," he added. Then he disappeared behind the polished wood door.

Marie offered Anna a dismissive shrug. "Come on, Princess. Let's go find some peas and get some good jumps in on that big bed of yours before Moody McOrnery Pants outlaws that too!"

****

The sunset streamed through Anna's massive bathroom window, and the sheers hanging on either side billowed with each gust of tepid wind, bringing with it the mild scent of decaying leaves and smoldering field fires.

The thrashing sound of tub water filtered through the bathroom.

"You okay?" Marie called over her shoulder, as she

unpacked her toiletries.

"Yup," Anna said.

"You done yet?"

"Nooope."

Marie looked at her watch. "Shouldn't that water be ice cold by now?" She'd threatened, bribed, and even dropped the temperature in Anna's room but nothing could pull that kid out of the tub.

"You get two more minutes," she warned.

"'kay."

Another thrash of water slapped onto the tile floor, and she hunched her shoulders. Two more minutes meant two things: she added an extra twenty in clean up time, and Anna developed a flair for negotiation. Mmm, wonder where she got that from.

Her parents had never been the negotiating type.

"Oh, suck!" She felt her pockets for the phone. "I still haven't called them back! Now where did I put that?"—her voice elevated—"Anna, have you seen my phone?" She shifted a moving box from the bathroom floor. "It's shiny and pink…."

"Like…a boat?"

"No. Not a boat." She scanned the countertop before looking to Anna and the new pink submarine at the bottom of the tub sending tiny distress bubbles to the surface.

"Oh, Anna, no!" She scooped out the drowned phone and frantically scrubbed it with a thick bath towel. "Princess, this has a battery in it."

Anna's frown for the loss of her toy altered to round, watery-eyes and a lowered bottom lip. She spouted a whimper.

"Here. Let's try something else." She dragged a

bucket of water toys over and unloaded them one by one.

Anna looked to the basket, then to Marie and back again, as if holding out until the last toy sailed into the tub. With the bucket empty, Anna thrust out her hand to take that, too.

"Girls?" a voice from the bedroom called.

She stuck her head out from the bathroom to find Quenton strolling into the room.

He frowned. "It's seven o'clock."

"Yep. I'm on it." She set the cell phone on Anna's dresser and jerked open the pajama drawer, trying to ignore the nervous energy stirring in her stomach. "Do you mind if I borrow your phone?"

"What's wrong with yours?" He reached around to pick up her phone before she could answer. A drop of water ran down the edge and fell silently to the lush carpet.

The heat of her embarrassment warmed her cheeks. "It gets a little emotional," she explained.

Quenton sighed as he turned the phone over and pulled out the battery. "House phone's in the kitchen. We'll let this dry out a few days. See if it's still functional."

"Thanks, I owe you one." From the corner of her eye, Marie caught the tilt of his head.

"One what?"

She lifted her shoulder. "One…. I don't know. It's a figure of speech."

"You know, I have a weakness for fair trade."

Electricity charged over her skin when she set her eyes on him, confused at his statement but too afraid to ask its meaning.

"I dooone," Anna sang. She stood in the open doorway wrapped neck to toe in a large towel. Her blonde hair plastered to her cheeks.

"Okay, bedtime," Marie replied.

When she approached with Anna's pajamas, the little girl threw back her towel like a magician's cape and scampered out of her reach. She squealed in delight, streaking around the room as Marie chased after her.

Quenton abruptly spun to face the wall and fixed his eyes on the ceiling. "So, I'll a—I'll see you two in the morning."

****

In the kitchen, Marie tapped out her father's number and activated the speaker button, before setting it down on the cherry wood table.

It rang once before her father picked up.

"Hey, Dad," she called.

"Hi, honey. You all right?" The concern that flowed over in his otherwise brusque tone soothed her.

"I'm fine. It's been a while, and I know I missed a couple of calls. I wanted to check in."

"Do you have me on that speaker phone again? You know I hate that damn thing."

"Yes, sir." She switched off the speaker and pressed the phone to her ear. "Sorry. I just like you better that way. It makes me feel like you're in the room."

His voice softened to a grumble. "You know if you want to come for a visit, you're welcome any time. It's been quiet for us these last few years."

"Thanks, Dad. That's sweet but you know it's better for me this way."

She leaned in close to the polished wood table. "Maybe when you guys get back to the states I'll visit for a day. It's too unsettling to travel that far. I'd turn into a complete basket case. You know what a pain in the butt I am when that happens."

"If you'd quit being so damn stubborn and take your medication, it wouldn't be a problem."

She rolled her head from side to side. "Yeah, I know, but enough about me. How's work?"

He sighed. "Same old thing. We'll be in Rome for another few weeks, so your mother has us busy taking in the sights."

She cringed. That was code for her mother dragging him all over the country, not leaving any historical landmark unmarred.

"And what are you up to," he prompted. It was more an accusation than a question.

"Things here have been a little busy."

"Busy how? You got a boyfriend?" She gave an absent tug on the strand of pearls around her neck, sliding her thumb and index finger down the silver chain and over each iridescent gemstone.

"A little wishful thinking there?" she asked. They both knew her relationships with men were extremely predictable. Boy meets girl. Boy makes his move. Boy gets rejected. Girl leaves. End of story.

He laughed. "Well, I figured since I wasn't there to scare 'em away you might have a fair shot."

The face of Russell, her first real boyfriend pulled to the forefront of her memory, but his features blurred. For a split second, Russell's pointy features, with ears he hadn't quite grown into, morphed into the haggard sneer of a much older man. The one that haunted her memory. Pale blue eyes became dark and beady, and the golden complexion turned ruddy, and pock marked.

With a mental shudder, she pushed him back, and Russell's face bled into view again before she wiped the memory away all together.

She wrapped her arms around herself and released a heavy sigh. "No Dad, this has nothing to do with a guy. I'm taking a new job. I have to leave the condo behind for a while, so I don't want you to be alarmed if I'm not home."

"Is that what's bothering you?" he asked.

"Well, of course it bothers me but it's just a job. Why do you keep insisting that something's wrong?"

"Because you're calling me. I'm the one that calls to check in, remember? You only call when there's a problem."

"Oh," she said.

"It must be a pretty good job. I know your mother and I couldn't have gotten you to leave that place if we set fire to it. Sounds like the change would do you some good."

It didn't surprise her that he hadn't asked exactly where the job might take her. For him, location was irrelevant as long as she still carried her cell phone.

"How's Mom?" she asked.

He sighed. "Crazy as ever. You know she nearly ran down one of the locals with her Vespa this morning? I keep telling her to ease up on the gas, but you know how she is."

She smiled at the thought of her mother's lavender-tinted hair and wide grin barreling down the sidewalk at breakneck speed, her silk scarf waving behind her like a fashion-forward pirate.

"She's lucky to have you keeping her in line."

"Yeah, speaking of that, I'd better go. She's got us booked on a daylong wine tour, and she's already hitting the bottle. She'll be under the table before the train even pulls out of the station."

"All right, tell her I said 'Hi.'"

"Will do. Love you, honey."

"You, too."

When she disconnected the call, the room settled into thick silence again. She sat tapping the phone on her chin.

How did a person like her ever come from such courageous parents? There they were, taking the bull by the horns at every opportunity, and here she sat gored in the rear by not only a good-for-nothing uncle, but an absentee father too.

Not exactly the most comfortable situation, and unless she wanted the pain in her ass to become a permanent one, she needed to take control of her situation.

She ventured up the stairs to wind around corners and down long hallways. For her, moving to a new place meant even the scant amount of sleep she normally got became a thing of the past. It often took her months to find a somewhat normal sleep rhythm again, so hopefully the library could offer her some useful tool for her bedtime arsenal.

The russet stone tile flecked with copper and the complementing cream walls were a constant, making her navigation even more confusing. Luckily, all the bedrooms were located on the main hall. Easy to find her way in and out, provided she didn't go wandering too far off course. At the moment, off course seemed like a huge understatement.

Quenton made the navigation of this house seem simple as he marched down the hallway throwing out gestures this way and that like a mime on meth.

An extra hulky, extra irritated mime on meth.

Was he deliberately trying to keep Marie from snooping around?

"Yeah, like he could stop her," she grumbled. In fact, it only made her more determined to explore every inch of the place, including the study that apparently served as the Blake brother's version of Fort Knox.

She ambled around another corner and breathed a sigh of relief when she met her destination. Shelves climbed to the ceiling with history, biography, and religious literature, all covered in varying hues of yellow, brown, and gold. Only one section on the far wall stood out among the others, all lovingly bound in indigo leather.

She turned to the anomalous collection in search of her reward. The books were all duplicate copies of the same volume in varying degrees of disrepair. One book in particular had several pages dog-eared at the upper corners.

"A True Account of Greek and Roman Myth."

Tonight this book would fit perfect. One, because she found the subject matter just boring enough to whisk her away to sleepyland, and two, Tobin didn't look the part of a bookworm. She figured the creased pages were more Quenton's style—worn and cryptic to their intended purpose.

All that oh-so-inspirational advice had to come from somewhere, right?

She padded back down another staircase and

through a series of halls until she found herself back where she started. She stopped to listen at Anna's door. All was silent.

While continuing to her own room, her eyes fixed on the study at the end of the hall.

She'd seen Tobin enter the room not long after Quenton, and they'd been bellowing at each other ever since. With the amount of time they spent confined in that room, she wondered how much longer the walls were going to hold.

As she neared the door, her ears perked to the thunderous growl of Quenton's voice. She frowned. The oak panel doors were thick, but his voice carried easy.

How was anyone going to sleep in this house if they kept this up all night? It was a lame idea to send Anna to bed this early to begin with in a strange place an hour ahead of schedule. The least he could do was keep it down so she could sleep.

She marched forward with her fist raised to pound on door but paused when the room cut to silence.

Did they hear her approach?

She held her breath.

If they were talking about her, she shouldn't want to hear it, but these guys had her life over a barrel. Any information acquired on them might work to her advantage. Pushing aside her better instincts, she continued to hover at the door when their conversation struck up again.

****

"Keep your hands off." Quenton demanded.

Tobin lifted both palms in innocence and grinned at his brother. "Hey, this is all Anna's idea, not mine.

She's off my radar unless she creates unwanted attention." He let his body fall like deadweight to the oversized chair. He propped his polished Italian shoes on the ottoman. "But she's got your full attention, so why haven't you screwed her yet?"

Obviously, because I'm insane.

Back when the spunky brunette with tight curves strolled into the hospital, ripping away her coat like amateur night at the Strip and Sip, an unexpected craving wrenched him to attention. He wasn't just smitten, he was determined, already envisioning what flavor she might be. His tongue flicked over the roof of his mouth, and his pulse thrummed with the excitement of domination.

A pull like that wasn't common, even for a Muse as old as he was. He had an attraction to countless people over the ages, but this was far beyond the norm. At his first opportunity, he captured her gaze, gathering the tiny pin pricks of light from her pupils to unveil the brand of her soul. He knew that soul.

You're mine, he thought.

She'd backed away twice. After witnessing her defensiveness, he felt her level of difficulty ratchet up from tough catch, to all out conquest.

In that moment, the urge to overtake her became primal. The aching sorrow that crippled his soul pulled free. Leaving a hollow chamber that flooded with the need to reach inside her and claim what was rightfully his—to draw on her energy until she healed him completely.

The problem came when he summoned his power to tug at the barrier of her subconscious, testing her boundaries for a weak point that would allow him access.

She seemed to work through the thin mist of pleasure he'd woven over her and jerk free as if she'd been burned. Something most women were incapable of. It made him feel…cautious. An instinct he never took lightly. Bad things happened when he didn't heed to caution.

His attention turned to the decanter of scotch resting on the side table. "Not your concern."

"Meh, with all that pent-up sexual frustration? You'll tear my house apart."

"You mean *my* house?"

Tobin put his hands behind his head and searched the enormous dome fixture above his head. "Whatever. My point is, she could have stayed in any of the rooms here but instead you gave her the one with a view."

"The logistics are better. She's closer to Anna this way."

"Really? And it has nothing to do with my impeccable decorating skills?"

Quenton snorted. "Hardly."

"So I guess you won't mind if I keep the key then?"

He let the trickle of his pouring drink answer for him.

"Damn you! You already palmed it." Tobin threw his hands up. "You're torturing yourself here, man. You won't be able to keep her that close without cracking. You're not a saint!"

Quenton glared at him over the rim of his glass. "Have you always been this obnoxious? Go find yourself some cheap entertainment. Pick up one of your regular girls, or whatever it is you do. Just get the hell out of my hair."

"I'm going to need at least three of them before setting foot back in this house. You people bore me to tears."

"Yeah, you need that low hanging fruit to level the playing field for your IQ."

Tobin hoisted himself up from the chair. "You forget who you're talking to. For me, there is no fruit unreachable."

"Yeah, sometimes it pays not to have a gag reflex." Quenton muttered under his breath.

Halfway to the door Tobin spun to face Quenton. He lurched sideways to keep his balance. "Tell you what. I'll even bring you back a sweet little peach, just to show you what a good brother I am. Something to sink your teeth into. Maybe then you'll come to your senses."

He threw the study doors open with such force they slammed against the wall, then recoiled to half-closed as he left.

Chapter 5

Marie clutched the book to her chest, closed her eyes, and let the back of her head thump against the wall once. Twice.

So stupid.

When she heard Tobin's nearing footsteps, she rushed to cover as much ground from the door as possible. She veered away from her own room, fearing she'd get caught passing through the door. Instead, she hid in the shadow of an intersecting hall.

Some ninja! She mushed herself against a blank wall with nothing to hide behind. Her eggplant tank top clashed against the cream and copper surroundings. She couldn't have felt more ridiculous if she were wearing a lamp shade on her head. Luckily, Tobin was too focused on where he was headed to notice her. Or maybe he didn't care.

She leaned against the cold wall and waited until the front door clicked shut, signaling his departure.

Around the corner, Quenton's dark profile loomed in an oversized chair. The sleeves of his shirt were rolled up to expose massive forearms. His once loosened tie disappeared. He sat in silence, studying the contents of a half-empty glass held loose in his hand.

She pressed her back to the wall again. *I am so screwed.*

After a deep breath, she put her head down and

slunk into the hall, taking slow measured steps on the balls of her feet. It wasn't the sound of her steps plodding across the stone tile which worried her; it was the unavoidable *swish* of her cotton pajama bottoms. Having lost elasticity over repeated washings, they hung low on her hips, leaving a three-inch margin of bare skin above, and a puddle of fabric at her feet.

She kept her gaze on the tiles in front of her, every step cautiously placed until she reached her destination. She fisted her hand to stop its trembling, and then advanced the knob a bit at a time. The door eased open, but just as she released the handle, the latch made a prominent *click.*

"Suck!" Her body froze with an inward cringe.

The lift of surprise in Quenton's voice sounded less than genuine. "Still up?"

She lowered her head and pivoted to face him. "Oh, you caught me trying to break curfew. What can I say. I'm a rebel at heart. Don't go to bed for anyone until at least eight-thirty."

"Come. Let's talk."

She turned, anchored the book to her hip, and strolled into the room. "But this is your personal, off limits, no touchy study."

His voice edged with annoyance as he nodded to the chair angling his. "Just sit."

She plopped into the warm leather chair.

His gaze flicked to the book cradled in her lap, then returned to her as he swirled the remnants of his drink around the bottom of his glass. The smoky caramel scent that wafted from it reminded her of the type her father drank.

"You like scotch?" she asked.

"Among other things, but tonight it fits the bill."

She opened the cover of the book and let it fall closed again. "Hard liquor and Greek mythology. Sounds like a party."

His broad chest jumped with a quiet snort as he tipped the glass to his lips. Silence stretched out between them as the book cover lifted and fell. Lifted and fell. Some ice breaker. The thing wasn't even worth its weight in confetti.

He leaned forward and something in his tone eased. "You surprised me at the hospital. I didn't expect that you would be…."

She raised her chin to face his shadowed features. "What?"

"Anna's nanny."

"Were you expecting some seventy-year-old broad with bifocals and a hunch on her back?"

"Actually, I was."

"Yeah, me, too."

"We didn't start off under the best circumstances."

"It's all good," she said, looking down at her necklace. "Water under the bridge."

He raised a dark brow. "Think so?"

She looked up. Her fingers still busy coiling and uncoiling the delicate chain around her neck.

"Yeah. Sure. Why?"

The faintest smile tugged at the corner of his mouth. "Because I'm still making you feel uncomfortable. We can't have that…"

"Don't flatter yourself. I'm fine."

"I have no doubt you will be, but until we leave here, your stay needs to be comfortable."

Her spine went rigid. "*We* leave here?"

"Yes. You included."

"We've been through this discussion before. Do *we* really need a refresher?"

His wrist continued its fluid rotation without pause, giving her the urge to pop the bottom of his glass with the heel of her hand.

"Maybe *we* do, because you still seem to think you have a choice," he said.

"The hell I don't!"

He flashed a patronizing grin. "Tell me, Marie, are you sitting in that chair by choice?"

Her jaw clenched, as the painful reminder of her decision to become the Nan-word gave her a mental noogie. She wasn't here out of convenience. She sat here because she'd been forced to stay in order to maintain a place in Anna's life.

Her mouth fired back without a hint of brain power. "You aren't really that conceited are you? To think I'll just follow you blindly wherever you go?"

Through the shadows she detected a smoldering challenge in his eyes.

"Without a doubt."

The defiant stiffness in her spine fizzled. He'd probably be delighted to force her into accepting the inevitable, and she had a feeling this battle wouldn't end in her favor.

But why? Her job carried an ample supply of little manipulators who excelled at pulling heartstrings. Yet, she successfully evaded them from day one. She even formed immunity to her own parents. They spoon fed her guilt for a solid month, trying to convince her to join them on yet another jaunt across the globe.

Once she set her mind on something, she knew her

decision couldn't be swayed. What sequence of events could have caused her defenses to buckle this time?

Marie skimmed through her memory until Anna's image materialized. Oh. Yeah. One golden-haired, knee-high princess managed to tear through her barricade with ease and left the gaping hole vulnerable to attack.

Anna's tender-eyed plea for her to attend, and that stupid blog entry lured her to the performance at the Governor's Ball. To an evening of torture by candlelight at the hands of Colorado's elite, and the suck-up, self-proclaimed stud muffin of an uncle.

Well, I guess we know where Anna gets it. She is but the student, and Quenton, the master.

Childcare options were easy to come by in this small town, not to mention the infinite supply he could find elsewhere. Why was he so determined about getting her to accompany him? Secretly, she felt flattered that he had value in her. A large part of her didn't want to dilute that, but this was all coming at her too fast.

She couldn't leave, not for some guy she barely knew. No matter how compelling. On the other hand, she couldn't see her life without Anna in it.

"Why do you suddenly want a part in Anna's life? Why do you want to take her away?" she asked.

His eyes narrowed to match the edge in his voice. "There's nothing sudden about it. I've always wanted a part in her life."

"Well, then why—"

"—it was Christie's wish to keep me out of the picture, not mine. She didn't want Anna to grow up with my lifestyle."

She sat back in her chair. "Children need stability, that's true. And even as resilient as Anna is, the constant moving would take its toll."

He tipped the glass to his lips but pulled it away again. "That's why we have you. You help her adjust, make her comfortable. You're a priceless resource for Anna. And me. Don't think I don't know that."

She shook her head. "Look, I don't want to say you've picked the wrong person for this job—"

"Then don't."

She threw her hands in the air and surveyed the room. "But you don't need to drag her all over the world. Why not keep her here? You have a beautiful home."

The molasses-colored upholstery and mahogany tables made the study feel comfortable and well-worn, with the exception of two doors sitting side-by-side. She could tell by the glossy finish on the wood, that they weren't part of the original construction.

"It's not suitable for Anna to stay here long term. Tobin's taken the liberty of fixing the place up—if you call this fixing. He's turning this place into his personal circus."

She smirked. "Well that explains the scouting for women with caked-on makeup and cherry red lips. So how many *can* he fit into his car at one time?"

Pressing his fist just under his nose, he cleared his throat. "About the women…."

She rolled her eyes. "No. Really. I get it. He's an eligible bachelor. He has a reputation to uphold for his fellow man."

"That's quite a pigeonhole you've—"

"What I'd like to know, is where's he going to put

the bearded one? I'm sure he'd want one of those, too. I mean, you've got to complete the collection."

"Marie." He gave her a dark frown.

"Oh, do you have a tower? Maybe he could keep her there! Then she could grow her beard *really* long and he could pretend to—"

"Enough!" he yelled.

She jumped back in her seat, and snapped her mouth closed.

"Don't try calling him out, even in front of me. You're a fundamental influence on the way Anna views this family, and I won't let you disrespect anyone in it."

Brushing off the nervous energy that scampered through her stomach, she folded her arms. "Boy, this takes me back. I haven't had a lecture like this in years. Makes me feel all nostalgic inside."

"Doesn't surprise me." He looked to her exposed navel, and the contour of her breasts. "You look like you were a handful."

"And you were a perfect angel, right?"

He splayed a brilliant smile before taking a deep swallow from his glass. "Nope. Nannies tremble at the sound of my name."

As if this one didn't? Her cheeks warmed. "Good thing I'm not *your* Nanny."

The sultry promise that lit his emerald eyes caused her heart to quicken.

"That depends on the perspective," he said.

She found it difficult to swallow when her line of sight trailed from masculine features to the frame of his open shirt. The faint dusting of hair that crept into view left her wondering just how far it traveled beyond her line of sight. His personality may be abrasive, but she had a feeling his skin would be something more like velvet over stone.

"So we have something in common. We're both troublemakers," she said.

He canted his head. "No. There's one fundamental difference between the two of us."

"And that would be?"

"Deception."

She pulled her brows together.

"I already have a handle on you, but you have no idea what kind of trouble I can cause," he explained.

He had her there. Reading people wasn't one of her strong points. She didn't do subtlety. In fact, it really got on her nerves. True intensions always shine through eventually, and it felt pointless to waste time erecting a giant masquerade, just to tear it away later.

That's why she loved working with children. The ways of the world hadn't corrupted them into hiding their identity. Of course, the mid-afternoon nap felt like a godsend for someone who never slept through the night.

She fought to keep her voice from sounding slighted. "You think you have me pegged that quick? How much could you possibly know? Apart from what I've already told you."

"Everything."

She tipped her head to the side, sending loose curls cascading over her shoulder. "Is that a challenge?"

His eyes glittered with amusement. "I wouldn't *dare* challenge you."

"I think you just did." She slid forward to perch on the end of the chair. "All right, bring it."

"One request." The amber lamp light spilled over

him, as he leaned forward. So close that their noses nearly touched. She forced herself to breathe in more slowly as that overwhelming scent swirled around her.

"Depends on the request," she said.

Her skin flushed under the feel of his fingertips caressing her chin, tipping her face up to meet his.

"Don't look away," he said.

Her heart jumped when Quenton fixed his eyes on hers. Staring into him unleashed an intoxicating sensation that overtook all her other thoughts. She savored the feeling of contentment that fell over her, even as her head began to spin. Her body pulled forward.

He parried her forward motion by easing away to deter any physical touch. His voice sounded cool and unaffected. "You thrive in an environment of your own creation. You're vibrant and imaginative…." His voice trailed off as she felt herself slip away into subconscious thought.

****

It took a fraction of a second to ensnare her attention. This time he only allowed the barest thread of his natural sedative to seep out. Soon her eyes were transfixed.

With little time to waste, he seized his opportunity.

His soul filtered out from his own body to pluck at her mind until the fabric of her subconscious gave way. Not large enough for him to pass through, just enough to push his voice inside.

"Let me in, Marie."

He had to find out what made her tick beyond the simple brand that he could read in her eyes. If he could just get close enough to reach her, he could find what she needed from him. They all craved something, and they always looked to him for it.

It gave him a rush to stalk through the dark labyrinth of their subconscious, wiping out thick bands of inhibitions, and leading them into uncharted territory. To keep this civic duty interesting, he often wiped away a little extra purely for his own entertainment. A simple task and one he was happy to fulfill, because they always came back for more, offering their endless supply of spiritual energy at the same time.

He knew the thread of pleasure he spun over her senses carried an intoxicating effect. It was impossible to resist, and the moment any human had a taste of it, they were hooked. This being her second dose, the odds that she would continue to come away unscathed were rapidly decreasing.

He waited for several minutes, but he could find no ripple of movement along the barrier of her mind. She wasn't coming. The reaction on the outside seemed obvious, with her practically falling into his lap, but he couldn't reach her soul without force.

He pushed out an exasperated sigh and dropped the magnetic hold on her then tore his spirit free.

Her mouth dropped open, and she sucked in a deep breath. She blinked.

He pretended not to notice. "You also get your feelings hurt easily. You have a brutal stubborn streak and you're a tad mouthy."

Her voice wavered. "As if that last one wasn't already obvious."

He leaned back in his chair with his arms crossed. "So how was that?"

She brushed the bangs from her forehead with a shaking hand. "Honestly? A little unsettling."

He snorted. "Unsettling, huh?" He downed the rest of his drink with one large gulp.

****

A racket from the hallway caught their attention. Marie didn't hear the front door open, but the clack of heels on the stone tile echoed through the entire house. Two women appeared, fresh off the runway with low-cut dresses draped over sculpted bodies. One a platinum blonde, the other a warm-honey brown. Tobin sandwiched between them.

When the trio entered, she got hit with a sickening-sweet fragrance, and Tobin's sneer. "What are you doing keeping *her* up so late?" he asked.

Tobin motioned to the women with a sweep of his hand. "Trixie, Roxanne, this is Sister Marie. She is our new Nanny and part-time apostolate."

Roxanne flung a tendril of brown hair behind her shoulder. "Aposta-what? Is that some kind of Italian food?"

Tobin released an impatient sigh, and then made a vague gesture with his hands. "You know she's like religious and stuff."

Marie ignored Quenton's puzzled expression. No use explaining that comment. Long story, short on patience. She shot Tobin a glare.

When she rose to her feet, she realized the book in her lap had vanished. She scanned her immediate surroundings, and then rounded her attention to Quenton. "Did you take my book?"

The moment the words were out of her mouth the realization hit. He must have kept her distracted so he could reclaim the book. Irritation bubbled inside her until her blood ran hot.

She wasn't sure whether the silent curse she uttered was for her or him, probably both. She moved to search the area around his chair but didn't get far with Roxie blocking her path.

She looked down her nose at Marie, as though at any moment the claws would come out, and the fur would start to fly.

Fortunately for Marie, Tobin's remark stoked her temper enough to overshadow the threat. With Quenton's tongue lashing about "respect" conveniently forgotten, and her new title as part-time aposta-whatever, she couldn't resist putting on a convincing show.

She clicked her tongue at the two girls in disappointment. "Well, I can see I have a couple of extra souls to pray for tonight! And what on earth happened to your clothes? You must be freezing! Honey let me get you a jacket. Its autumn, you know. Tobin, you need to take better care of your guests."

Tobin slid into Marie's vacant chair and pulled Trixie down to straddle him. She let out a startled squeal.

"Don't worry your little head," he said, looking into Trixie's eyes. "I'm going to take good care of them."

Marie tried not to gag when she heard Trixie's muffled giggle pressed to the curve of Tobin's neck. Apparently she liked to put on a show, too.

She crossed herself and gave a disgruntled huff. "Poor Tobin. Son, you still haven't figured out that you can't be God's gift to women if you have to buy them outright. And you really should take her out of your mouth, dear; you don't know where she's been."

The two women turned to Marie with a deadly gleam in their eyes.

Her attention made a quick shift to Quenton, but his tensing posture caused her throat to constrict, and her gaze fled from him the moment their eyes met.

Tobin snapped his fingers in front of Trixie's nose. "Over here" he called, with an overlay of mild irritation. When she continued the undulating, back and forth motion in his lap, his tone lightened. "Not just God's gift. As far as these women are concerned, I *am* a God."

She snorted but the two women made no reply.

Tobin paused. His attention snapped to the ceiling in a mock epiphany and he slapped the arm of the chair. "Oh my *self*! Does this mean you've devoted your whole life just to worship me? How fortunate!" He checked his watch. "But you'll have to wait in line 'cause I won't be through with these two until at least tomorrow afternoon."

Quenton's glass crashed down on the side table with enough force to shatter it. Tiny shards of glass flew out in every direction.

Both of Tobin's women let out a startled cry, and she stood frozen in shock.

"Now, don't be so sullen, Quentie," Tobin chided, as he pulled Trixie back to the crook of his neck. He nodded to the woman left standing. "Here. I've brought a tasty little snack to cheer you up. So be a good host and offer this sinfully talented woman your attention."

The woman looked to Quenton, to the broken glass, then back to Tobin.

Marie raised her brow. *Sinfully talented? She's not even skilled enough to think for herself.*

Quenton threw his head back, gritting his teeth. "Get lost Tobin. Now."

"I'm sorry. Does this bother you?" He ran his fingers down the woman's bare spine and thrust his hand into the backless dress to grab her ass.

Marie could tell from Quenton's deadly expression he was about to erupt. He worked his jaw back and forth as if grinding over bone.

Being bested by the conceited Casanova and his "two for one" special, she was in no mood to witness yet another rousing game of *Family Feud*. She decided to leave the room but not without the last word.

"You know Tobin's right. I'm really not much of a night owl. I think I'm going to go."

"Marie—"

She cut Quenton off, batting her lashes at the two women. "It's really great to meet you two." *Or not.* "And I'm glad you're here. It gives those poor farm animals out back some peace and quiet for one evening."

Quenton jumped to his feet before Tobin could unseat the woman on his lap.

"All right, let's go." He grabbed her by the wrist and tugged her from the room.

She bubbled over with glee on the inside, but her outside remained all innocence. "And, Quenton? Maybe we could continue our discussion tomorrow?"

"You got it."

She slipped him an impish grin as she neared her bedroom door. "Have a good evening with your she-clowns. If they offer you a handkerchief…run."

"There goes that mouth again."
She glared at him. *Jerk.*

Chapter 6

Marie took a long shower in attempt to clear her head but thoughts of Quenton persisted. The scent of wild orchid soap infusing the steam around her did little, except leave the room stifling and uncomfortable.

She'd been around enough men to know the power he possessed was something more than ordinary. He sent her away someplace inside her mind that she'd never been. Some astoundingly tangible dream-like state where she felt herself drift free from the physical limitations.

Only the dream wasn't hers. She wasn't in control. He was. Losing her hold on reality was one thing she could never allow. She just didn't function that way. She even refused to take medication aside from the half dose of Advil here and there for pain; because she hated the way it clouded her control.

She pulled on a thin cotton tank top and matching pants, and combed through her damp hair, which dripped down to cool her shoulders. She crossed the room to the single window and opened it wide, hoping to catch the cold evening breeze.

A mass of singing insects greeted her as she peered into the darkness. Her memory rounded again to the conversation between Tobin and Quenton. They called this the "room with a view," but the moonlight provided enough evidence to see the view was far from breathtaking. Just a faded lawn segmented by a winding dirt path. The mountain backdrop was obscured by the rest of the house and the tall pines framing the lawn. There weren't any x-ray specs on the pillow at turn down, so beyond pure sarcasm there wasn't any reason to call this a good view.

The dirt path had potential though. It snaked along the rolling landscape and disappeared behind a moderate slope. She made a mental note to wake extra early for a little exploration before her appointment with Quenton. Unless he didn't take her invitation seriously.

Her attention flew to a dark shadow creeping along the side of the house. The muscles in her chest constricted with surprise. She watched it move across the grass. It advanced in complete silence, as though its feet never touched the ground. With the broad shoulders of a man, her first thought was of Quenton, but why would he lurk outside in the dark? He moved past the light cast down from her window, and her suspicions were confirmed.

She backed away from his line of sight, hoping he hadn't already noticed her. When she found the courage to lean out and search the perimeter again, she caught sight of him slipping into a side door.

Quenton was right; she couldn't read him very well at all. She'd watched him run through a full spectrum of emotions tonight. From casual to flirtatious to threatening homicide. He slid from one to the next, and back again before she could blink. He always kept her guessing.

Whatever the case, she found him to be a valuable ally in the war against Tobin. Aside from one awkward hand-napping and a lecture that turned her to a shrinking violet, she was actually starting to admire the big thug.

She spun away from the window. "Wait a minute. What am I saying? The only reason he approached me tonight was to get the book. I can't go gaga over some guy because he read *Hypnotism for the Dummy* and memorized this morning's horoscopes. I mean jeez, how desperate am I?"

"Hummm let's see" she murmured, feigning her best gypsy accent. She held up her palm and traced its branching lines with her index finger.

"This is your love line." She *tsked*. "Woefully inadequate."

"Ah and here is your life li—" She peered closer. "Wait! Where did it go? Oh, I guess you don't have one of those."

She wound through the room in an aimless pattern as she stared into her hand. "Yep. Uh-huh. Here it is. You see this line? This is your *moron line*. Surprisingly long for someone your age."

Given her brief encounter with him, why did she keep having this obnoxious compulsion to take him at face value? Although the book *was* technically his to begin with, he stole it from her, and from his conversation with Tobin, he obviously had something to hide. Nothing about him said trustworthy.

When she looked up from her hand, she found her reflection in the massive mirror. Due to her running shoe-clad therapy sessions, her five-four frame was toned with just a little curve in most of the right places. She turned this way and that. Admiring how the cotton top clung to her damp skin.

She couldn't flaunt her figure, but she had enough to consider herself appealing. The two women left in Tobin's study were certainly more expressive with their wardrobe than she could ever be, and she had to admit their appearances demanded attention.

But not Quenton's attention.

When his brother offered one of them on a silver platter, seasoned to taste with an entire bottle of perfume, he didn't even notice. Instead, he chose to sneak around outside the house collecting eye of newt, or whatever he was up to. If he wasn't attracted to that clowny kind of woman, then what kind did he like? What kind of female fascinated him? She pulled the plunging neckline of her top lower to reveal a fair amount of cleavage and smiled in the mirror.

It might be kind of fun to look into that.

She spun away and shook her head, half expecting to hear something loose rattle around in her brain. She plopped down on her bed and snapped off the side table lamp. "I think I better sign myself up for a CT scan."

It was getting late and her mind was wandering to ideas she shouldn't entertain. She just met the guy, and Quenton was Anna's father! They couldn't be more than friends. For her own hormonal preservation, she had to stop trying to convince herself he was a good guy. Start considering how bad it would blow if any potential relationship with him went sour.

Anna came first, not her hormone-laden fantasies, and even if he did seem larger than life, he was still a flesh and blood man. No more. No less.

She tossed and turned, seeking out a position where she could force herself to sleep. Damp hair stuck to the back of her neck and face. She flicked it away with an impatient brush of her hand, only to have it flop forward again.

She threw back the covers and stomped off to the bathroom in search of a hair clip. Once she had her tangled mane fastened securely, she laid back down again, only to sit up in bed a moment later with a growl.

Argg! Forgot to brush the teeth.

She threw off the covers yet again and traced back to the bathroom. "Sure. Why not add a big dollop of obsessive-compulsive disorder? The perfect finishing touch to the steaming pile of crap that is my life."

After brushing, flossing and rinsing for good measure, she shuffled half-way to bed, then whirled for the bathroom again.

Face cream. Hand cream… Cream of OCD, right here!

Deep down, she knew it wasn't her repetitive nocturnal habits that frustrated her, but the way she worked so hard to maintain only a simple appearance.

Her thoughts went back to the two women, who were no doubt waist deep in the throes of passion by now. They couldn't possibly need all this to look good. Even through their caked-on makeup she could tell they were naturally stunning. Put them in some old tattered drapes and dump a bucket of water on them, they could still turn heads.

Although, she wouldn't mind giving it a try just to be sure.

****

After nearly twenty minutes of pacing like a caged animal in his bedroom, the wild moans of his brother's slutty companions had filtered through the walls. Spiny pricks of rage had needled at his temper until he nearly ripped the door from its hinges. He barreled through the study and down the hall. He had to get out.

His angry strides had crossed the length of the hall with his focus set on the front door. A long drive might help to clear his head, and he planned to keep on driving until he could think straight again.

As he passed Marie's room however, his pace had slowed and thoughts of her diverted his path. He continued down the hall, and out the front door, but changed course, quietly advancing the length of the house until he came upon the side door.

Marie had slipped away for the second time in so many hours which felt both infuriating and powerfully enticing. He didn't want her to run off, but the only thing keeping her here was his daughter, not him.

Agreeing to live under this roof meant a big adjustment in the near future. It seemed best for her to take everything in a bit at a time. She didn't need any more reason to fear him.

The thought of her running scared made the muscles between his shoulders knot. He wanted her always as open and eager as she had been tonight.

A slow smile crept across his face at the memory of her staring at his open shirt.

He passed through the weighted door on the exterior of the house, plunging into the darkness. Quenton stood in a stone cell surrounded by the smell of mildew. Strange how such an uninviting place offered more contentment than any other room in the house.

The remaining distance to the other side of her two-way mirror became an internal struggle.

She deserved her privacy and his trust. He worked

his way up the chiseled steps. Slick stone walls flanked either side, but he didn't bother sticking close to them. With eyesight as powerful as his, he didn't need to use his sense of touch.

She isn't hiding anything, and even if she were, her own thoughts and actions are none of my business.

Sound reasoning, yet he continued to advance a few steps more. He reached the top of the staircase that fed to a long hallway.

Even with as open as she seemed in tonight's conversation, she still wasn't going to reveal everything, but he wanted everything: mind, body, and soul. This would be the safest way to feed his curiosity and maintain a safe distance. He knew it was wrong.

But I've already come this far….

His path dead-ended at a barren cell lit by the glow from her side of the mirror, the only separation between this room and Marie's.

The moment he caught sight of her, he froze in place. Her playful character and candid discussion with the mirror fascinated him. Even now, as he watched over her sleeping silhouette, he felt unable to pull himself away.

His eyes roved over the curves of her body, draped in nothing more than a pair of thin pajamas. Curled up in a ball, she shivered from the loss of the blankets she punted off the bed hours ago.

That bed looked far too large and uncomfortable for her. She needed something cozier, like his bed. With him in it.

A husky groan, one too real to be his imagination, pulled him back to reality.

The last pillow on Marie's bed slumped to the floor

when she turned to the side. Her movements seemed less frustrated now, more…pleasurable.

A second, prolonged groan brought all thoughts to an abrupt halt. His ears primed and a throbbing heat flowing to his groin.

Dreaming, finally. Apparently the erotic kind you'd kill your alarm clock over.

He should be a good host and retrieve the pillow for her. She wouldn't sleep long without it, and given the chance she did wake up, he'd be more than happy to lead her back into those fantasies.

He gave himself a mental shake. *No, bad idea.* He still couldn't get a handle on her tolerance level and wasn't willing to risk feeding her too much of his sedative. She'd already consumed her fair share for one day. For tonight she'd go without his intervention, however difficult that may be.

But only for tonight.

Chapter 7

Marie's footsteps punched out a quick, gritty tempo. She packed down her fatigue in every step. The fringe of tall grass brushed her legs as it bent and swayed in a crisp autumn breeze.

Her pulse drummed pain into her temple with every beat. The end result of seven hours spent tossing and turning while her mind played keep away with dreams of large, mysterious men in impenetrable sunglasses. And nothing else.

The two aspirin and three cups of sugared coffee hadn't taken effect, but they would…any minute now.

She followed the trail along a dry ravine for about three miles, until her path abruptly dead-ended at an old wooden bench.

The two wide slats that made up the bench seat were ten inches thick and grayed with age. The surface cracked and split over time but the iron spikes holding it together looked sturdy enough to last another ten years. It must have seen its fair share of use, she guessed, because its location offered a rare, unobstructed view of the morning sunrise.

When the full circumference of the clearing came into view, she spotted Quenton and her feet faltered to a gradual stop.

He emerged from the surrounding trees and approached with purposeful strides that carried him soundlessly across the clearing. A look of irritation tugging the corners of his mouth proved he wasn't expecting to see her either.

"Funny, you don't look like much of a Marine," he said. His gaze trailed over the emblem printed on her chest.

Her father often told her it was a symbol to wear with pride, and he believed she'd been through more than enough to earn it. But with the look on Quenton's face, it may as well have said "Pink" or "Juicy."

Or "Screw Me."

Her voice quivered with nervous energy. "What are you doing out here?"

"Bird watching."

She didn't have to be proficient at reading people to know he lied. He didn't look like the bird watching type with those massive shoulders and labor-callused hands. Any chickadee in a three-mile radius would drop dead from fright.

"No, seriously. What are you up to?"

"How did you sleep?" he asked, changing the subject.

"Oh, like a rock." She could play the evasion game, too. "How about you?"

"It was a rough night."

She shrugged. "You play, you pay." Her feeble attempt to brush off last evening's entertainment was short lived, given the surprise in his raised brows.

"Oh, not me. Tobin likes to go all night, and with my room next to his, the noise carries easily," he said.

The image those words brought to mind made her cringe. *Did he really have to use the term "go all night?"*

He nodded to the small receiver clamped to her waistband. "What's that?"

"Baby monitor."

He frowned. "She's not a baby."

"She still needs to be monitored."

He started toward the bench and motioned for her to join him. "What makes you think that cheap contraption will work clear out here."

She studied the matchbox sized speaker. "Best one on the market. It covers up to three miles."

"You're at four-and-a-half."

"Well…I guess I should be going then."

He waved the suggestion away. "Anna's fine. Tobin's watching out for her."

"Oh, I feel *so* much better." She turned back for the trail,

His voice hardened. "He's her uncle. You may not like him, but you can trust him."

"I don't thin—"

"Didn't ask you to think. I'm telling you she's fine. Sit." He motioned to the bench again. "Tell me about yourself."

She half covered her mouth in feigned surprise. "You mean there's something you don't already know?" Her attempt for sarcasm didn't fly far.

His brisk tone smoothed with a low chuckle. "Humor me."

She took a seat and closed her eyes for a moment to compose herself. Being in such close proximity turned her into a tightly coiled ball of nerves. She cleared her throat. "Well, I like to make dramatic entrances in hospital rooms. Apparently I have missed my calling to a religious lifestyle, and I'm gainfully employed to work with children for a living."

His lips twitched. "Try again."

She sighed in mock-defeat and turned to face the pale gray sky. The strewn clouds were just beginning to take on a rosy hue.

"I love coming out to catch the sunrise. It's like witnessing the rest of the world come alive."

She cast a tentative glance in his direction.

Amusement tugged at the corners of his eyes. "You're serious?"

"Sounds pretty lame when I say it out loud."

"Very optimistic." He gave her a reassuring pat on the knee, which surprisingly enough, had the opposite effect. Her hands became shaky, and her palms pricked with moisture. She gripped the edges of the bench until her palms burned and forced her attention back to the rising sun.

"And I'm a glutton for early morning exercise," she said.

"You like to walk then?"

"I like to *run*."

"Of course, you do. Feel the wind in your hair."

She nodded. "Well, that. And I figure if I ever come across some stranger with a thirst for blood, I'd like to outrun him."

He cocked his head to the side. "Wait. Did you just say you'd like to be chased?"

"No! That's *not* what I said."

"I have to admit that's something I didn't know."

"But that's not what I meant."

"What did you mean?"

She threw her hands up. "It's a self-defense tactic. The best way to escape your attacker is not to fight, but to run."

He snorted. "You couldn't outrun me."

She raised her brow. "Yet another challenge? This one won't be as easy as last night's."

"Well, see how confidant you are once I chase you down."

She flushed at the mental image of him hunting her down like a wild animal, his gaze penetrating and feral. She stole a quick glance at the large bands of muscle in his thighs. No, she didn't think she could outrun him, and she would no doubt be powerless to try.

"Speaking of chasing, how long have you known Tobin?" he asked.

She looked up. Surprised at his abrupt change in subject. His face remained a mask of calm and control.

"I only met him on the night of the accident. At the Governor's ball. I wasn't there for the politics. Christy had negotiated a performance with Anna's Ballet class. I was there for Christy and Anna."

"Yeah?"

"Yes." She drew the word out expectantly. Was it really so surprising she'd have a life after the center's closing hours? Okay, maybe she didn't, but it's completely beside the point.

"Tobin show you a good time?"

She clenched her jaw. "How's that any of your business?"

His tone was level and expressionless. "You're my employee. It's important for me to know if you have a history with my brother."

"Well, I don't, okay? He made some lewd comment that night, about having a wicked vice for teasing pretty girls. He begged me to "save him" with a little candle-lit confession at his place. Apparently, he has a thing for hot wax? I don't know...." She knew she was rambling. Keeping up the conversation gave her no time to focus him, or the chaos he caused on her heart rate.

"So I told him I left my crucifix at home, and unceremoniously blessed my drink before throwing it in his face."

He nodded. "That's my girl."

Hardly, she thought as another unexpected flush colored her cheeks. "I feel kinda bad about it really." She used a polished nail to toy with the frayed edge of the bench. "One, because I'm not even Catholic. I hope I didn't unintentionally commit some kind of grave sin. And two, because I wished I had something more potent than water in that glass."

She looked up from the bench to his chiseled profile, and her breath hitched in her throat. The glow of the morning sun cast light across his rugged features. He appeared almost angelic, which fell in stark contrast to his sultry green eyes, coaxing her closer with every beat of his dark lashes.

She wasn't sure why she let her hand veer off course to reach for the curve of his face. But when his line of sight shifted, her heart leapt into overdrive.

What am I doing?!

She forced her gaze back to the horizon, and her hand once again clamped onto the bench, biting into the wood. *No touchy remember?*

She felt him still smiling down at her but refused to look in his direction.

He snorted. "You were saying?"

"I was?"

"About the ball?"

"Yes. As soon as Tobin and I met, it was obvious I wasn't his biggest fan, and I'm pretty sure after the water incident, the feeling became mutual."

He nodded slowly. It seemed more a gesture of acceptance than understanding.

"It was like pulling teeth to get this job. I honestly didn't think he'd give me a chance. Not that I'm incapable." She rushed to assure him.

"Tobin's protective."

"Protective? You're kidding right?" She could easily imagine Tobin as a pretentious prick, but *protective*? That one threw her.

"Protective of his family. He knows we're the one connection in his life that will last. He hates when outsiders influence his family ties."

His voice shifted to the same cautious tone from the night before. "That feeling you get when he's around? Listen to it. Don't mistake it for excitement. And be careful…not to push him."

The last four words were dealt slowly as if to ensure she understood their full weight.

She frowned. "You mentioned that last night."

"It bears repeating."

From her heated confrontation with Tobin before leaving the hospital, she already considered him a force she didn't want to reckon with. Quenton's warning only validated that he was capable of much more than idle threats.

She dipped her head and brushed her fingertips across her temple, sweeping her bangs to the side, and shielding her embarrassment.

It had been years since someone put her in her

place. Quenton may have tried to do it with an air of compassion, but the fact still remained that she'd just been scolded—twice now—by the most attractive man in Sterling Springs. She stared down at the bench, wishing it would open up and swallow her whole. She pushed out an exaggerated breath. "All right!"

He laughed. "That's cute. You and Anna have the same expression when you get in trouble."

And there it was. Marie's perfect excuse to escape from this awkward situation.

"Oh, that reminds me, I've gotta get back!" She jumped to her feet. He followed her lead.

He looked to the monitor on her hip. "Anna won't come around for a couple more hours. What's your hurry?"

"Oh, I still have to get ready before she wakes up."

"For two hours?"

She stared.

"You mean you spend *two hours* getting ready every day?" He rocked back on his heels. "You're surprisingly high maintenance. These little tidbits just keep on coming, don't they?"

"I am not. Just because I take care of myself doesn't mean I'm high maintenance."

His smile never wavered. "Sorry if I struck a chord there. I think it's great you try to enhance your appearance with all the exercise and the primping. And it's inspiring that you can sacrifice half your life to do it."

"Really?" she drawled.

"In fact, I think you've inspired me to do a little maintenance myself."

"What's there to maintain? I think you're looking

pretty fine on your own."

She snapped her mouth closed. *Just said that. I just said that!* And from the look on his face, he hadn't missed it.

"Actually, I was thinking about a morning run tomorrow. Do you think you could keep up?" he asked.

Her eyes narrowed with mischief. "Hmmm…a duel of the feet at oh-dark-hundred? You're on!"

"Before you go, here." He pulled the phone from his front pocket and handed it to her. She turned it end over end, feeling the warm weight of it in her hand and thumbing the corner where she'd marred it with nail polish. The gouge where she'd dropped it on the cement, all of it gone. It looked brand new. "Thanks. I—"

"You owe me one. I know."

****

Marie left him at the old bench and raced for the house. A seductive grin curved Quenton's lips as he watched her go. His gaze followed the hypnotic sway of her ponytail, down the taunting curve of her back, to rest on the tight ass that switched back and forth with each stride she took. All of those motions fused in perfect harmony, begging him to follow.

He tossed his head back in frustration. It would be a long couple of weeks cooped up in a house with that woman. She'd put up quite a fight, and Tobin would expect him to keep her in line. It was a delicate balance to maintain, getting close enough to gain her trust without losing his resolve.

She faded into the distance. The sun spilled over the mountain top and directly into his eyes. When the light made first contact he sucked in a cold breath at the searing pain.

He whipped out his sunglasses, slid them into place, and retraced his steps into the shadowed forest.

Mindful of dead branches and fallen leaves, he moved slow and silent, winding around jagged rocks and tall pines with his ears primed for any unusual disturbance.

The insects hummed, and the sporadic rustle of underbrush meant the smaller forest inhabitants continued their business unfazed. Overhead, large fox squirrels scampered up and down tree branches, chirping and whistling to each other, grooming their ashy-brown coats.

He followed a network of narrow deer trails for over five miles until he came upon the prints. They were long impressions barely perceptible in a bed of pine needles. He bent down and traced two fingers over the narrow footprint. *Human—or was human before the Shade took it over.*

He pinched a few pine needles and held them under his nose. The sharp smell of decay told him the body couldn't be more than a few days old.

Did Tobin know they were venturing this close so early in the season?

He followed the tracks for another mile, but their course continued uninterrupted.

One set of prints. Only one.

Was it safe to assume the Shades weren't desperate enough to squabble over the single body? Or did the Shade inhabiting it possess too much superiority to risk a challenge? He looked up at the irregular jigsaw of pale blue sky and towering trees. He searched for an answer.

The being who took down his ex-wife must have been powerful, and if it found any indication of Anna's potential as a Muse, it would come after her.

He'd been hunting those roaches from hell for as long as he could remember, and that was a damn long time. He had no doubt they'd stick to their old routine. With the days getting shorter, they'd be seeking out more of their "food source," for lack of a better word. Their numbers would increase as they migrated south to warmer climates.

Time was already running short. He had to draw out this Shade before he became outnumbered. The only effective way to do that was with bait.

Marie wouldn't be safe running around out here on her own, unguarded and unable to defend herself. He didn't like the idea of putting her in harm's way. Not on any level. But he needed her to create the temptation.

If he could stake one of Tobin's bimbos to the ground out here he would, but the Shades didn't work that way. They liked the hunt. No other way around it. Using Marie was the fastest way to complete this mission and keep his family safe.

Chapter 8

Late the next evening, Marie slumped on Anna's floor like one of Anna's plush toys who'd lost all her stuffing. She smoothed moisture from her forehead with the back of her hand.

"You, go here." Anna crammed an orange, stuffed cat on the shelf beside the bed. It tipped forward from the bulk of stuffed animals consuming the space and cartwheeled to the floor the moment Anna released it.

Marie climbed to her feet. "Here. We'll put it higher." She could feel the weight of Anna's stare as she stepped back to admire her handiwork. "There. Better?"

"Where's mommy?"

The warmth drained from her face and her heart rate quickened. "She's…in heaven, Anna."

"She come back?"

Marie tented her brows in sympathy. "I'm sorry, Princess. She's not."

Anna seemed to consider her words as her motions slowed and she turned back for the box of toys. This new environment wouldn't be easy for any of them.

The unsettling ache in the pit of Marie's stomach grew with every box she unloaded. Doubt crept in from all sides about whether she'd made the right decision coming here.

It shouldn't matter if she was in Colorado or not.

Away from home was away from home, regardless of the distance. And how could any place be worse than this one?

High-class living aside, she couldn't get passed the thought that she slept—or tried to sleep down the hall from the most repulsive human beings she ever met. Okay, only one of them was repulsive, but one was more than enough.

Tobin couldn't hide his casual relationships forever. The man was too careless for that. Sooner or later Anna would see it. Marie didn't think she could stomach the questions the little girl might pose.

How could she paint Tobin in a favorable light, and deny her distaste for him? Even for Anna's sake?

For as much as he wanted her to trust Tobin, Quenton wasn't putting on a very convincing show. He seemed to gauge every movement Tobin made. Like he didn't trust him either. Odd how all that glowering over them actually put her at ease. Having some muscle in her corner worked to her advantage.

Anna moved to the next box.

"Who knew such a little girl could accumulate so much stuff?" she moaned.

Anna went up on her toes to reach into a three-foot moving box filled to the brim with more animals.

"Not little," she snapped.

She blinked. "Anna, the attitude needs some work."

Anna grabbed stuffed animals by the fistful and threw them over her head to rain down behind her back like oversized tufts of cotton candy.

"*You* work." She shot back.

Marie's hands went to her hips. "Don't talk that

way, or you'll find yourself in time out. Is that what you want?"

Anna ignored her and strained to reach the inside of the box. She watched as a startled squeal erupted, and Anna tipped into it headfirst. Her legs kicked out in a wild panic. She could scarcely hide her smile as she lifted Anna out by the waist and set her down on the floor.

"You okay?" she asked, stifling a laugh.

Anna's face contorted with rage. She let out a defiant grunt and slapped at Marie's hands.

"You're mad at me?"

Anna curved her lower lip into a pout, and she crossed her arms over her chest.

The little one seemed to be healing at an unexpected rate. The anger thing was completely new. But then, Marie didn't have a lot of experience with children grieving the loss of a parent. She looked down at her watch. *Shoot.*

Dinner time escaped her. Bedtime was fast approaching. Her lack of adhering to the chief's schedule would be the first strike against her. Probably not the last. "Okay, clearly you're tired and hungry, not to mention emotional. Let's find you something to eat." She reached for Anna's hand, but the little girl slapped again.

"Uhh!"

She frowned. "You're not allowed to hit or to negotiate. We're not turning into monsters today." She didn't have time for this. She reached for her again only to be slapped away a second time.

She pushed out a deep sigh and snatched Anna by the wrist. She pulled her forward, bent low, and hefted

Anna over her shoulder. She staggered to her feet under Anna's weight before making her way to the door.

Anna's initial shock wore off the moment she left the room, and a long screech rang out in Marie's left ear.

"Apparently we *are* turning into monsters today."

Anna pounded her fists on her back and kicked like a wild animal.

"This isn't helping either one of us!" Marie called out. But her voice was lost in the all the noise. The commotion amplified through the hallway, and by the time she reached the kitchen she felt pretty sure she'd lost an eardrum.

"What the hell," Quenton shouted. He stood in the kitchen, a large glass of ice water in one hand and a plate heaped with sandwiches in the other.

"What?" she called back over the howling. She stepped forward as Anna's hands latched on either side of the doorway. She pushed again with more force, and Anna lost her grip.

The sudden give caused Marie to stumble forward into the room. She would have crashed into the counter if Quenton hadn't caught her by the arm. Her face flushed with humiliation. *Oh this is great. Don't I just scream professionalism?*

"What's her problem?" he asked.

She set Anna down in a kitchen chair, but the screaming didn't stop. Anna's face turned fire engine red, and she bounced up and down in her chair like a tiny rocket ship about to blast off.

Marie held her hands over her ears to buffer the noise. "Temper-tantrum. She isn't usually like this…"

His expression became impassive as he watched

Anna for several seconds, and then carefully slid the plate under her nose. Anna instantly shoved it away, causing slices of bread, cheese, and cold cuts to tumble off the plate.

"She can't go on forever, eventually she'll wear herself out," Marie assured.

She wasn't sure which of them she wanted to convince more. She'd heard a thing or two about traumatic brain injury. It did change people. Not always for the better. What if this outburst became the first of many?

She couldn't tell how much of her statement filtered through the racket, because Quenton's eyes never left his daughter. He held his glass of ice water high above her head and tipped it until the cold contents spilled over the rim.

Anna's scream rose to a high-pitched shriek that lodged in her throat. Her body clenched as the water ran from her head over her shoulders in frigid rivulets. Her mouth fell into a pronounced frown. Her chin quivered. Then a new sound came, a long, pitiful wail.

"Wa—what'd you do that for?" Marie stuttered. She reached for a kitchen towel that lay on the nearby countertop. "You can't just dump water on her it's...it—"

"It worked," he said.

Chapter 9

After a clean change of pajamas for Anna and a five-minute lecture about appropriate behavior, Marie sat her back down to the kitchen table.

Quenton polished off half the plate in their absence but slid the rest of it back under Anna's nose. He brushed the remaining crumbs from his hands as he looked down at his daughter. Anna glared back, mirroring the same stubborn set of his jaw. When he dropped his elbows on the table and leaned into her, Anna spun to hide her face in Marie's pant leg.

She reached down to smooth the damp hair on Anna's head as the doorbell rang.

Quenton glanced up. "Why don't you get that?"

Her gaze fell to Anna's huddled form. She didn't agree with his somewhat unethical methods for dealing with the little girl but couldn't argue with the results.

He was her father, and if he chose to intervene she didn't have any authority to say otherwise. She tried to dam the irritation venting into her bloodstream, threatening to heat her face a pretty shade of pissed. She gave Anna's shoulders a reassuring squeeze. "Be right back, Princess. No food fights while I'm gone."

At the front door, she found a slender, blond man with freckles that dappled nearly every inch of his face. The shaft of harsh light casting over the porch made his features appear gaunt. He looked up from a small note pad and pushed back his wire-rimmed glasses.

"Are you Marie Durrant?"

She wrapped her arms around herself to guard against the evening chill. "I am. How can I help you?"

The badge he flipped out from his back pocket, glinted in the porch light. "My name's Detective Farnell. He gestured to a second man approaching from behind him. "This here's Detective Stewart. We're stopping by to ask a few questions about Heather Magnotti. I understand you were familiar with her?"

Her mouth fell open as Dr. Scott's last passing statement pulled into her mind. "Yes. She works at St. David's Hospital. She's still missing?" Marie felt a cold lump of guilt lodge in her throat and she looked from one detective to the other. She hadn't once thought about trying to contact Heather since leaving the hospital.

Farnell's shoulders shifted back. "She hasn't been seen or heard from in over forty-eight hours, and the circumstances surrounding her disappearance—"

"What circumstances?"

He tucked his badge under his notepad. "She hasn't missed a single day of work until now, and we found her vehicle still sitting in the hospital parking garage."

A sickening weight dropped into her stomach. "God, I hope nothing's happened to her. She didn't seem like the kind of person that would just wander off without telling someone. She wouldn't just disappear."

"Who?" Quenton's gravelly voice met her ears in the same moment she felt his hard chest pressed against her back. She jumped forward a step but not before a shiver ran over her skin, a shiver that had nothing to do with the cold. She whipped around.

A polite smile played in his eyes. "Would you step farther outside so I can close the door? I don't want Anna to hear."

Marie's words galloped from her mouth at a frantic pace. "He's here about a missing person. Heather's disappeared. She used to visit Anna all the time, and we became good friends."

He leaned back against the closed door with the same impassive expression he'd given Anna only moments ago, which made her thankful she hadn't been a good enough host to offer drinks. The next drink in the face might have been hers.

Farnell thrust out his hand to Quenton. "You're Mr. Blake, right?"

"One of them," she said.

Stewart shifted from one foot to the other. "Would you mind, Mr. Blake, if we stepped inside? Asked Ms. Durrant a few questions in private?"

Quenton ignored the second man and took full assessment of Farnell before offering his hand. "How long has she been missing?"

"She was last seen leaving the hospital with you."

Quenton released the man mid-handshake. "When was that exactly?"

Farnell absently flexed his hand. "Are you telling me you don't know?"

The two detectives exchanged a glance.

Marie's voice quivered from the encroaching cold. "He's thinking about Tobin, not you. He has to be."

Without taking his eyes off the detective, Quenton raised one finger to silence her.

She lifted her brows. *Did he just shush me?*

Farnell pulled a pen from his notebook and

scribbled down a quick note. "What was your relationship with Heather, Mr. Blake?"

"Nonexistent," he replied.

Marie let out a silent huff of indignation. He must be referring to Tobin, and she wasn't about to let Quenton's evasiveness hamper the investigation.

"He took an immediate interest in her from the moment they met," Marie offered, deliberately forcing the words against Quenton's one fingered gesture. It wasn't the bird, but it may as well have been.

"He'd been brushing her off I think. Maybe she was too much effort for him. He prefers fast women," she added.

Quenton raised his hand again, this time, using two fingers to silence her.

Again the compulsion to submit to his request slapped her across the face, but the tiny shot of adrenaline racing through her veins was powerful enough to overthrow it. Her heart rate kicked up.

"It was against company policy for her to date him. And I hate to say I'm relieved that they didn't hook up, but I am. That may sound like I'm trying to save him for myself, but I'm totally not. Forgive me for saying this, but the guy's a man-whore."

Farnell glanced up from his notepad with a look of profound shock. And in the moment of silence, Marie's mind raced for what she could have said wrong. Quenton's attention rounded on her slowly and he raised a dark brow.

The sudden epiphany crowned her with a mental dunce cap. Did they still think she was talking about Quenton?

"Tobin. I was talking about Tobin. Heather barely

got to meet Quenton."

"Because you were saving me all for yourself?" he asked with a smirk.

There was nothing pretty about the deep red blush of embarrassment that seemed to warm even the roots of her hair.

Stewart spoke up before she could force a response through her chattering teeth. "Did you notice anything odd about her behavior the last time you saw her? I'm sorry. Would you like to borrow my coat?"

Her answer died on a startled squeak as Quenton pulled her against him and briskly rubbed his hands up and down on her bare arms. The calloused ridge of his palms sent heat skittering along her bare skin and into places she didn't even know she had.

"She'll be fine," Quenton said.

It was nearly impossible for her to compose rational thought when he touched her. Not that she wanted him to stop. She looked down at her necklace, rolling one of the pearls between her thumb and forefinger as she tried to steady her voice. "She mentioned that she was seeing Dr. Scott off and on. That was kind of an odd revelation but that's all it was. Honestly, she seemed fine."

He snapped his note pad shut with a tight smile. "And is Tobin here?"

"He left this morning on business," Quenton said.

Farnell retrieved his billfold and offered Quenton his card. "When he returns, have him call me. We'd like him to stop by the station for a few questions. Thank you for your help, Ms. Durrant. Mr. Blake? We'll be in touch."

"You will let us know if you find her right?" she

asked.

Farnell's eyes dimmed in mixture of sadness and foreboding. "We'll let you know."

****

"This whole thing just makes me feel sick inside," Marie said. She closed the front door and turned the deadbolt.

Quenton called back to her from the hallway with a hint of annoyance. "I could tell. You were all but throwing up on the guy."

She marched after him. "I was only trying to be helpful."

He grunted some indistinguishable response.

Which was more than you were doing by the way, she thought.

"And what's with the charades? You were seriously counting at me? What happens when you get to three? Going to turn me over your knee or something?"

He stopped cold before reaching the kitchen and turned in the doorway to face her. Embers of warning glowed to life in his green eyes. "Don't push me, Marie. Or my knee will be the least of your worries."

Her heart fluttered wild in her chest even as she stepped forward to challenge him. Her eyes narrowed on his as she opened her mouth to speak, but the words got lost in her throat.

The delectable smell coming off him paired with the urge to melt like butter spun a covert web around her better judgment.

Quenton's gaze fell to her parted lips just before covering them with his own. His lips crushed against hers as he explored the liquid heat of her mouth. When the tip of her tongue stroked against his in cautious reply, he pulled her close in an iron grip and angled his mouth to take in more of her.

A faint moan of pleasure resonated from low in her throat and he jerked away. She staggered to regain her balance as he brushed by and continued down the hall.

"I'll let you put Anna to bed," he called back.

His voice sounded oddly impassive, but what should she expect? That kind of behavior was customary around here. Perhaps he wasn't so different from his brother after all. She could tell he dismissed that kiss the moment it ended, leaving her with a bitter taste of the one feeling she hated most.

Being forgettable.

****

As soon as Marie tucked Anna in and snagged a sandwich from the kitchen, she wandered back to her room and met yet another moving box. She thought she'd finished the last one, but like an old penny, the damn things kept showing up. She swiped her phone from the bedside table before she sagged down beside it.

She scrolled through the phone numbers until she found Dr. Scott and touched on his private cell number.

While waiting for the phone to connect, she gave the box a smirk when her fingers came in contact with its rough sequined contents. Erring on the side of vigilance, she had packed every article of clothing she owned, including some long-forgotten outfits that rebelled her current trend of dress. She plucked the first article of clothing from the box and held it to her torso with one hand.

From the Valentine's dance of her junior year in

high school, the dress was a strapless, venetian red with a hemline that met mid-thigh. She fished out the tag sewn into the back. "Mmm…bet it still fits."

"Scott here," his voice crackled over the background of muffled voices.

"Dr. Scott, it's Marie. Anna's nanny."

His tone lightened. "Oh, hi. How's the little one?"

"She's good, I guess. A little agitated today but—hey, do you have a spare minute to chat?"

His response came with a faint rustle of movement. "Yeah, hang on. Let me get to a quiet spot. I'm due for a break, so this is good a time as any."

When the phone went silent, she tossed the little red number back inside the box and pushed it a few feet away. The hands of time may have little effect on her figure, but wearing that dress was a rare act of bravery the first time. Not something she felt like repeating.

Dr. Scott's voice came back on the line. "Okay, so what's up?"

"I have to apologize about our last conversation. You mentioned Heather was missing, and I didn't give you the attention you deserved."

There was a brief pause on the line before his voice lowered. "There was a lot going on. It's understandable."

"Have you heard any good news? Any other clues about where she might have gone?"

"No. You?"

"Not really." She lumbered to her feet and approached the box again. "A detective stopped by tonight to ask a few questions, but I wasn't much help."

"The detectives act like her trail's going cold."

"I know. They came tonight asking for Tobin, but

he's not here. He's on business."

Scott snorted. "Convenient."

"He didn't speak to me or leave a number before he left, but I get the impression he won't be gone long…." Her voice trailed off. Talking wouldn't find Heather. They needed answers right now, not whenever Tobin decided to show up.

"Why don't you ask his brother?"

She gave a half shrug as she folded the stiff cardboard flaps over to seal the box. "Quenton talked to them tonight but I don't think he knows anything. He didn't spend any time with her."

Dr. Scott's voice rang loud with outrage. "Bullshit. They knew each other. They met. They must have!"

She looped an obstructing tendril of hair behind her ear and pressed the phone closer. "You're serious?"

"Hell yes, I'm serious. And if he's keeping quiet about it, it's because he knows something."

"God, she never told me. In fact, she flat-out lied to me. Do you think they were in some kind of relationship? She said that's against company policy."

"So do you think dating *me* was any less against company policy?"

"Oh, this sucks!" She chewed on her lower lip. Her memory scanned back to the detective's visit when Quenton pulled her into his chest. Was that jealousy? Or was he deliberately trying to distract her—to shut her up? Or both?

He never denied having met Heather. Didn't have to. Marie's ignorant, loudmouth did all that for him. She perpetuated Heather's lie and didn't even know it. She brushed her bangs aside and cradled her forehead against the dread that washed over her. Her stomach rolled, threatening to offer up the turkey and Swiss she had eaten.

"I'm sorry. I had no idea."

"I know," he replied bitterly.

She blew out a deep sigh. "Well, I'll try to get whatever information I can until Tobin comes back."

"Just be careful."

After disconnecting the call, she hefted the box into her arms, carried it to the back corner of the closet, and let it crash to the floor. She gave it a few extra kicks for good measure.

How could she be so stupid? How could she be attracted to a man who's an accessory to kidnapping? Or worse, the kidnapper himself! And if that were true, the possibility of him having murdered her wasn't too far off.

When she walked back into the room, her movement in the mirror caught her attention. Her clothing looked rumpled and dingy from carrying boxes to and fro, and her hair had come partially unraveled from its ponytail. A stark contrast to the vision she had of herself ten years ago, sauntering around in that sassy red Cupid's target. She remembered how grown up and sophisticated she felt in that dress.

This is how it's supposed to be, she'd thought, *a stable life with a stable boyfriend going to a dance like any other red-blooded American girl*. Of course, that was before her father announced for the hundredth time, that they would be relocating in two weeks.

He never informed her why or where they were going, and she was "encouraged to forget" the friends she left behind. She vowed then and there, she would fight to live a normal life the moment she turned eighteen. She'd met that goal until now.

Nothing about the life she forged for herself felt normal. It was disturbingly predictable but not normal.

In another strange house for who knew how long, while her friends were being ripped away. All of those old fears were manifesting themselves, and it was becoming more and more difficult to keep a clear head.

She couldn't let them turn her sense of security upside down, not if she had any power to stop it. And if knowledge was power, she needed to find whatever she could without wasting more time.

She glanced to both ends of the hall.

All clear.

With tentative steps on the balls of her feet, she made her way to the study. The doors were open wide for a change, inviting her in like a magnificent spider's web waiting for the next passerby. The scant amount of amber lighting pulled long shadows from the corners of the room.

She didn't want to flick on the large dome light overhead, afraid it might draw too much attention. Instead, she stood motionless waiting for her pupils to adjust and her breathing to calm. A quick survey of the room found nothing out of the ordinary.

The first adjoining bedroom door opened without a sound. Mirrors affixed to the walls reflected the large black armoire, dresser, and a king-sized bed. She looked up.

Yup. Mirrors there, too.

The dim glow from the study bounced off the mirrors and the stainless-steel stripper pole in the corner. Just enough light to navigate the furniture without bumping into anything. The air grew thick and humid inside with the spicy tang of sex and cheap perfume.

Like one giant trophy case, it boasted countless odd shaped, metallic objects littering the floor and tabletops, some of them still in their boxes. *Sex toys*, the thought occurred to her, as her eye caught a thin metal chain glinting in the mirror's reflection.

She wrapped her arms around herself, not willing to touch what she couldn't readily identify. *Or anything she could, for that matter.*

The plum silk bedding looked rumpled and pulled free on one side. It cascaded over the foot of the bed, partially melting over a large black chest. She knelt down, and after brushing the sheets away, tried to lift the lid.

Locked.

If Tobin was bold enough to store his toys in the open, she wasn't sure she wanted to know what he hid under lock and key. She scanned the rest of the room, but her surroundings were too dark to identify with much clarity. Maybe she could get back in here during the daylight and find a key to the chest.

She got to her feet and tried to pick her way out of the room. When she stepped on a ten-inch cylindrical object, it rolled. Her feet went out from under her, and her butt hit the floor with a bone-jarring thud.

The silver object rolled across the hardwood floor emitting a low buzzing noise until it tinged against the metal stripper pole at the far end of the room.

The guy's got a flair for matching his accessories I'll give him that much. She scrambled after the vibrator, put both hands around the beveled shaft, and fumbled for the switch to shut it off.

Ew.Ew. Ew!

She gritted her teeth, running her hands along the device until she found what appeared to be the switch. Hopefully it wasn't the "go faster" button.

She flipped it and the buzzing died off, then she flung it toward the bed and scrubbed her palms over her jeans.

She wanted to race back to her room but chickening out wasn't an option. With the commotion, she'd get caught. And if she was already screwed, she wasn't going to face Quenton's wrath for nothing.

She made a hasty pass into the second room where she found identical furniture and a neatly made bed. It was missing the chest and mirrors, making it seem smaller without all the reflections, more casual, and Quenton's familiar scent lingered in the air around her.

Heat threaded through her veins at the thought of being in his room, knowing at any moment he could return to find her. Her impish thoughts cheered her on. Fueled by flames of excitement, they danced around in her mind as if coaxing him to materialize out of thin air.

She ran her shaking fingertips along the surface of his nightstand until she came in contact with the worn edge of a leather-bound book.

Good enough for now, she thought and tucked it under her arm.

Nearly home free.

She spun to the door, but her breath caught in a gasp. Quenton's massive silhouette slipped in front of her, and Marie braced herself against the doorjamb to keep from running into him.

He seized her wrist before she could pull away. Not a painful squeeze, just catching her and holding her in place. He stood as a solid, unreadable blockade of darkness. But the heat in his touch filtered into her skin, causing a rash of goosebumps to race up her arm and across her chest.

"Let me guess…learning disability?" he asked.

She banked the fear that gripped her and pulled her wrist free. She crossed both arms over the book. "I—"

"I told you to stay out."

"I want to talk to you about Heather."

He stepped forward, backing her into the room. "First things first. Why've you come to my bed?"

Fast. Think fast. "Not your bed. Your room. I was looking for…for the book." She rushed to explain.

"This isn't the library, sweet thing."

"I want this one. The one you stole from me."

He canted his head. "Overlooking the fact that it wasn't yours to begin with, why?"

"It's…it caught my attention that's all. Why did you want to keep it from me?"

"That book is extremely rare. There are only twelve copies known in existence. It's worth more than ten times your salary. Take it, but it's going to cost you."

"You know I can't afford that! And I don't want to buy it anyway. I just want to borrow it for an hour."

"What'll you give me for it?"

"If you want me to spend an hour…on etiquette lessons for Anna, I'd be happy to barter. Otherwise, I don't have anything to give."

"Leave the etiquette but I'll take the hour."

She shifted her weight to one side and jutted her hip. "An hour with the book for an hour…of what?"

"That's for me to decide. Deal?"

How much trouble could one hour be? If this was his book, the fact that he would mar it by turning down the pages meant its content held more value than its monetary worth. He had already taken it once. She wouldn't let him do it again.

"All right. Deal."

"Good. Your clock starts now."

She dropped her arms to her sides. "Wait a minute. You still have some explaining to do about Heather."

His hand moved to her shoulder, curling a finger inside the V-neck of her shirt, and began a slow descent to the hollow between her breasts. "You want to prepay? I'm fine with that. Or maybe you don't want the book at all. Whichever the case, you don't need to make excuses to stay."

Her nipples pearled, straining against the thin material of her bra. The heat she felt in her cheeks couldn't be detected in the dark room but if he continued in his wayward direction, her breasts would be an irrefutable proof to the effect he had on her.

She provoked a collective harrumph of injustice from her naughty thoughts when she lifted his hand off her chest and dropped it to his side. "You're right. I don't need to make excuses. Because I'm not staying."
So put that in your pipe and smoke it, big boy.

Chapter 10

Victory ballooned within her when she shut and locked her bedroom door. She vaulted to the bed stomach first.

The book was far too large for reading cover-to-cover, so she decided to scan over the dog-eared and weather-beaten chapters. She leafed through the stiff yellowed pages, savoring the smell of ink and stale cigars.

The volume indicated a common theme: following the sporadic lineage of the Greek Muse and three keys to their power. They could lure mortals in, sedate them, and push suggestions into their head. Most disturbing, was their ability to rip open the fabric of a mortal's subconscious to feast on their soul.

The book told of Mozart, Picasso, Shakespeare, and countless others, all under the influence of a Greek Muse. All being fed on, a bit at a time.

The origin of these creatures came from the first Muse, who sold—not his soul but his body to Hades. Paying the toll to enter the underworld and find is mate. His one and only chance to become whole. Since when does the devil deal in flesh and bone? Since the Muse's soul was broken and useless in the first place. What more could he barter?

Apparently, that didn't end so well for the Muse.

Great pains were taken to document their notoriety

for inspiration, and about the payment of a human soul for the "gifts" they dealt.

With every page, her mind wrestled the warped information, and her stomach churned. It wasn't difficult to recognize a trend between a Muse's influence, and the power Quenton seemed to wield over her. She shook her head, thrusting the very thought from her mind.

"Not possible." She slapped the book shut with a frustrated sigh. "What a joke."

A heavy wrap on the door jarred her thoughts, and her attention flew to the doorknob.

Quenton. First he lied about Heather, and then he swindled her out of an hour of her time. If she compounded it with the absurd notion of him being a Muse, her paranoia would set all kinds of new records.

Should she answer it? Invite him in for a piece of her mind? Or lock the door and make a break for the window. Where she would no doubt plummet to her death?

"Better him than me." She shoved the book under the heavy pillow top mattress and stomped to the door. She wrenched it open to find him standing with a compelling smile and two glasses of milk.

"What are you doing here?"

"My turn." He handed her a glass as he brushed past into the room.

"It's getting late. Maybe I could pay up tomorrow?" she asked.

He scanned the room. "I figured you could use a night cap to settle your stomach. I don't sleep well in new places and figured you might be in the same boat."

"Ah. Thoughtful." She cooed into the glass. "Could

have used something stronger…but how do I know you aren't trying to poison me?"

He stopped next to the bed. "I'll offer any service to see you well rested, but poison would be overkill."

He looked at the wrinkled bedding where she lay only moments before then back at her. He inclined his head, and his gaze swept the length of her body. "You sleep in your clothes?"

"No!"

"Go get changed. I'll wait." He sat on the bed and propped his feet up.

Marie's hands went to her hips. "I thought authority over bedtime was in *my* job description. Not yours."

"No, I'm the authority, you're just the enforcer."

"No, you're the *advisor*. And I can take it or leave it." With a sugary smile and nod of her head, she gestured to the open door. "I think I'll leave it."

"I'm not leaving."

After a pause, she growled and snapped the door shut. "You know what? Fine. You have some explaining to do anyway."

"Why else would I be here? Now quit stalling." He jerked his chin to the bathroom door.

She shook her head in disbelief as she weighed what little options she had. She *should* send him on his way. On the other hand, she needed this time to get any answers she could. The best way to drag information out of him was to do it while she still had the nerve.

Every hour Heather remained missing was another mountain of odds stacked against her. Besides, she owed him. She may as well get it over with so he couldn't hold it over her head.

She slammed her glass down on the nightstand, sloshing milk over the rim and onto her hand. She flounced off to the bathroom. As soon as the door shut, her mind began a pinwheel of deliberation. In front of the mirror, she released her hair from its messier than messy up-do, then pulled it away from her face into a loose ponytail.

Being shut in a room with a possible accomplice to Heather's disappearance should make her want to run for the hills but it didn't. It was her growing bond to him that did that.

Attempting to make herself at home left her feeling more heartsick than a mutt in a pet shop—an all too familiar feeling.

It plagued her as a child. Always the new kid that never quite fit in. Desperate to find a connection. Quenton seemed to know more about her, than she did—and how was that possible? The concern that kept popping up made her want to cling to him like a new best friend.

But clinging was only good for koalas and cellophane wrap.

Situations like these led to trouble. Drinks never came free, and his plan to offer any service meant he had at least one in mind. Most likely the kind that would leave a girl feeling anything but well rested.

The mere thought of him seducing her brought back the memory of that hot, jarring kiss, and her imagination conjured up all kinds of services she'd like him to offer. Maybe if the situation were different, she could give those plans full reign.

But with Anna's father and her boss? She should know better. She grimaced as she forced her frisky little imagination back onto its leash.

"That kiss didn't mean anything. Not to him. And it shouldn't mean anything to me."

"Which one of us are you trying to convince?" He called from the bedroom.

She bit down on a washcloth to stifle her moan of embarrassment.

She turned the faucet and shower on full force to dampen any more noise before scrubbing her face and brushing her teeth.

Even if he did see her as seduction worthy, she'd be crazy to fall for it. He was the kind of guy that would drop her like a rock at the first sign of reluctance. To put herself in such an awkward situation with Anna's father would have some painful and long-standing side effects.

She gave her reflection a determined nod. "Not gonna happen."

If his actions were anything less than honorable, he'd require a willing participant to execute them. As long as she kept things strictly nonphysical, she would remain in control. She'd pulled free from his hypnotic gaze before. She could do it again if she wanted to.

She slipped into a pair of teal pajama bottoms and matching tank, then pulled a thick terrycloth bathrobe over top.

Deep breath.

Showtime.

Her mouth went dry at her first glimpse of him stretched across her bed. His eyes were closed, and both hands rested behind his head. She picked up the glass of milk from the nightstand and drained its contents, wishing he'd laced it with something a little stronger.

"Thanks for the milk."

"My pleasure."

He frowned when his eyes lowered to her tightly cinched robe. "Cold?"

"A little," she replied, thankful her voice still sounded even.

He let out a small sigh, stood, and peeled back the down comforter.

"Oh, you don't need to bother."

He matched her even tone as he continued to pull on the sheets. "Marie, I'm not leaving here until you're asleep."

"Hey, we only agreed on an hour."

"I'm betting it won't even take that long."

"That boring, huh?"

He paused with a pillow gripped in his hands. She could almost see him fighting the urge to whack her with it. He tossed it into place instead.

"Besides, these walls aren't *that* thin. I wouldn't keep you up. And there's no way I'd fall asleep with you here," she said

The stern look showed her the issue was no longer open for discussion. "You asked about Heather. If you want answers, you'll work with me."

"Don't you ever get tired of playing this game?" she asked.

"I could think of a lot better games to play, but this works." His lips twitched. "Get in now, and I'll answer five questions."

Seriously, why was she arguing with him? She needed information, and she needed it now. This slumber party was but a small price to pay.

"Four questions."

She shot him an indignant glare.

"Three."

"I'm going." A bubble of panic rose inside her as she reluctantly climbed onto the bed. When her knees sank into the cushy mattress, her aching joints nearly collapsed in relief.

She slapped both palms down on the comforter. "All right, questions. First, why didn't you tell me you knew Heather?"

Quenton sat down on the edge of the bed and untied his scuffed leather shoes. "You didn't ask."

Her anxiety jumped when she saw him bent over the same spot where she crammed the book between the mattress and the box spring. "What are you doing?"

"Is that one of your questions?"

"No!"

"Next question." He slipped off one shoe then the other.

Her eyes narrowed to tiny slits, boring into his back. "The detectives asked if you knew her, and you lied to them, didn't you?"

"No. They asked me about my relationship with her. I didn't have one."

"Okay, so if it wasn't a relationship, what was it?"

"She was an acquaintance from your blog. That was three."

"When do I get more questions?"

He sighed and gave a patronizing eye-roll. "That would be four. You were only allowed three. Now you're in debt."

She fisted the nearby pillow until her knuckles ached. "We never discussed terms."

"Again, you didn't ask." He ducked as the pillow

sailed over his head and stifled a chuckle.

"Great, so now what?" she snapped. "And don't say that's five because it doesn't count."

"My turn," he grinned.

He leaned back on one arm. "When was the last time you slept? I mean a full night's sleep."

She swallowed. A charge of energy skipped between them. "Why?"

He tipped his head in challenge. "Answer."

"I don't remember."

"And why don't you sleep?"

She looked down at the knot in her robe. She didn't want to talk about this. He already had enough control over her mental and physical state. Muse or no Muse, he still had power over her as an employer. His plans to traipse around the world with her in tow would have a profound effect on her mental well-being. Knowledge of her inability to cope would leave her vulnerable.

"Pass. Next question."

"You don't get a pass." He laughed.

She blew out a frustrated breath and searched his eyes for some hint of mercy but his unbreaking stare told her not to waste her time. "I don't know, they say it's some form of post-traumatic stress or something like that. There. Ya happy?"

Silence stretched between them.

He used his fingertips to trace a lazy figure eight on the back of her hand.

"I suppose you want me to elaborate now but you're not going to get any freebees. You have one question left, so fire away," she said.

"How can I help?"

The words came in nearly a whisper, and with such

simple compassion it left unshed tears stinging the back of her eyes. She knew she had a problem but how could he have known? How did he manage to pick up on her worst flaw so easily?

The cold compresses and eye makeup masked the dark circles under her eyes. The three cups of coffee every morning kept her perky all day. She didn't want to explain to him as far as sleep deprivation went, she was a hopeless cause.

She blinked the tears back as quickly as they formed, then feigned a thoughtful gaze at the flat white ceiling.

"Um. Going away might help," she offered.

He shook his head. "Really. I want to help with this."

"Why do you care whether I sleep or not?" she asked.

He stared at her, his expression unreadable. If she didn't get a handle on the situation, she'd crack. She needed a distraction, to lighten the mood before he tucked her into an emotional breakdown.

"How about a good bedtime story? You can tell me the one about the vanishing nurse."

His leveled her with a weary look. "You're a little old for that don't you think?"

She gave a small shrug. "Hey, I'll take my information wherever I can get it. If you're just going to sit here and stare at me while I try to find my way to dreamland…I figure you could at least offer a little entertainment."

He rounded to the other side of the bed, mumbling under his breath. "Oh, I'll give you a story…."

She slid her legs under the covers and smoothed

the sheets around her waist, biting back a smile of retribution.

"You can't sleep sitting up, Marie," he chided as he stretched out beside her. The bed dipped under his weight, and she felt her body tilt toward him. Her pulse raced.

"You okay?" He asked, "Do I make you uncomfortable?"

"No." *Yes!*

"Do you want me to go?"

"Yeees."

"Then lay down."

"Okay, okay…sheesh." She sank down until the comforter touched her chin.

"Ready?" he asked.

She closed her eyes and nodded.

The gritty edge of his voice fell to a low rumble which had a surprisingly smooth effect on her harried thoughts. The tension in her shoulders fell away as she sank deeper into the feather pillow.

"Once upon a time, two young angels were hopelessly obsessed with each other."

"That's not the story I'm looking for here," she said in perfect deadpan.

"This one's better."

"The man was known far and wide for his great strength and stamina. The size of his lady-pleaser gave him a reputation that all the women begged to sample…"

"What!"

"And beyond the girl's rare beauty, she was gifted with such enthusiasm and imagination for love making, her reputation *nearly* rivaled his."

"Quenton!"

His brows shot up his forehead. "What?"

"I hope these aren't the kind of bedtime stories you've been telling your daughter."

"Isn't this the way all of the good ones go?"

"Uhhhh, I don't think so."

"Well then." He flashed a mischievous grin. "This one will be just for you."

She tried to cover her smile with a yawn, but the warmth of her cheeks couldn't be hidden. "You are officially on probation. The only stories you get to read are ones rated with *The Cat in the Hat* on the binding."

"Since I'm already being punished, I may as well finish this one."

"Fine. Just tone it down okay, Fabio?"

He rose on one elbow. "Am I deflowering your virgin ears?"

"The status of my ears or any other body part for that matter is none of your business. Thank you very much."

He snorted. "I think the death grip you have on those covers speaks for itself. But we're getting off track…where was I?"

He tipped his head to the ceiling. "Oh yeah, When the angels were called away, they would say goodbye to one another with one brief kiss."

"Why a brief kiss?" she asked. Her eyes closed, and her voice slurred with fatigue. "Why not one of those long steamy kisses that love stories are so famous for?"

"The brief kiss was an unwritten contract. It meant that like the kiss, their time spent apart would be brief. They would save the good, long, steamy ones for when they were reunited."

She let her breaths come in slow and deep. She knew sleep wasn't far off. Succumbing to it while in such a vulnerable situation would only invite more problems but she couldn't ward off her exhaustion.

"You still with me?" he asked.

She managed a slow nod.

"Should I keep going?"

She nodded again.

"One day the young man was given an enormous task; sent down to Earth to live out a lifetime of human experience. The angel tried to assure his lover the time they spent apart would not be long…but when he left, she fell into misery.

"The time and distance became unbearable for her. So the girl sat down on God's knee and begged him for comfort. He told her that to comfort her meant to take away the love she felt for her man. To deprive her of true love was something he wouldn't do. Instead, she asked to follow him down. To seek him out on her own.

"God warned her time and experiences on Earth can leave angels unrecognizable, and her search wouldn't be easy…." Quenton's voice trailed off.

She leaned into the feel of his warm calloused hand caress the side of her cheek, and a silent moan parted her lips. When she realized what she was doing, her eyes cracked open with uncertainty.

"Sweet dreams," he said. Her eyes fell closed, and she sank down into a heavy sleep.

****

Marie's full body stretch began at the tips of her toes and ended with a blissful curve of her lips. She blinked up at the ceiling, waiting for the dreamy glaze to clear from her eyes.

A full night's sleep. How fabulous was that? What time did she finally go to bed? She remembered unpacking, and the unsettling call to Dr. Scott, then Quenton—

"Oh, God!"

She bolted upright in bed and glanced down to where he'd been the night before. She figured pretending to fall asleep would deter any bright ideas he may have about servicing her. It worked like a charm. In fact, it worked so well she actually *did* fall asleep. It seemed like mission accomplished on both fronts.

She went to bed as expected, and he didn't try to bed her *as expected.*

What were the odds that Quenton, who could make her short circuit with one sideways glance, managed to cure her insomnia? She caressed the faint impression he left in the comforter, wishing the simple motion of her hand would conjure him up again.

Her hand paused. *It was still warm.*

Her mind whirled with the possibility of him spending the entire night by her side. And she didn't even notice?

Should she confront him about it? Yeah right. *Excuse me but did you happen to notice whether I had the pleasure of drooling on your chest last night?*

She grimaced. On second thought, maybe it would be best to forget it ever happened.

She pulled herself out of bed and dressed for her run with slow, reluctant motions, then clipped on the baby monitor. Quenton challenged her to a race yesterday, and she would probably meet up with him on the trail.

She had no idea what to say to him. Her mind begged to ask about his connection to the book and confront him about the strange powers. But that would be even more painful than asking if she was a good snuggle partner. No, better let that one slide, too.

On a whim, she snaked her arm between the heavy mattress and the box spring.

She couldn't find it.

She slid down farther along the side of the bed and reached for the book again.

Nothing.

He took it. Again. She sighed and made her way to the front door. Who cared? Let him have the stupid thing. Unless it had a magical spell to cure her obsessing over him, it wasn't of any use anyway.

The frigid autumn wind blowing across the valley whipped her ponytail from side to side and rustled the grass as it bowed low under the weight of accumulated rain. The sparse clumps of leaves that still clung to the trees looked soggy and fatigued as they swayed along to the tune of her rhythmic pace.

The rain came down in a slow drizzle. She hoped the worst of the storm would hold off until the end of her run. Small icy drops pricked at her skin. The cold ate into her fingertips until they were painfully numb. At least the path lay closer this time. Well within range of Anna's baby monitor, and convenient enough to cut short in case of a downpour.

She wound around small puddles of rainwater as she pressed onward. Despite the sting of cold air in her lungs, she amplified her stride in a vain effort to produce more warmth.

The impending fall season set upon her more

quickly than she anticipated. Her surroundings were noticeably murky compared to the morning before, causing an eerie sense of foreboding to torment her imagination.

She speculated about what kind of creatures might be hiding in the forest beyond the trail. She quickened her pace, as she passed through a dark canopy of trees.

Suddenly, she wished she hadn't gone out alone.

"Unfamiliar territory puts you at a disadvantage." That's what her father used to say. "Lack of visibility leaves you playing in the enemies' hands."

A flock of tiny black birds erupted from the trees a hundred yards in front of her, careening through the spindly pines and darting for the sky. Something must have scared them.

She quashed the notion as quickly as it had formed. Her gaze swept the landscape for any sign of Quenton. As the pathway turned for its final stretch, she saw the old wooden bench.

He was nowhere in sight.

"Figures."

A twinge of disappointment slowed her progress. Regret, not only for Quenton's absence, but also for herself having believed he'd be there.

In the past, her father had chastised her numerous times that she would fare better if she could bring her head back down to Earth. For most circumstances, she would wholeheartedly disagree, but this moment was an exception.

"What am I? Twelve?" Why did she have such a fascination with Quenton? Why did she feel such an intense connection after only a few days? She knew better than to give in to guys like him, why the sudden lapse in judgment?

Her ears perked at the sound of rustling bushes behind her.

The wind or *a small animal. It has to be*.

The justification did nothing to help the fear closing in around her. As though a swarm of dark tree shadows came to life, consuming the space between her and whatever made that noise. Panic gripped her heart, causing it to beat frantic in her chest. A cold chill ran up her spine as she turned.

Standing in the clearing a hundred yards away, an ashen figure draped in filthy gray scrubs reached out to her. The set of its mouth seemed so similar to Heather's, but the height was all wrong. The body looked stretched and willowy, more spider-like than ballerina, and the spine hunched like a hunting bow stretched tight.

Strands of dark hair clumped together with grime fell over the creature's forehead and about its ears, having come loose from a ponytail fastened at the nape of its neck. Its eyes were large, round, and dark, boring into her with a feral intensity.

"Youuu," it said.

The voice was Heather's. There was a harsh metallic strain over the tone, but she recognized it, nonetheless. The hairs on the back of her neck stood on end. Terror shuttered her mind from all logic and rendered her immobile.

Before either of them could take a step, Quenton sprang forward and slammed into Marie mid-air.

A high-pitched scream ripped from her throat as the force of the collision sent them flying off the trail into a ravine that flanked the path.

The lush overgrowth didn't break much of the fall. Lights flashed behind her eyes when she struck the ground. Her chest seized on a painful gasp.

A solid mass of taut muscle and bone pinned her from the hips down. Quenton's chest heaved against her, the hot vapor of his every exhale fanned her chest. His crown of wild black hair tilted down, obscuring his features.

"Knew you couldn't outrun me."

He took one look at her, and his smile dropped. "I didn't mean to scare you that bad."

She swallowed hard to recover her voice. "It's not just you. There—there's something else out here. I think it's Heather. My God..." She shoved his chest with both her palms but couldn't budge him.

"What did you see?" he demanded.

"I don't know. Like a ghost or a—a zombie. A gourmet zombie."

"Gourmet zombie?"

"Yeah, you know, like a regular zombie only...gourmet. It was tall, white, and it freaked me the hell out. Wearing scrubs and everything. Let me up!"

When she tried to sit, he pushed her back down into the soggy undergrowth.

"Don't move. Stay here," he said.

It wasn't a request. It was a command, and the tone he used to issue it, had the needle on her freak-ometer tilting to hysterical. She gripped his shirt. Her words ran together so quickly, they were almost unintelligible to her own ears. "You are not going to leave me here by myself. What kind of idiot do you take me for?"

He shackled her wrists together with one hand. "I don't have time for this. Either you stay here and be quiet, or I'll tie you to a damn tree." When he released, he gave her one last warning look before disappearing over the edge of the ravine.

Chapter 11

Moving slow and methodical, Quenton tamped down the surge of fury growing to life inside him.

He spiraled out from Marie's location until he found the Shade's path of retreat. He crouched down. His shirt pulled tight against the enlarged muscles of his back and shoulders.

The muddled collection of elongated footprints formed in soft clay, all traveling in the same direction without any concern for covering the tracks. There were three, not counting the rest that were probably still shopping for a body—Marie's body. Shades moved in packs and their population had been steadily growing for years. Like rats.

He didn't want to lie to her about the Shade coaxing her into the clearing, but he would. What choice did he have?

If he wasn't so utterly pissed about the attempted ambush, he might have smiled at the memory of her sneaking into his room last night. Standing in a darkened corner of the study, he watched her wander first into Tobin's room then his own. She wasn't like him. Her attempted stealth wasn't worth a damn, and she could find herself an awful lot of trouble in these woods.

Quenton prevented any attempt for the Shades to engage Marie when he took her to the ground. It blocked their decoy and sent a clear message that she was guarded. She belonged to him. The Shades seemed to get the message.

For now, he reminded himself, because his action also proved Marie wasn't dispensable. She was important to him, which made her a valuable player in their game.

Suddenly his brilliant plan to use her as bait didn't seem so brilliant after all. These creatures didn't normally reveal themselves to their prey, but these Shades weren't typical. They were more conniving, more aggressive, and they approached her with a vehemence that caught even him by surprise.

Marie said it. They were gourmet. And now that they had a taste for her, he knew the surprises weren't going to end there.

Apparently, even in hell the glass could appear half-full because history proved this near miss would whip the Shades into a frenzy. Soon they would become more persistent.

He rolled his head to the side, kneading the stiff cords of muscle in his neck. Life was about to get a lot more complicated.

****

Ten minutes later, Quenton crouched down beside her. He just appeared there.

"Don't move yet. Are you hurt?" he asked.

She cringed when he pushed her back down into the slick foliage. He ran his hands along her ribcage with motions that were disturbingly unrushed.

"A little soggy, but fine. Did you see it?" she asked.

"No. There's nothing out there now."

He laced his fingers through her hair, tugging under her ponytail to massage the tender spot at the back of her head. A sharp pain branched across her scalp.

"Ow. *Stop*."

"You said you weren't hurt."

"You're *making* it hurt."

He muttered something about her being a big baby, but she chose not to acknowledge it, too distracted by the feel of his warm hands working down the back of her neck. The touch sent little crackles of electricity shooting through her system.

"I swear I'm not crazy."

He kept his voice level as he worked down her shoulders. "It wasn't Heather."

"She would have called to me, right? She would have called my name."

"It didn't know your name. It wasn't her."

"So, you did see something?"

"No—"

"What the hell was it?"

He closed his eyes. "Marie, I didn't see anything. You did. And with as fast as it disappeared, a ghost couldn't be that far off. But it's gone."

He turned over her hands to reveal the angry red scrapes on her palms. She dismissed the mild sting, but with the scolding frown he gave her, she could have been hiding an amputated finger.

"It doesn't hurt. I didn't even know it was there."

With eyes fixed on her, he lifted each palm to his lips. His hot breath against her skin and the soft caress of his lower lip sent her rational thoughts skittering into hiding.

"Anywhere else?" he asked.

Is it too late to conjure up a fat lip?

She gave a numb head shake. "Just my nerves."

In a matter of seconds, the rain grew to fat droplets that splattered her upturned face. The sound drowned out everything except the hum of energy between them.

"We need to go back," he said.

Her skin flushed under the feel of his thumb gliding down her cheekbone to the curve of her jaw.

"You ready?" he asked.

He offered his hand to help her up.

She grabbed his wrist, tethering him down instead of getting to her feet. "No. I'm not."

If that thing spawned from her own twisted imagination, she'd take a stand right now. She wouldn't let her fears control her. Not anymore. And if taking that stand meant dropping a bomb over all things terrifying, what better place to start than here? With him?

Apart from the cold, the rain, and her commonsense firing back for escalating this situation into dangerous territory, something inside wanted him. To test the connection, she couldn't ignore and whatever came from the end result, for this moment she wouldn't feel alone.

A small part of her cried out. The risk she took for one fleeting moment of security would only cause more pain.

She didn't care.

She couldn't see past the fear that gripped her, and the knowledge she had nothing in her life—in this moment—to tie her to reality. She needed this. She needed him.

****

Quenton felt a rush of heat course through his veins. He could feel her mind opening up to him and asking for something more. The urge to take hold of her grew, and this time he refused to stop it.

He fed the sweet, weightless elixir to her slow, until her body went limp and her mind let go of awareness.

His entire body charged with arousal when he pulled at the veil of her subconscious and it tumbled down like falling silk.

He didn't need to call out this time. He could feel her spirit already standing there. Expecting him.

He welcomed the thick sensation of his soul pulling away. Being caught between his body and the outside world caused a frigid current to sweep through him. He wasted no time moving into the warmth of her mind. To locate the part of her nestled in the darkened pool of her subconscious.

"Come to me," he said.

He watched her image rise up from its dormant coil and stretch out to him in timid wisps of light. Her hair lifted and flowed in a lazy current around her bare shoulders.

He locked his arms to his sides, letting her spirit use its whisper-soft touch to explore him. A flash of white-hot energy shot through him on first contact. It was a sensation that should have come easy, but it still managed to stun him. The shock faded to a subtle pulse, chanting low, and building up a desperate need to feel the rush again.

"Closer," he said.

Her lazy exploration continued without a response,

as little ripples of heat lapped into him.

"I can give you what you need. Just tell me."

She gave a weary shake of her head, and the imploring tendrils of vapor withdrew from him. She started to fade back into the shadows.

Desperation clawed at him to follow but he couldn't. He was too afraid he might hurt her. Forcing her to give her spirit over to him could cause irreparable damage if he unknowingly drained too much of her energy.

"Damn it! Don't leave. Just tell me!"

She continued pulling away and became nothing more than a thin outline.

"You can't hide, Marie. I will take you."

He guessed he should have taken more care with his word choice, because in an unexpected bout of rage, she shoved him back with both hands.

His breath hitched in his throat as searing heat bolted through him. The light from her contact blinded him, and he felt his spirit sailing backward from the momentum.

Without anything to hold on to, he could do nothing but wait until the backward motion gradually slowed. When it did, and his vision returned, he gathered enough composure to reorient himself. He found himself at the edge of her subconscious again, Marie nowhere in sight.

"I can't believe you hit me!"

He didn't bother trying to find her again, even if she didn't have far to go. She needed time to cool off. Besides, he got what he came for. A single word suspended in the energy she pushed into him and it echoed in the corners of his mind.

"Safety."

Safety?

He tipped his head back with a sigh of frustration.

Shit!

Chapter 12

Fuzzy splotches of color pulled into focus. The smell of brown sugar and winter frost baited the air. The tranquil current of sound that lulled her only moments ago, grew louder and more frantic as she regained consciousness. It was then she realized the escalating tympani was the sound of her own heart.

"Don't ever do that to me again." She gasped, fighting to catch her breath. Her tongue felt so thick she had trouble getting the words out. When she sat up, her surroundings tipped and spun, forcing her head down between her knees.

"What did you do, drug me?"

Quenton got to his feet. "It's more a power of suggestion than a chemical."

"You're—" She looked up at him, afraid to speak the word.

He nodded, urging her on. "I'm…."

"Not a political advisor. I'll give you that much."

"Yeah, and you're a Scorpio but we can overlook our differences."

She glared up at the hand he offered her. "Why did you do that?"

"You asked me to."

"You can't just go around knocking people out!" she sputtered. "That's illegal. You'll go to jail for that." *I think.*

The soft green in his eyes darkened. He snatched her by the wrist. He jerked her up with such force, it pulled on her socket. She locked her knees to keep from collapsing.

"Look, I'm sorry. You wanted my help. Don't deny it," he growled. "If you can't handle the consequences, be more careful what you ask for."

She wrinkled her nose with disgust. "I wasn't asking you to drug me."

"Then what were you asking for?"

Her mouth opened to reply but the words caught between rejection and the excitement of his threatened consequence. Shouldn't it be obvious she wanted him? Wasn't it the first thing that came to mind when a woman looked at him like that?

Of course it was. He had to know exactly what she wanted. He wanted to hear the words come out of her mouth. To savor the victory of having one more notch on his bedpost. Her chin inched up in a defiant tilt, and she snapped her mouth shut. Her teeth clanged together, sending a shock of pain up her jaw.

He cursed under his breath, snatched her wrist again, and gave her a tug toward the house. He let go as soon as she walked without resistance, then stormed ahead without looking back.

When they approached the house, a dusty yellow cab idled outside the front entrance. Roxie staggered to the car. She wore the same dress she had two nights ago. Her cheeks were sunken and pale with lines of mascara streaked down her face. She gave a polite smile, but it didn't reflect in her eyes. Her expression seemed haunted and desperate.

Marie made a move toward her but the firm grip on

her upper arm kept her at a distance. The woman climbed into the back seat of the cab and rolled away. She glared down at her arm, then to Quenton, then back to her arm again.

"I think you have something that belongs to me." She jerked free.

She marched to the front door with him close behind. Tobin leaned in the open doorway, watching the cab pull away.

"What'd you do? Put her in the closet for safe keeping while you were gone?" Marie asked.

Tobin snorted. "I don't do leftovers."

Her nails bit into her scraped palms, sending sharp pain through her hands. "Is that how you treat all your women? Send them off looking like they'd just been through a war?"

"She did all that to herself. Some people just don't know when to say when. She was pounding on the front door when I got home and scaring poor Anna to death."

He gestured at the gravel drive with a careless wave of his hand. "But as you can see, I sent her on her way."

Hot anger built inside her, threatening to erupt. So it's already begun. Less than a week went by, and Anna's innocence was tarnished by some lust-crazy harlot.

"Where's Anna?" she asked.

"Inside. Where else would she be?"

She didn't bother asking him to move, just ducked under his arm. "Someone wants to talk to you about Heather's disappearance."

"So I hear."

She spun to face him. "And what do you have to

say?"

His eyes narrowed. "I have to say that it's none of your damn business."

"When one of my friends goes missing I make it my business."

"You better watch that holier-than-thou attitude before I'm tempted to really put the fear of God into you."

The look she gave him could have cut steel. "Don't you dare threaten me, you walking talking STD."

"Stop!" Quenton shouted. "Marie, go take a cold shower. Tobin, if you ever threaten her again, I'll tear your head off and hand it to you."

Marie turned her glare to Quenton. "Oh, you can just butt out! I don't need you to fight my battles for me."

Quenton barreled through Tobin's doorway blockade and came nose to nose with her.

"Go. Now."

Her chin jutted up. She spun around so quickly, her damp ponytail bitch-slapped him across the face. The twinge of justice did little to ease her anger as she stomped down the hall to her room.

****

Quenton rounded the corner into the kitchen to find his daughter precariously scaling the shelves of the pantry. One foot poised mid-air, and a hand stretched above her head.

With a slow exhale, he pushed back the hitch in his throat.

"Hey, Anna." He drew the words out to conceal the waver in his voice.

His steps were slow and vigilant on the balls of his

feet. Ready to dash under her should her foot slip from its narrow span on the shelf.

His calloused hands swallowed her tiny waist. He lifted her overhead to the top shelf. As soon as she came within reach; she grabbed a vibrant, orange and red bag of corn chips, and pulled them into her chest.

He paused at the familiar crinkling sound. He hadn't paid much attention to what she aimed for, but now that he knew, he felt the need to second guess his gallant effort.

Even *he* knew that potato chips didn't fall under the recipe for a breakfast of champions. What would Marie think if she came into the kitchen only to find that he, the new Father of the Year, had been feeding his daughter a fist full of nacho cheese chips for breakfast? His gaze dashed skyward, and he pushed out a deep breath as he lowered her to the floor.

"You know why we put that stuff on the top shelf?"

Anna turned around, craning her neck to look at him. The color drained from her face. The bag crackled again as she tightened her grip. She shook her head.

"Maybe you can guess?" he prompted.

"Cause-cause they're not good breakfast," she mumbled, barely moving her lips.

"Well, partly because they aren't healthy but mostly because Uncle Tobin can't reach that shelf either."

Anna remained frozen and ever watchful as he reached back inside the pantry. He pulled out a box of cereal, and then wandered around the kitchen collecting bowls and spoons.

He reached into the refrigerator for a carton of

milk. "How do you like your new home?"

"It's okay." Her voice came at a near whisper, lost in the sound of rain pelting the large kitchen window.

"Just okay?"

"Not much fun." She looked down at her chips. "Kinda scary."

He frowned as he set his items down on the table and motioned for her to join him. "Are you scared of your new room?"

She took a seat next to him. "Out there." Her index finger extended, gesturing through the rain sleeked glass. "It's not safe."

"Because of Tobin's lady-friend this morning?"

She gave him a patient look as if her mind had moved ahead several steps and waited for him to catch up.

He stared out into the grouping of trees shuddering in the wind.

True, this world could be a scary place for a young girl who lost her mother. Forced to leave her home for one completely different. Not to mention cared for by men she had rarely seen. But she indicated something more.

He knew what lurked out there.

He would prefer to explain away her fears, but it was imperative to her safety that she knew the truth, too. When he pulled his gaze from the kitchen window, he found her staring at him.

He blinked and looked again.

Her eyes were a periwinkle cauldron of old-world knowledge, and pure trust, and upon deeper inspection, the tell-tale marking of a Muse in the making. Her irises speckled with white so faint it was undetectable to the untrained eye.

"You have your father's eyes."

Her lips splayed in a wry grin. "Marie doesn't know."

"Well, I know…." he reached for the bag of chips she held captive, pulling it open, and popped one in his mouth, savoring the sharp flavor that exploded on his tongue.

"Not from mommy?"

He paused. "Your mommy gave you other things…." Like a normal life and friends. How could he compete with that? "You miss her, don't you?" he asked.

She offered a somber nod.

He looked back to the table. "I'm sorry, Princess."

A quiet sadness pulled through the room until he felt a warm hand on his elbow. "You like Miss Marie.," she said.

"She's a very nice lady, don't you think?"

"'cept when she says to do stuff."

He sifted out a handful of chips and set them in front of her. Her eyes followed the scoop of his hand from bag to table and back again.

"I'll bet she's pretty fun to play with," he said.

"Oh, she-she's fun."

He put the chips back in the pantry. When he returned and reached for Anna's pile of chips, her hands dropped down on either side to corral them away. He sighed, and then reached for the cereal box instead.

"You can play with us," she offered.

He knew exactly the kind of playing he wanted to do with Marie, but that kind wasn't meant for a child's eyes. On the other hand, he didn't see any harm in settling for a diluted version. He had never enlisted the help of another to get what he wanted. He almost felt bad for taking Anna up on the offer.

Almost.

Chapter 13

After Marie readied herself for the day, she went searching for Anna. She found Quenton keeping her company in the kitchen. Their conversation died off into silence when she entered. Quenton's smile faded as he stepped to the kitchen window.

She looked at the mounded cereal, the spoon in Anna's hand, and scanned the kitchen for puddles of spilled milk. "Did you fix that yourself, Princess?"

"No. Quent helped."

"Oh, that was nice…" she said.

He flashed a smile before strolling out of the room.

She shook her head, convinced that once again her personal brand of male repellant was free flowing. If only she could patent it as a spray. It'd make a killing in the self-defense market.

With a quick glance outside, she propped her elbow on the table, resting her chin in the palm of her hand. "I think we'll be staying inside today."

Anna frowned.

"Not to worry though. We'll find something fun to do," Marie assured.

Tinted milk dripped from her spoon as she paused it mid-air. "How about dress-up?"

Marie nodded. "Dress-up it is then."

****

Marie and Anna spent the better part of the day in a

makeshift beauty parlor surrounded by the scent of jasmine perfume, and the swing notes of ragtime jazz. She wrapped sections of Anna's hair into tiny pin curls and piled them high on her head, while Anna remained patient and surprisingly still.

When she circled the vanity chair to inspect her handiwork, she noticed Anna's face tipped up with her eyes closed and a hint of a smile resting on her cherry-red lips.

Her chest swelled with pride, knowing that for a moment, Anna found her home. The memories of Anna's mother were still fresh in Marie's mind, and she could only imagine what this frequent pastime must bring back for Anna.

She would never take Christie's place in Anna's heart, but she still felt honored to substitute from time to time. Anna needed her. This was her job, and even though Anna's melt down last night left her feeling more inadequate than ever, she had to press on.

"You look pretty as a picture" she whispered.

Anna blinked and took a long stretch. "'Kay, but we still need dresses."

She nodded and reached into the small cedar chest. Anna turned down each item with a critical shake of her head until the box lay empty, and Marie held nothing more than an expectant shrug.

"Do *you* have any dress-ups," Anna asked.

"Hummm." She pressed a finger to her lips. "I think we might be able to find something."

She took Anna by the hand as they scampered to her bedroom closet. They ruffled through an assortment of knee-length skirts, and Marie kept a cautious eye on the back portion of her closet. She hoped Anna would find something before they came upon her personal Pandora's Box.

She never should have doubted Anna's credentials as a dress-up expert because after scanning through the contents of her closet, she headed right for it.

"You wear this one," she announced. The ruby sequins gave Marie a thousand sultry winks. The mere sight of it made her cringe. *I knew I should have burned that thing.*

Anna continued to dig through the box until she pulled out a waterfall of blue velvet. She gave Marie a triumphant grin. "And I'll wear this one."

"You sure you don't want to trade?"

Anna folded her arms across her chest and stuck out her bottom lip for added effect.

"Someone up there has a really bizarre sense of humor," Marie mumbled.

Anna remained silent but her expression morphed to satisfaction. She'd won this battle before it even began.

Perhaps last night's temper tantrum held more power than what she gave Anna credit for.

They dressed quickly and spent a good deal of time posing in Marie's gigantic bedroom mirror. She was right. The dress still showcased her assets without revealing too many of her flaws.

A sudden stroke of inspiration lit Anna's face. "Let's go to my room, and—and paint nails."

"You got it!"

She watched Anna clomp ahead in her oversized gown. But her smile fell when she caught sight of the hulking man, headed right for her with a small silver tray of cookies.

Quenton stopped short and leaned against the wall. He gave a low whistle as she passed, fueling the heat in her cheeks. His gaze seemed to trail the full length of her body, taking his time over her breasts and the juncture between her legs. When he returned to her face, he raised his brows.

"Dress up party," she mumbled as she bowed her head and continued to Anna's room.

"I like the dress. It matches your face."

"You see the lengths I go for my job? I deserve a promotion," she groused.

The corner of his mouth twitched. "Are we talking about the length of your legs or the length of that dress?"

She turned to face him. "Neither."

"How about the length of time it takes to get you out of it then?"

She steeled away her smile with an abrupt chin lift. "Not in your wildest dreams."

He crossed his arms. "I happen to know for a fact, that you have some very wild dreams."

She gaped in horror, and her mind jumped back to last night. Did she talk in her sleep? Did she moan? It shouldn't surprise her since she couldn't even keep her mouth closed when she was fully conscious. "You're lying!"

"Would you believe me if I said I wasn't?"

"Are you?"

His mischievous smile held no discernable answer.

She hoped flouncing back into Anna's room would convey her irritation, but she knew she couldn't stay that way long. She was too pleased her appearance had an impact on him.

His footfalls weren't far behind. "I'd hate to see you two ladies all dressed up with nowhere to go. How about a little tea party?"

Anna pulled away from her and rushed for the doorway, snatching a handful of cookies as she passed.

Marie plucked a cookie from his tray and pointed it at his chest. "You just paid off my company, milk-and-cookie man."

"I don't bribe people for attention, but I had to give Anna a small token of my gratitude."

Her stomach danced with anticipation when his gazed locked on the cookie poised at the edge of her mouth. "For what?" she asked. Still managing to sound innocent despite the naughty thoughts leaping over their mental fence and doing a little victory jig.

"Well, for this." He gestured the full length of her body. "And for willing to be your chaperone."

"Two can play this game. I'm glad you're here because we have a *fabulous* pink feather boa with your name on it."

"Anything to keep you poured into that dress."

She headed down the hallway with Quenton following close behind, and her heart thumped against her ribcage. Her ears strained to catch the soft echo of his footprints on the tile, but she couldn't over the clip of her heels.

At the hint of warm breath on her shoulder, she stopped. Part of her willed him to keep his distance while the other dared him to pursue.

In an instant, the hard length of him was pressed against her from shoulder to hip.

She froze. "Oh, sorry!" She moved to pull away. His free hand pinned her in place.

His breath felt hot at the curve of her neck. "Don't be."

"It's these heels." She teetered from side to side.

"Then take them off."

"What?"

"Your shoes. Step out of them."

She straightened against him. "No, I'm good. Just takes a little getting used to."

His hand made a slow descent along the inner curve of her arm. "I'd hate for you to sprain your ankle. Force me to carry you back to your room."

Unwilling to allow herself a second night with him anywhere near her bed, especially with her naughty thoughts on the loose, she complied.

She slipped off one shoe and shifted against his body as her foot met cold stone.

"Careful." His voice rumbled low in her ear.

With a shaky breath, she kicked off the other shoe, and as her weight leveled, she felt his erection pressed against the curve of her backside. She tried to inch forward but his grip tightened. His lips brushed feather-soft over the shell of her ear.

"Are you trembling?"

"You jerk!" She jumped out of his embrace, snatched up her shoes, and stormed down the hall. Pretty sure she was blushing from head to toe.

"Funny though, the shoes don't seem to make much of a difference. You don't look any safer or more comfortable."

****

Anna and Marie were in full character until late into the evening, complete with thick proper accents and ramrod posture. Quenton sat just a few feet away, his elbows propped on the table, eyes glittering just over his laced fingers.

She worked hard to avoid making full eye contact with him. Every time she caught his penetrating gaze, she faltered out of character. She managed a quick recovery though. Even had the privilege of looking down her nose at Tobin, when he barged in with yet another strange woman in tow.

"I'm home!" he called out.

She couldn't suppress her eye roll. "Oh great, the prodigal womanizer returns." She sent Quenton an apologetic look. "I think I'm going to get Anna ready for bed."

He nodded, but kept his eyes trained on the woman under Tobin's arm.

Something seemed off about this one, Marie thought. The redhead was all sharp angles and dainty curves, and although she had a naturally pale complexion, it shouldn't have been that pale. Her arms were crossed at her narrow waist, crimping the hem of her white ruffled blouse.

Quenton sat farther back in his chair and gave his brother a reproachful look. "This is something new."

"A healthy change of pace don't you think?" he asked.

She painted on a smile and gestured to an empty seat at the table. "Do you like tea? I was just about to take Anna to bed but Quenton and Tobin would be happy to serve you."

"No need," Tobin interrupted. "Claire and I have a party of our own planned."

She felt a pang of remorse for Claire as Tobin wrapped his arms around her waist and tugged her to him. Claire's flinch was subtle, but it was there.

"Tobin, maybe you should ease up a little, huh? It wouldn't kill you to be a gentleman," Marie said.

"Don't blame me, the woman has needs. I already canceled my plans for the evening at her request. How much more gentlemanly can I get?"

He glanced down at Claire, who looked at her toes. "This one wants to be a musician. Isn't that something?" A smirk pulled at his lips as he turned on his way out of the room. "I know you're a little rusty Quentie, so I'll be conducting lessons in my room should you care for a few refreshers."

A current of desperation filtered into Marie and hardened her tone. "You know all this is meaningless don't you? After tonight, he's just going to move on to someone else."

Claire looked into her with what could only be described as plain certainty. She managed a tight smile. "I know but I need this."

"You don't need anything that bad." Marie took Anna by the hand and led her out of the room. "It was nice to meet you, Claire. I'll be sure to light a candle for you."

After putting Anna to bed, she marched beside Quenton to her own room. "That woman doesn't have a clue what she's getting herself into."

He was slow to reply. "No one made her come here."

"No, but that's not the point. He's bringing them here under false pretenses." She shrugged. "*I need this?* How could anyone need sex so badly that they're willing to have it with someone they can't stand to be in the same room with? Seriously, what makes Tobin so compelling to inspire that in people?" The moment the last word tumbled out of her mouth, the realization hit, and she spun to face him.

Her voice turned on a shrill note. "He's hypnotizing them, isn't he? Using the same power you used on me. That's how he gets them to come here?"

He stayed silent.

"Incredible!" she muttered.

Her cell phone chirped out from her nightstand as she entered the room. She left him standing in the doorway as she rushed to get it. She looked down at the screen.

Unknown Number.

She held one finger up to Quenton. "Excuse me. I have to take this."

She spun away. "Hello?"

"Hey, honey."

A delighted smile curved her lips. "Dad. Hi! How are you?"

"Good, good. I'm calling to tell you we'll be leaving for the states earlier than expected. We're just passing through, and I want you to come see us for a few days in Aspen."

She wandered around the room, absently twisting her necklace. "That sounds really great, Dad, but I don't know if I can make it."

"Okay, okay just one day then. That's not too much for your old man to ask."

She turned to find Quenton watching her. She tried to focus on her father's conversation but couldn't. An ember of intent grew in his eyes, one that captured her thought process and rendered it useless.

"I'll—a. I'll see what I can do." Though no longer

certain what she agreed to.

Her father's tone hardened around the edges. "You sound distant. How are you sleeping?"

"Good. Better than good." She tilted her chin to the flat white ceiling. "It's a miracle I know."

She didn't bother mentioning this particular medical remedy came by way of a mythical being who could knock her out with just a whiff of his mojo. Best to save that little token of knowledge for a more comfortable blood alcohol level.

"That's good news," he said. "Maybe you could spend a couple of days."

Her shoulders slumped. "Don't push your luck."

Her father's voice became rushed. "Yeah I know, just promise me you'll think about it, and I'll call you again to confirm."

The phone crackled a bit as if he'd suddenly taken off on foot. "I have to cut this short. Your mother arranged a gondola ride and she looks like she's about to—" His words cut off under the muffled sound of male voices yelling in panicked Italian and the faint splash of water.

He sighed. "I've gotta go."

She smiled at the phone after he disconnected. "She told me all those water aerobics classes would come in handy someday."

She lifted the phone at Quenton in a sarcastic salute before dropping it into the side table drawer and shoving it closed. Somehow the phone caught an odd angle, sandwiched halfway out of the drawer. She jerked it opened again and gave it a little jiggle before slamming it closed again. "My parents. They're going to Aspen in a few weeks and want me to join them."

"You should go."

She ambled around the bed to face him. "Oh, I don't think I could leave Anna."

"It's fine. Anna and I'll travel with you. I've got some business up there anyway. It'd be a great trial run for all of us."

She stood in silence, weighing her options. She didn't want to pass up a visit with her parents. With their sporadic travel schedule there was no telling when they'd be able to see her again. If his plans to leave were successful and they went on the road as well, it would make time with her folks even more infrequent.

She wasn't sure if she liked the idea of her mom and dad meeting Quenton. She knew her parents. They could find some pretty wild assumptions for why she had taken a nanny position with the young single father.

"If you don't want to go for your own reasons, consider it payment for your miracle," he said.

Payment.

The word hit low in her stomach as her memory reeled back to the leather-bound book she'd read. It documented payment of a human soul. Even as far-fetched as the idea sounded, it made something wet and cold slip down her spine. Yeah, as if anything in this situation was conventional.

If the book's accounts were correct, a Muse's influence was like a drug. If taken too often it would lead to an addiction she couldn't shake.

Like Tobin's Bimbo-clown, Roxanne coming back time and again for just one more fix, and bit by bit her soul would be eaten away with every pass, until she had nothing left to give. Remove enough inhibitions to get at the final bits and pieces of that soul, soon the basic necessities like food and water were no longer a priority. She'd waste away to nothing.

She remembered how it felt to have Quenton put her under, and she didn't like it. Her aversion for losing control might be her only saving grace.

But, there were more dangerous components at work.

She was attracted to him. That seemed more powerful than any mythical spell he could cast and the real key to her undoing.

How far would she let her attraction to him go before giving him her soul? If Tobin's women were any indication, she could already be up to her neck. Could Quenton be feeding off her without her knowledge?

She steadied her voice. "I never did thank you for helping me get to sleep. It really means a lot to me."

"Are you asking me for a second helping?"

She swallowed hard. "No. but there must be something you expect in return."

He pushed himself from the door jam and cupped her bare shoulders. "I won't take anything that isn't offered."

The weight of his hands sent a warm current flowing through her body, but she pushed it away with a flare of anger.

"You have got to be one of the most cryptic people I have ever met! First, you blow me off in the woods this morning, and then you brush up against me in the hallway this afternoon. Now you tell me you won't take anything unless it's offered?"

His voice became a low growl. "You didn't offer me anything in the woods this morning. You asked. You asked for safety, and that I can't give."

He used his thumb to trace her lower lip. "But what you offered this afternoon? That I can take."

Slipping his hand to the curve of her jaw, he pulled her close. His lips closed down on hers. The kiss advanced quick and deep when their lips parted, and he stroked his tongue against hers. He worked her back to the bed with slow, shuffling steps and lifted her up with one easy motion. Closing off her escape with his own body weight, he urged her onto the down comforter. The feel of him pressed against her hips made her nerves jump. Her body went rigid.

Quenton seemed to recognize her hesitation, and his motions slowed. His kiss found a hot syrupy rhythm that taunted and explored her until her muscles eased their tension. The kiss deepened again.

While his mouth was busy on hers, he pushed down the neckline of her strapless dress until both breasts were exposed. Nervous anticipation fluttered in her stomach as the cool air drew her nipples taut. Her hands snaked around to grip his massive biceps and urge him closer.

He slid the edge of his hands around the curve of one breast, drawing his calloused thumbs over her nipple. The friction sent sparks of pleasure dancing through her body. She arched against him when he dipped his head to cover her breast with his mouth.

His scent wafted around her and sent all caution into a downward spiral.

His hand roved lower and pushed the hem of her dress up over her hips. Her muscles tensed, but she lifted up to accommodate him. He played along the silky inner curve of her thigh as he wedged himself between her knees, pushing them farther apart.

Her grip on his arms tightened, and she pulled him down to reach the curve of his neck. The rough feel of his denim-clad erection rocked against the thin fabric of her panties. But not for long.

A low growl came from his throat when his hand slipped inside the thin fabric to brush the juncture between her legs.

"Smooth."

She froze and for a moment, uncertainty blanketed her arousal.

"Is that okay?" she whispered against his throat. Too afraid to see what might be written in his eyes.

"It's more than okay." He groaned.

She cried out when he reached one finger in to claim her throbbing core. Moisture pooled between her legs as he coaxed her to move with him. Her thighs trembled in tiny waves of pleasure when she lifted to meet the stroke of his hand. With each penetration, he brushed against her in a progressive tempo that sent her spinning toward orgasm. Her cries escalated when he inserted a second finger. She couldn't restrain the feverish panting sounds as her muscles contracted around him.

Her nails scored over his shoulders, and she tipped her head back with a frantic whisper. "Please! Quenton, please let me have—"

He shook his head. "Not this time."

She wanted to protest, to beg to feel him inside her but she couldn't vocalize any more rational thought. She wasn't ready to let go like this, to be the only one losing control, and for him to take it so easily.

The tight burning sensation of his third finger threw her over the edge. She shuddered against his hand as she came.

He held her until her breathing slowed and her heart found a steady rhythm. He threw a thick comforter over Marie before pulling her into his chest.

Even through the chrysalis of feather down and cotton, she could still detect his erection. But he wasn't about to move. In fact, with his hand pressing down on her thigh, she wouldn't be going anywhere either.

She stared at their reflection in the full-length mirror, but his face was turned away to the nape of her neck. A mixture of confusion and regret swam through her.

"You didn't…. Why didn't you—"

"Take advantage of your lapse in judgment?" The subtle vibrations from his bitter chuckle cut right into her.

"Because I can't," he said. "You're more important than that."

The statement lingered in heavy silence as if he were only stating the obvious. She pushed enough of the hurt aside to keep her voice steady. "Would you care to elaborate?"

"No."

The weight that came with that single word made it far from clear-cut. If he didn't want to have sex with her, then why was his lower half so happily pressed against her? She hadn't seen it in action, but it appeared to be in perfect working order. His problem wasn't physical.

It became apparent to her that the act served as a warning. A reminder that he was still her boss, still Anna's father, and still willing to drop her like a bad habit the moment he got bored. Her stomach kneaded at a sickening thought. She already knew what happened in her predictable relationship cycle. Boy makes his move. Boy gets rejected. Girl leaves. But what happens when the *girl* gets rejected? What then?

She brushed an errant curl from her eyes. "You can go now," she said.

He didn't move.

"I said you can leave. I have to get ready for bed, and I think your wicked stick needs some room to breathe," she said.

"Your bed is more comfortable than mine."

She pushed up from the pillow. "Fine. We'll trade."

His arm tensed around her waist. "You don't want to do that."

She grasped the edge of the bed and dragged her torso away. "Anything's better than staying here with you."

He locked his arm around her chest and pulled her back. "Is that so, snuggle bunny?"

Her biceps strained under the human tug-of-war, and her fingernails clawed into the seam of the mattress. "Yeah, that's so," she grunted.

His tension increased slow and deliberate until her hands ripped free, and he dragged her back. "You sleep better when I'm here. You can't deny it."

She pushed out a frustrated breath. "And why is that exactly?"

"My scent. It's harmless in small doses and completely involuntary unless of course I don't shower. Then I can literally clear a room."

"Something tells me that sleepy time pheromones aren't the half of it."

Silence stirred her curiosity but his obscured image in the full-length mirror didn't offer any expression. "What else do you do?" she asked.

"Haven't you heard?"

"Oh, I've heard it. Seen it. I think I may have even experienced it firsthand. I just don't believe it." She hooked her thumb under the long chain around her neck, working it back and forth under the pearls. "You inspire people. That's your job?"

Hearing his heavy sigh, she arched back, bumping up against him.

"Don't." He growled.

"Answer then."

"We can push suggestions to anyone, but the real work is tracking through the subconscious. Clearing out inhibition and blurring restraints from past experience."

She stilled. "You've been in my head? What did you see?"

He laughed. "Cobwebs mostly. Go to sleep."

"That's what people pay you for? Their soul in trade for something they had all along? Sounds like a bum deal."

Each of his words came measured and purposeful. "The relationship is symbiotic. We both need things. We both get them."

"I don't need anything from you."

"Really? Not even my…what did you call it?"

"Shut up."

"Oh, yeah, my wicked stick. The one you've asked for…what? Twice now in the last hour?"

Cinders of anger flared to life again inside her. "You love it don't you? Being crack dealer of the gods. All those women hanging on you. Begging for it. Well,

I'll tell you something, I had my taste, and I'm done. You can count me out from now on."

She could feel the heat of his stare boring into her shoulder. His fist tightened on the material at her waist.

His voice flowed through the room in an acidic rumble, barely audible under his breath. "I didn't sign up for this shit."

He jostled the mattress as he pushed himself off the bed and stormed out, slamming the door behind him.

****

Quenton watched the silent rise and fall of Marie's chest through the two-way mirror of his stone doghouse. A bittersweet pride warmed his chest, knowing he managed to ease her insomnia for the second night in a row without using any power over her.

Felt like cementing his feet to the ground after a lifetime at sea, but he had done it.

Better get used to it, too, he thought. *Because where I'm going, there isn't any amount of magic that can help me.*

His memory traced back to the message her soul slammed into him.

Safety.

Why not an artist? That was an easy one. Or a singer? He became world renowned for his ability to loosen a woman's vocal cords. *Even a goddamn ballerina would have been tolerable at this point.*

But safety?

The only way to get her to safety was to get her the hell out of Colorado which was the one place she didn't want to leave. No way could he force her to go and still have the odds in his favor. But they couldn't stay….

She already caught the Shades' interest, but as long as he didn't claim her soul, she shouldn't draw more attention than any other hot, athletic, twenty-five-year-old running through the forest like a scared doe.

He lowered his head.

Hell, who am I kidding? She's the pinup girl for Victims Monthly.

Rigging his plan with the perfect bait should've made him giddy with anticipation. And after what she said, she could use a slap on the ass.

"Crack dealer to the gods." Hadn't heard that one before and coming from her, it stung.

With the emptiness inside him stronger every day, he would soon find himself weak and unable to protect Anna. Time was running out. He needed to find an energy source soon and hated the idea of anyone else, knowing it would never be enough.

The first night, he was strong enough to reign in his power. That wouldn't happen again. He couldn't spend another night so close to her. Not after the little morsel she gave him in the woods. His hunger felt like a bottomless cavern and with her tempting him daily, the edges of his restraint eroded away as the hunger grew.

He didn't realize how close to the edge he stood until she touched him.

Hit him.

He hated to admit it but damned if he wasn't torturing himself as Tobin predicted. After waiting this long to find her and getting her comfortable enough to let him in, he still couldn't claim her.

He couldn't discern her threshold for the power he wielded and couldn't risk an addiction. That meant doing it without sedation. Not impossible just difficult.

He would only have one shot to get it right.

He had to get her out of these hills soon and by any means necessary.

She fit into a valuable place in Anna's life, and he didn't want to tear that apart. She would stay and care for Anna as long as she wanted, and for him, she would only serve one purpose.

Marie said she had enough of him. Fine. Once she filled him up, he would cut her loose.

No more wasting time. Deploy the bait, kill the Shades, and nail the girl.

Operation Inspiring Temptation starts now.

Chapter 14

Quenton stood behind the mahogany desk, watching dawn break over the clearing. The mist rolled in like a ghostly tide, making it difficult for him to see through it. His shoulders were clenched, and he swiveled his head to ease the building tension in his neck.

"I saw another one out there last night. They're swarming," he said.

Tobin glanced over his shoulder to Claire before closing his bedroom door. He lowered his voice. "What else is new? It's business as usual this time of year." He plopped down into an oversized chair and brought his feet up to rest on a nearby coffee table.

"It didn't seem to keep you from frisking the nanny."

Quenton braced his palms on the windowsill. "You know she's more than that."

"Anything more draws too much attention, and I for one value my home and family too much to let that happen."

He glared. "I know."

"And if you continue to let yourself waste away, they're going to take you just as easily as they will her. Where will Anna be then? Those two females—Anna and Marie—are all we have left. You can't afford to take up martyrdom now."

Quenton gave a noncommittal grunt.

Tobin tucked his hands behind his head. His brows drew together in mock contemplation, as he searched the giant pendant light above. "What you need is to go into town and feast on some busty beatniks. Marie won't know the difference…or care for that matter."

"Get your damn nose out of my business and back to where it belongs."

Tobin lifted his shoulders in a careless shrug. "Would love to but sweet cheeks in there can't keep up with me. She's called a time out. I told her she needs to conserve her energy but damned if the poor thing keeps getting carried away. Especially when I turn her upside down and—"

Quenton slammed the chair into the desk. "I don't want to hear excuses. I want you to do your job. Help me find Christie's Shade."

"First the glassware, now the furniture? You need a therapist man. A young one with long legs and big tits."

Anger heated Quenton's face as he rounded the desk. "Tobin, I swear to God—"

Tobin held up an undersized throw pillow in a feeble attempt to shield his face. He jostled it like a trembling leaf. "Look, we have too little to go on and with those detectives breathing down my neck, it isn't getting any easier."

"Take care of them then. In the meantime, I'm calling in reinforcements."

Tobin's head snapped to attention. "When?"

Quenton smacked the pillow out of Tobin's hands. "I'm putting in a call tonight. I'm finding safe haven for Marie and Anna, too. We can't lock them inside without cause, and they aren't safe out there."

"You want to leave?" Tobin scoffed. "You can't outrun them. This place is as safe as any. It's our home. Marie's too. Making her leave will only drive her away from you. You can't afford that. We're staying."

"If we stay, you've got to stop bringing innocent women home. Anna and Marie can't be exposed to that."

Tobin raised an indignant brow. "Marie's a big girl. What makes you think she needs sheltering? Besides, those women approach me looking for an experience in life. Why shouldn't I accept their proposal? Unlike you, oh, patron saint of chastity, my gift comes without limitations. No other will minister to them. Because the only other Muse is…Well. You."

Quenton dropped into the adjoining chair. "It's careless," he bit out.

"If it makes you happy, I'll sew my wild oats in a different patch until spring. But I've got to tell you that Claire has me tempted to keep her around a while."

Quenton took his brother's distant expression with an air of caution. "Yeah, I noticed that about her."

"She's close Quentie, real close. Full and ripe and…."

"Not close enough."

The sudden tension in Tobin's jaw disappeared with a wry smile. He sucked in a breath. "Harsh words. It's a good thing I don't follow your standards. I'd never get laid." Tobin launched to his feet and headed back to his room. "Give me another hour. I'll take first watch on the evil shadow puppets since I have a feeling you'll be doing a little sightseeing of your own."

****

The simple bronze doorknob fit nicely in Marie's

palm, but she clamped down on it with both hands. Turning bit by bit until the latch pulled free and the door swung open with only the faintest whisper across the carpet.

Last night's confrontation with Quenton had left her on edge. She may have sunk down into a dreamless sleep but the moment she swung her legs off the bed, all of her frustration waited for her.

She needed to get out. Clear her head.

Midway down the hall, a distinctive *click* rang out behind her.

She clenched her fists and kept moving. She wanted to stomp back and beat the stupid thing into submission. Of course, that would only result in three bleary eyed, ultra-ornery Blakes to answer to.

Nervous energy coiled in her muscles as she advanced to the front door with tender steps.

When she stepped outside and took one look at the foggy landscape, her perky optimism withered in defeat. After yesterday's paranormal encounter still fresh in her mind, she'd rather play the hamster, running laps around the house than risk spraining her ankle out in that soupy mess.

And who knows what freakish ghostie might offer her a hand up.

Off the front porch, the sound of tires rolled up the gravel drive. She peered through the fog until a silver sedan loomed into view.

Detective Farnell and Stewart emerged with their heads down and shoulders hunched against the cold. Puffs of breath trailed after them.

"Good morning, Detectives. You here for Tobin?"

Farnell extended a tired smile. "He called an hour

ago, said he'd be leaving town again, and this was the best time to meet. Are you just heading out?

"For a minute, yeah." She moved aside and motioned for him to follow but he didn't move.

Marie frowned. "Any news?"

Farnell's eyes dimed with regret. "I wish I could say it was good, but the fact remains that we're racing against time. Heather is diabetic. All her insulin is accounted for. If she doesn't have access to medication, she won't last long."

She tugged on her necklace, urging herself to maintain composure. "There was something wrong with her insulin pump the day she disappeared. I remember it beeped."

He nodded. "We're not ruling out the possibility of diabetic shock. Maybe she got confused and wandered off. Either way, she wouldn't have gotten far."

An icy hand wrapped around her spine at the thought of Heather out in the woods alone. With the cold and rain over the last few days, chances were slim even an experienced person could survive. But the detective was not even giving Heather a slim chance.

Ghost or not, that thing in the woods looked so contorted and grotesque, she did not want it to be her friend. She would rather cling to the thought of Heather slipping away from cold and shock. Her body lying somewhere out in the woods, untouched and frozen in time.

Stewart fished through his inside pocket, pulling her away from her thoughts.

"I'm sure you've already seen the papers, Ms. Durant. We have another missing person."

He handed her a folded copy of the front page. A

twenty-something blonde. With heavy mascara stared back at her. Droopy, jewel-encrusted earrings nearly met her shoulders.

"Her name is Roxanne Loftus, have you seen her around?" he asked.

Marie closed her eyes. "Yeah, with Tobin and another woman on my first night here but that was before he left town. She came back a second time, but she didn't look very good."

He pulled a notebook from his back pocket. "How do you mean?"

"She was distant. Haggard. Not like the first time I saw her. She didn't stay long though."

Marie did not bother mentioning how the woman went from the epitome of glamour to a burned-out addict in a matter of days. How was she going to explain that Tobin turned her into a distraught nymphomaniac? Even an imagination guru like herself had trouble swallowing that one.

She ushered the detectives to the study but before she could knock, the doors swung open wide to reveal two scowling Blake brothers.

"Good morning guys, you have company." She brushed past Quenton into the room and flounced into an oversized chair, slapping her palms down.

Quenton gave her a hard look. "Marie, could we trouble you for some coffee?"

"Well, you could but I think it should wait till I hear what you two have to say."

Farnell looked to the men then Marie. "Coffee sounds great, thank you."

Tobin grinned. "I'll take a grand mocha latte with extra cream and sugar if you don't mind."

"I do mind." Marie blasted all four men with a narrowed glare before marching to the kitchen. She bypassed the pot of fresh roasted coffee sitting on the warmer, heading straight for the economy sized can of instant. She put three heaping scoopfuls into each glass, and five into Tobin's for good measure, and then filled each cup with lukewarm water. Except for Tobin's, his was cold.

By the time she reached the study, Farnell, Stewart, and Tobin were sitting in the adjoining club chairs in deep discussion, and Quenton lounged on the couch behind them.

Any other man might have looked relaxed with one arm draped over the back of the couch, and his ankle crossed over his knee but the heat in Quenton's stare threatened an attack at any moment.

She tried to brush off the ten-point tumbling routine her stomach performed as she set the tray of coffee on the table. She divvied out the cups and sat beside Quenton to take in the show.

Stewart went first, taking a tentative sip, and then set his cup back down without any noticeable change of expression. "Just to be clear, we'd still like to invite you to the station for an official statement."

"Sweet offer. Really. But for now, we do this under my terms."

Farnell exchanged an unreadable glance with his partner then cleared his throat. "All right." He flipped the page on his notebook. "Security cameras show Heather leaving with each of you on the day in question. Quenton in the afternoon and Tobin that evening."

Tobin smirked. "What a slut. I thought I was her

one and only. Well, except for Doc Scott, and that guy in the gift shop. But Quenton…." He shot his brother an accusatory glance. "Never saw that one coming."

Marie opened her mouth but Quenton gave her knee a warning squeeze.

She needed to keep her emotions in check. Including the parade of hormones that danced gaily through her body when Quenton's hand moved from her knee to caress her inner thigh. Did he really think she was dumb enough to fall for his distraction twice?

She glared at him, even as the moisture pooled between her legs.

"What time did you leave Heather?" Farnell asked.

"Oh, I don't know, after a few hours the action fizzled out, so I left her at my place and scouted for something better. I forgot all about her until the next day," Tobin said.

Marie erupted. "How could you possibly forget about a woman you left in your bed? Even for someone with the attention span of a goldfish."

Tobin looked to his brother. "Put a muzzle on that thing will you? Where's all this pent-up hostility coming from? You aren't suffering from some kind of penis envy are you?"

Farnell and Stewart both looked to her with raised brows.

Marie wanted to jump up and introduce his penis to her size six-and-a-half shoe, but she couldn't with Quenton's hand locked on her thigh.

"Enough playing around Tobin, we haven't got all day," Quenton said with a calm that made Marie want to kick him, too.

Her gaze darted to Quenton's coffee cup as he took

his first sip. The moment the liquid met his lips he frowned into his cup, threw back his head, and downed the rest. Marie grimaced with a sympathetic gulp. He shoved the cup back to her and leaned in close to whisper in her ear.

"Could you get me a refill? Now."

Her eyes narrowed on him as she swiped the cup away and stormed out of the room.

Several moments later, she returned with a smile and a cup full of gloppy sludge that probably would not move, even if Quenton turned it upside down. She absently handed it to him as she took in the sickening display laid out before her.

Claire, in the same rumpled clothes from the evening before, sat glued to Tobin's side.

"Claire spent the rest of that evening with me, and we've been together ever since," Tobin said.

"Oh, you have got to be kidding me," she groaned.

Tobin gave her a wounded look. "Why do you take such issue with our relationship Marie? You're not being replaced. No matter how close Claire and I get, I'll always wipe my feet on you."

"That's enough Mr. Blake—" Stewart said.

Tobin ignored him and turned to Quenton. "She's really putting a damper on the chemistry in here. Can't you bore her to sleep or something?"

Shock slammed into Marie, quickly followed by hurt as her attention flew from Tobin to Quenton. "You told him about me?"

Quenton didn't look at her, which in part was a good thing. Claire gave her a distant smile. "Marie, I understand that you lost your friend, but you can't just go around blaming innocent people."

Marie's jaw hardened when she saw that all eyes in the room were set against her. Even the detectives weren't arguing. They sat stone quiet, staring into Tobin like men lost in their own thoughts. The same haunted expression she saw in Roxanne before she disappeared.

Her mind pin-wheeled into a panic, and she jumped to her feet. "Tobin, what did you do?" Quenton reached out to snag her wrist but she jerked away and staggered toward Farnell.

"Detective?"

Farnell gave her a puzzled frown. His thin lips parted, and he stumbled over his words, sounding as if he couldn't even remember his own name. Let alone hers. "Yeah…sorry I got distracted." His face reddened. He looked to his partner then ducked his head over the notebook. "Go ahead, Mr. Blake, I'm listening."

"As I was saying, gentlemen, you've hit a dead end here. Time to go back to the drawing board."

She turned her fury on Tobin. "You're not getting away with this. If I have to hunt the truth down myself, you're going to rot in hell for what you've done."

The solemn tilt of his eyes drove cold fear into her veins. "In that case, it'll be the last thing you ever do."

Chapter 15

Marie chose to bide her time outside after Quenton assisted the absentminded detectives to their car. She had watched Farnell stagger away as Quenton helped Stewart into the passenger side before Quenton redirected him. It would be a miracle if they made it back to town.

Quenton must have offered some choice words to his brother afterward, and Marie wasn't anxious to be next in line for the hot seat.

With the detective's hands mentally tied, she knew it would take a lot of manpower to bring down someone like Tobin Blake. The town wasn't big. Local authorities weren't exactly hopping up and down to stake out one of the most influential families in Sterling Springs.

Everyone knew about the Blakes' heavy hand in town politics, hence their invitation to the Governor's ball. For all she knew, he could be paying the police to look the other way, or worse, hypnotizing the entire police for to their whim.

She needed to find proof and waggle it under the detectives' noses until they had no choice but to go after him.

She bee-lined to the side of the house, around overgrown ivy and wilted climbing roses, to the door Quenton passed through on her first night in the house.

She found it camouflaged, carved into the stone exterior. Undetectable to anyone that didn't know where to look for it.

She jerked back on the crude iron handle once. Then propped her foot against the wall for more leverage and jerked again. The cold handle bit into her hands but it wouldn't budge an inch.

She shook her hands until the sting faded, evaluating the door's placement on the wall. The fresh chisel marks on the stone told her this feature wasn't original to the house. It looked like a shallow storage area, but her intuition told her something more.

Quenton wouldn't come here to converse with the gardening equipment. If Tobin was turning this place into his own personal funhouse, anything could be behind there.

Her skin burned on contact when she pressed her ear to the frosted door.

Silence.

Prisoners? Not likely. Why would he keep a woman under lock and key if they willingly clung to him anyway? And she never saw him approach this door. It would require him to make repeated trips through the entrance if he were working to sustain life.

But death on the other hand....

She squeezed her eyes shut. No, she didn't want to go there.

In any other magnificent home in a land far away, she might assume this door led to a dungeon for the pet dragon. But Tobin's lair was far off in the study—nowhere near this entrance.

After the threats she made in the study, Quenton wouldn't offer her information about this door or anything else. Her only option was to sneak into Tobin's room and find a key that could unlock the door.

Tobin had plans to leave for a business trip tomorrow, so keeping track of two Blake men would no longer be an issue. With any luck, Tobin would take his young fling with him. If Marie sent Quenton off on a few errands, she could have all the time she needed to explore.

****

While her brain whirred, forming the details of her plan, she set about her daily routine. She and Anna spent most of the afternoon outside, raking up leaves scattered around the yard and launching themselves into them. The fog didn't thin out much as the day wore on, leaving an eerie haze along the tree line and damping out the sunlight.

"Take it in while you can, Anna. Cooler temperatures are coming, and you know what that means?"

Anna threw an arm full of leaves in the air. "Snow!"

Marie offered more of her preschool patented enthusiasm. "Won't that be nice to see this whole valley covered in snow?"

"Yeah, 'cause it's safer. 'Cause you can see tracks."

Marie twirled a giant maple leaf between her thumb and forefinger. "Animal tracks?"

Anna stopped backstroking through the leaf pile to study Marie. "Yeah. If you don't see tracks, that's bad, 'cause—'cause they're coming. If you see tracks it means they go away. 'Cept the dead ones, they don't go anywhere."

"Oh. That's comforting," Marie said.

"Are *we* going away soon?" she asked, resuming her strokes.

"I don't know, Princess."

Her plans for convincing Quenton to stay here were drifting off course. With Tobin's bad influence, women disappearing all around them, and freaky creatures hanging out in the woods, she'd be crazy to recommend that Anna stay here.

In the beginning, she'd waged this battle to protect her from an unsettling childhood. One she found painfully familiar.

But maybe she didn't need to.

Maybe the only problem came from the hopelessly maladjusted nanny. If so, she couldn't hold Anna back. She had to let Anna leave, even if she wasn't able to follow.

****

I could be warm and cozy in bed right now. Full and drowsy and content. But noooo.

Tobin entered the clearing and glared over the collar of his wool coat. Ice crystals suspended mid-air, needling at his skin. Going out in weather like this felt more than uncomfortable, it was just plain stupid.

The fog hung so dense, his gaze couldn't penetrate more than fifty feet in front of him, which said a lot for someone with his visual acuity. He was completely exposed, and not in a good way, with no telling how many little buddies the Shade had tagging along behind her.

He paced back and forth, covering the length of the clearing and bypassing the old wooden bench with every turn to keep his body heat up and his mind focused.

Dealing with this Shade really got on his nerves. He should've destroyed her the moment he cornered her in the hospital morgue.

With his hand locked around her throat, he'd lifted her off the floor. Her fingernails dug into his wrist like tiny hot pokers as she tried to claw her way free. His palms slicked with moisture over cold, waxy skin. His grip started to slide.

Draped in an oversized hospital gown, Christie had looked so small and helpless. The way her legs dangled limp in mid-air made his stomach clench.

"Please, please don't hurt me!" she croaked.

He squeezed his eyes shut.

Just one quick jerk would end it all, but no. He had to get all sentimental, then she'd opened her big mouth.

It wasn't so much the words she spoke but the sound. The sound of Christie's voice ensnared his brain. It refused to break the connection between her voice and the memory of her precious spirit.

Christie's soul had already moved on to the great shopping mall in the sky, or whatever she liked to do. The moderately functional shell became the only thing left behind; minus the eight pints of blood she left in the totaled Bentley which particularly sucked because he loved that car.

Christie's body would be mutilated as well. This murdering shithead decided to take up residence and planned to do a little redecorating.

It compacted itself inside her corpse for the time being, but eventually it would stretch and pull her to fit its own form. Then strut around like a bag lady in a new mink stole until her body's usefulness decayed away.

At which point, the Shade would move on to bigger and better accommodations.

He couldn't let Christie's body be used like that.

"Sorry, no vacancies," he said.

"Please, I'll do anything! I can help you. I can. Just don't hurt my body."

He clenched his jaw. "It's not *your* body."

"Oh come on! This is the best one I've ever found. She didn't need it anymore. I can't let it go to waste—"

"You're breaking my heart."

Its black orbs grew wider, overshadowing sunken cheeks. The Shade spoke in desperate pants. "Yes…heartbreaker! That's what you are, yes? I know what you want. Know how to get it too. Just don't hurt me."

"What the hell are you talking about?"

"Your—a. How you say? Device. It's broken, yes?"

"What!" he roared. He wrenched the body to his hip, catching its head under his arm, poised to snap its neck.

"You're broken," it cried. "Missing pieces! I can find your missing pieces."

At last, a bargain he couldn't refuse.

Shades were about as prevalent as fleas. They hid all over the country in forests, mountain ranges, and corn fields. Where they could easily stalk their prey. They had an intricate social system that maintained close contact during migration. Most importantly, they always hunted people like him, and any potential mate he met.

The vicious cold brought him back to reality, and he kicked at a rock with the toe of his shoe, sending it skittering across the clearing into the trees.

With his kind of luck, she wouldn't even show, and he spent the evening freezing his ass off for nothing. He shoved his fists into his pockets.

If she still lurked out there somewhere, her time was running short. Pretty soon her pack would have gorged themselves on all the bodies they could find, from every morgue, funeral parlor, and wake, then the encroaching winter would drive them all south. When that day came, he would make sure she did it without her trophy. He knew he'd made a mistake to let her go the first time. He planned to fix that the moment she gave him what he wanted.

He jumped at the slight rustle in the brush behind him and spun around to greet the gangly silhouette standing only a few feet away. "You better have something new to offer me." He growled.

The Shade spoke with a raspy metallic strain over Christie's voice as it sulked in the shadows. The glitter of tiny ice crystals floating around the creature's head and shoulders were the only discerning characteristic.

"I have information," it said.

"Have you found her?"

"We know where she is."

Tobin sucked in a slow breath. "Tell me."

"Not so fast, heartbreaker," it chided. "We've not yet settled our terms."

He gritted his teeth at the endearment. "You know the terms. You get me information. I let you keep your head."

"But your brother makes things difficult. He's posing a threat."

"I'm not here to talk politics. Your cronies can eat

it as far as I'm concerned."

The Shade shifted its weight from one foot to the other. "If you choose not to honor my comrades, I can't ensure their loyalty."

"I'll survive."

The body creaked and groaned as it moved into the clearing, making his stomach turn. Its limbs were stretched thin and teetered awkwardly on the edge of their sockets. Its choppy blonde hair matted with dirt. There wasn't much left that reminded him of Christie, except for the delicate curve of her jaw. He forced his gaze away.

"You don't like the way I look?" it asked.

"The hospital gown makes your ass look big."

She turned to check her back end, and the moment he saw that the gown had come untied, he held up both palms. "God! Don't turn around. I don't want to see that!"

What was with Shades these days? They always managed to pick bodies in varying degrees of wardrobe malfunction. Even the ones swiped from the funeral parlor had their clothes slit up the back to make dressing the bodies easier. Didn't they ever get cold? Frostbite? Laser hair removal?

Apparently not.

Christie might have been a hot momma in life but in death she looked more like pulled taffy. She'd be a whole lot better six feet under where she belonged.

The Shade cocked its narrow head to the side. "You're not as detached as you like to appear."

He yanked his fists from his pockets. "Keep it up, and I'll show you detached!"

"Can't find your one mate, can you? You do not

feel drawn to her, and so do not wish to be drawn to others, yes?"

"I don't need a psychologist, I need answers. Speak, or I'll tear out your tongue."

The Shade took a hesitant step back and bowed its head in submission. "It's rumored that your mate resides in Iowa."

"Find out where. And if any of you so much as cast a shadow on her, I'll spare no expense hunting you down."

"I cannot find answers without resources."

He crossed his arms over his chest. "Not my problem."

The Shade's head tipped down as if she were scoured the frozen ground for answers, afraid to look up. "My sources ask a payment. They want the woman. The common one."

He cast his eyes to the billowing fog that curled over his head. "Tell you what, I'll get my brother off your back, and you can hunt her your damn self. In the meantime, you'll go to Iowa and find my mate."

"It's difficult for us to travel north so late in the season."

That's precisely what he counted on. He didn't trust the Shade to make good on any deal without profit. If they knew about his mate, nothing would keep them from trying to take her. He had to find and relocate her before they could do her harm.

"Go back to your source. I want her location and proof she's unharmed."

That ought to buy him some time. If they were too busy trying to prove she's alive and well, they wouldn't be able to hurt her. And the only Shades left in the area would offer a trail right to her.

****

Fresh from her morning shower the next day, Marie clicked through her playlist, and then slid up the volume. A sexy concoction of urban rhythm and pert violin solos carried through her room. The swivel of her hips kept time with the thumping base as she sauntered around collecting her clothes. Feeling empowered in nothing more than her pearl necklace, she took her time slipping on a black lace bra and matching panties.

"Perfect for a woman on a mission," she said.

Tobin had left hours ago, hopefully taking his redheaded patsy with him, and that left just one more opponent. The biggest and most powerful of the three but today she wasn't worried. She could take him.

She stretched her arms skyward and let her torso slither and sway to the beat like a charmed snake.

Facing off with Quenton over the last few days, she recognized she couldn't bend him with her size or her blunt logic. She needed to take a more underhanded approach.

"Dur. *How* long did it take to figure that out? Why ask permission when I can beg forgiveness? I'm weak and insignificant, so clearly he would take pity on me. Or punish me. Bypass his knee and show me all those more fearful body parts."

She pulled a rust colored sweater from the dresser and draped it around her shoulders like a feather boa, sliding it back and forth across her shoulders. "Quenton...you are in so. Much. Trouble."

Anna went down for nap time at 11:30 a.m. If she sent Quenton out for groceries, she could have the entire house to herself for at least an hour. She would search every nook and cranny until she found a key to fit the lock on Tobin's trunk or the one to the side door.

If she was lucky, both.

With the light in her favor this time, she could triple glove her hands and bag any incriminating evidence from Tobin's room. When Anna woke, they could make an impromptu field trip to the police station.

"Piece of cake," she said, shimmying into a pair of dark indigo jeans.

"And if Quenton comes home before we get back?" She shrugged. "We went for a drive to see the leaves."

Following the beat of the music, she turned in a slow circle belly dancer style. She toyed with her necklace and flashed her best come hither expression as her memory locked on Quenton.

He thought he could dismiss her so easily, but boy, did she have a surprise for him.

She slid her hands over her breasts, causing her nipples to strain under the thin fabric of her bra. Her memory spun back to the feel of his touch over her skin. He may have forgotten but her body had not, and within these four walls she could freely admit it.

Her palms roved to the curve of her hips, and her mind to their brief encounter in her bedroom; to that moment that sent her sailing over the edge of insanity. Her groan sounded barely audible over the thumping beat of the music.

"Nothing wrong with fantasies provided they remain…fantasies," she reasoned. It gave her the liberty and power to choose when she lost control. No one else could make the decision for her.

"Come here big boy, it's my turn now," she said.

"For what?"

On a shriek, she whirled around to find Quenton glowering in her open doorway.

"Get out!" She used the arms of her sweater to cover her chest. A pretty futile attempt to hide, standing in the middle of the room heated from head to toe like a giant blinking light.

He snorted. "Sure you don't want to invite me in?"

"Get. Out!"

"Your music is up too loud."

She stomped over to the music and clicked it off. "Anna doesn't seem to mind, she's still sleeping. Don't you knock?"

"I did. You were distracted. Finish getting dressed; I want to talk to you." He nudged himself away from the doorframe and disappeared down the hall.

"I locked this door."

"No, you didn't," he called back.

She slammed the door shut and flipped the lock. "Yes, I did." And how did he manage to get it unlocked anyway?

A bolt of enlightenment struck her. Tobin mentioned a key when she overheard him that first night. At the time, she thought they were referring to her room but the lock to her door had no slot for a key. The key they referred to must belong to the outside door.

Quenton was last seen out there. He must have the key. That narrowed her scope a bit but didn't eliminate the problem of getting him out of the house long enough to snatch it.

She lifted her chin to her reflection. "All right. This

can be good for me."

She tried to smooth over the frayed the edges of her confidence. Quenton's interruption made her stumble right out of the gate but the race wasn't over yet. She could still win, if only she could rise above her emotions and take action.

She pulled on the sweater, added a few bangles for flair, and marched to the kitchen in knee-high boots. Hopefully it gave the illusion that she held her head up after being caught wallowing in the gutter.

She dropped two slices of bread in the toaster and pushed down the lever. "All right, what's up?"

He stopped scrolling through his phone and tossed it on the kitchen table. "I just finished making plans for our stay in Aspen." He gestured to the window. "I'd like to leave today but as you can see that isn't going to happen."

She gaped at the large windowpane crisscrossed with delicate threads of ice crystals and the winter wonderland beyond. A thin layer of ice covered every branch, rock, and blade of grass. The most beautiful yet horrifying thing she'd ever seen.

"Tobin called from the airport. The ice fog warning is no longer in effect, but the damage is widespread. Travel is being restricted. He's staying in Colorado Springs for a few days to wait it out," he said.

"But what about food? We need to pick up some more peanut butter for Anna. You know it's the only thing she ever eats."

"We still have a little, and this shouldn't last long. Maybe a day. I thought you of all people would be thrilled. Locked away with nowhere to go."

The toast popped up, and she smeared the warm

slices with a thick layer of orange marmalade. "It all depends on who I'm locked away with."

His glacial stare rivaled the view outside. "If you don't like my company, there's always Anna and Claire."

She stopped tapping the stray crumbs from her toast. "Claire's still here?"

He nodded.

She muffled out her words from a mouthful of toast. "Okay. Why?" The tart nectar of the marmalade slid down her throat, and her shoulders sank back in surrender. She couldn't remember the last time anything tasted this great. Normally, the multiple cups of coffee she consumed hampered her appetite for anything else. With insomnia long gone, she could welcome breakfast.

He narrowed his gaze on her mouth. "Tobin left late last night. I guess he intended for her to leave this morning—you've got a little something...."

"Here?" The tip of her tongue darted to the corner of her mouth.

He closed his eyes. "No, the other side."

She used her tongue to trace the seam of her lips. Was her action really having an effect on him? *Interesting.* "So when exactly are we set to leave?"

"Tomorrow."

"And why the rush?"

"Staying in one place makes me stir-crazy and I have some business to attend to."

She readily agreed that Sterling Springs wore on him. The light in his eyes gradually dulled as days passed, and the faint crease between his brows looked more pronounced. "You look like you need a vacation.

We should book you for a day at the spa. You need replenishment."

He gave a silent snort.

The conversation froze as a battered Claire stumbled into the kitchen doorframe. Too busy cradling her head with her hands to watch where she was going.

"Coffee?" Marie asked.

Claire winced. "And some Aspirin please."

"How was your night?"

Quenton gave her a do-you-really-want-to-know kind of look.

He was right, she didn't. And thankfully, Claire didn't elaborate.

"I think I'm going to bundle Anna up and take her outside this morning. You're welcome to join us." Marie suggested.

Quenton's eyes followed Claire as she shuffled to the kitchen table, looping tufts of fiery red curls behind her ears.

"The fresh air might do you some good," he said.

Marie offered the woman her second piece of toast with the coffee. Quenton pulled it away just as quickly when Claire's pasty complexion turned green.

"Don't worry, it'll pass," he said.

Why was he being so nice to her? He didn't care about any of the other women Tobin brought home. Why was this one so special? Was this just another convenient method for stoking his masculinity? Being the hero by cleaning up after Tobin and saving the damsel in distress?

If that's the case, what did that make her? Another mended doll he patched up and put high on the shelf?

Her chest constricted. No. She was on a different

playing field because at least around other women, he was willing to let his guard down. Quenton probably didn't have any qualms about having sex with other women. Being his brother's…brother and all.

Claire's head lifted from her hands, her eyes pleading. "Do you think you could give me a hand?"

Quenton stared at Claire. "Marie, is Anna awake yet?"

There was a hungry gleam in his eyes. Wild and focused. It didn't last long, but long enough for her to catch it.

He seemed just as needy as Claire did. His expression was starved as if he were barely clinging to the edges of control. Looking to take as much from Claire as she was willing to give. And the woman didn't mind one bit.

She clenched her jaw. "Nope. Still sleeping."

"Why don't you go check on her?"

"Nice try."

Would he seriously agree to put her under? To fill her with the sweet overpowering elixir he gave her only days ago? She couldn't explain the sudden possessiveness that engulfed her. At the time, she hated how it felt to be robbed of her control. She told him she never wanted it to happen again, but she hated the thought of their intimate moment tarnished.

Hurt and anger welled in her chest. She turned to the kitchen sink before anyone could see it in her face.

"I'm not leaving. If you want to get down and dirty, you'll have to do it in front of me."

Claire canted her head to shoot Marie an offended look but Quenton grasped her jaw and forced her back to him. He blew a quick puff of air in her face. The breath passing through his lips didn't make a sound or even stir a single strand of hair on her head.

Claire's eyes remained open, but her expression wiped clean. She dropped forward, heading nose first for the kitchen table. Quenton swiftly caught her forehead in his palm before it hit and eased it down to the polished wood.

All sound sucked out of the room, except for the splat of Marie's toast, landing marmalade side down on the tile floor.

He flicked his gaze to her. Rage and disgust twisted his mouth into a scowl. "What do you take me for?"

Her hands shot out in broad gesture to the heap of red curls. "I don't know. I don't even know what the hell that was!"

"She's been up all night, so I put her to sleep. This is Tobin's—"

A bitter laugh boiled up from her throat. "Oh, that's right. I forgot. You guys don't like to share your toys."

Quenton's chair shot across floor. The bellow of wood scooting across the stone tile made her heart clench. She managed one step back before he pinned her against the stainless-steel refrigerator.

"You're asking for it, sweet thing."

Her shoulders pressed against the cold metal, and her courage took a rapid descent. Panic wavered over her voice. "I think you've been charitable enough for one morning, don't you?" She slid to the right, but his hand slammed into the fridge, blocking her escape.

Her heartbeat hammered against its vise, urged on by a fear so ingrained in her memory, escape became her singular thought.

"Let me go," she said.

He shook his head slow, and his anger melted to impassive observation.

"Let me go!"

His image rippled and curved like a carnival mirror through the moisture brimming in her eyes.

He rocked back on his heels and caught one of the tears racing down her cheek. "Care to tell me what this is all about?"

"You're the mind reader. You figure it out."

"Can't read your mind. If I could, I wouldn't have to ask."

She lowered her head. "That's right. You wouldn't ask. You would just take wouldn't you? Like you take everything else."

Seizing her opportunity, she shoved past him out of the kitchen.

Chapter 16

Marie spent the better part of that afternoon breathing through her emotion until her teeth ached from the cold. The piled leaves on the lawn were crusted with ice until the sun filtered through the trees to give them life again.

She ambled along the perimeter of the yard, watching Anna dive into them. Soon Anna would grow tired of the same outdoor routine every day. Marie sighed. She needed to up her game. The frosted lawn crunched beneath her feet, the only sound apart from Anna's playful murmurs.

Without the sound of birds chirping or the occasional rustle of leaves, the forest was ominous and silent. The weather posed a significant problem for her plans. The sun started to thaw the ice. Not fast enough though. Maybe she could still convince Quenton to head into town with a list of supplies for their trip.

If the thaw wasn't timed right, he may try to drag her along on their way out of town.

Maybe she could convince him to take Claire home and that might buy her something. But from the way their gazes were locked on each other, he didn't seem in any hurry to send her packing. Another ache wrenched at her chest, but she pushed it back with a sharp intake of cold air.

Men suck.

Her head snapped up at the sound of a second pair of footsteps behind her.

"Sorry, I didn't mean to startle you," Claire said, falling in step beside her.

"Oh, you decided to join us…." *Greaaat.*

Marie's gaze swept the sprawling landscape until it narrowed on Quenton. Crouched down next to Anna, wearing a faded leather jacket she hadn't seen before, and those predictable dark sunglasses. When he looked at her, she lifted her chin and pulled in another stinging breath of cold air.

"Feeling better?" she asked Claire without bothering to look in her direction. She told herself she didn't care to hear the answer, even as her ears primed for a response among the crunching sound of lawn beneath their feet.

"A little. Quenton was right; the fresh air helps."

She quickened her step. "Yeah, he's just waiting for frostbite to set in so he can come to your rescue."

"Do you know how critical you sound?" Claire asked.

She glanced back. Claire was wrapped in Quenton's wool coat, and the subtle smell of him was overpowered by her cheap perfume. Another pang of hurt slammed into her stomach.

She jerked her gaze back to the horizon. "I can't afford not to be. Stupid females are quickly becoming an endangered species around here."

She heard the scuff of Claire's feet stopping short. "Stupid is someone who doesn't know a good thing when she's got it. You're throwing away a chance of a lifetime, but I'm going to take this ride as far as I can, for as long as I can."

Yes, and with every man she'd find along the way. To Marie, Claire didn't seem anything like the woman she met a few days ago. All hints of uncertainty were gone, and in its place, pissy determination set in those narrow shoulders.

"Maybe you don't realize just how short this ride is," she countered. "Roxanne only knew Tobin for a few days. Heather? A week tops. Your number's coming up fast, and the only thing keeping you alive is…I don't know, maybe a trip to jail? Do you realize you're making yourself an accessory to murder right now?"

"Don't you threaten me!" Claire stepped close. "I've found more inspiration over the last few days than I have in my entire life. I've needed this, and you don't know Tobin like I do. He wouldn't hurt me."

She threw her hands up. "He just ran off in the middle of the night, leaving you with a bunch of complete strangers. You're telling me that doesn't hurt?"

Claire tossed the hair from her eyes with a flick of her head. "Yeah, it hurts, but that's life. My life. And you can stay out of it."

Claire stomped off into the woods but didn't get far. Her foot caught on an exposed tree root, and she went down—hard. Marie cringed at the heavy thud of Claire's body hitting the ground.

"Are you okay?"

Claire struggled to her feet as a raspy metallic moan slithered through the trees overhead. The acrid smell of sulfur infused the air. Alarm bells went off in Marie's head when sound grew more intense and dropped lower around her ears.

A rush of cold air shot behind her, flinging loose curls over her shoulder.

Marie yelped and flipped around but only caught a smoky blur. The force of the wind that cut along behind it lashed across her face, stung her cheeks, and made her eyes burn.

Claire's shriek pulled her attention back to the woods. The woman cowered in fear, surrounded by a swarm of the dark shapeless blurs. They spun around her with such ferocity Marie couldn't make out her profile.

The metallic sound escalated to a deafening screech. It drowned out Claire's screams as it pushed her to the ravine. She watched Claire slam into the frozen ground when her feet slipped over the edge of the embankment.

Marie staggered. Her legs weighed down with terror. She stole a backward glance to Quenton, but her line of sight cut off by a tall wraith-like figure. She gasped and spun to face it.

The screeches cut off to dead silence, followed by an eerie creaking sound as the figure drew into a menacing crouch.

The creature's limbs were unnaturally long and slender just as she remembered from days ago. Filthy, tattered scrubs—like Heather's—hung loose on her skeletal frame but nearly three sizes too short for her length. Her head tipped slightly as if trying to understand Marie's sudden change in behavior.

Heather.

The emaciated figure stared back at her with eyes the color of midnight.

"Run," it said. "Run!"

The sound of Quenton's roar ripped through her fear. "Marie!" He crashed through the dense trees lining the yard, headed straight for the creature.

The creature's head snapped up. It sprung deeper into the forest edge and left Marie swaying on unsteady legs.

Quenton grasped her by the arms, digging his fingers into the tender flesh. "Take Anna. Get her inside." She opened her mouth to respond but couldn't force the words. He wrenched her arms in a brutal shake. "Go now!"

She gave a choked whimper and a jerky head bob before he raced off in the creature's direction.

Once she broke from the forest, her heavy legs found their rhythm and picked up speed. Her vision tunneled to Anna as her feet clamored for traction on the frozen ground. She couldn't seem to move fast enough. Her frustration and fear mounted as she sprinted across the lawn to where Anna stood with a frozen expression, her hands still clutching the leaves.

She snatched her up but plowed into the ground from the sudden strain on her momentum. Her knees and left wrist took the brunt of the fall.

She dismissed the pain that shot through her knee and scrambled to her feet again. Her arm clamped around Anna's rigid torso. She charged up the front steps and into the house, slamming the door shut behind her.

****

The drumming in Quenton's head escalated. His vision spotted over with red. His muscles bulged and expanded. His clothing pulled taut, causing the neat seams at his shoulders and thighs to pop free.

His gait fueled with bloodlust as he ate up the distance between himself and the creature, driving her deep into the woods until he could no longer detect sight or sound from the house. With a quick sprint, he overtook his enemy, knocking her to the ground.

"Where is she?" he bellowed at the gangly form sprawled out on the forest floor. The Shade thrashed around like a wounded spider, flexing and stretching her awkward limbs until she successfully folded them in place again. Impervious to any pain.

She narrowed her eyes in appraisal and poised herself for attack. "Tell me, Muse, is this your place to govern?"

He ignored the question as he circled his enemy. "Tell me where your leader is, and I'll let you keep your ass long enough to kiss it good-bye."

The Shade looked up and down the length of his body. "You're weak, Muse. You have a common one with you, and yet, you do not feed. Why? She is special, the one who travels freely and dangles herself before us. She and the small one make a most unusual pair."

He could tell the creature was fishing and advanced again with murder in his veins. His powerful snap kick struck the Shade square in the chest and sent her flying into the trunk of a massive pine tree.

The body collided with a sickening thud. The strike alone was delivered with enough force to kill a human but unfortunately that heart stopped beating long ago.

"This is my land, and everything on it belongs to me. You will not hunt here!"

The Shade was slower to rise this time and looked to each limb with her thin purple lips pulled into an angry pout. She got to her feet, unable to stand her full height.

Broken back, Quenton thought. With bodies in short supply, this Shade would hold on to it as long as she could. But without mobility and all five senses, the corpse shell would quickly lose its value.

Despite the fact he'd just broken the Shade's favorite toy, she seemed to gain confidence with each passing minute. When he heard the sound of rustling branches and a low moan echoing through the clearing, he knew the rest of the creature's pack circled to find their missing member.

He grinned inwardly. *Gather around kids, this is going to be fun.*

Coming into this battle without a weapon didn't bother him. Having refined his talent for disposing of Shades centuries ago, he preferred to use his hands. More amusing, less mess, and a hell of an effective means of communication. These creatures weren't the smartest of Hades' brood. They seemed to learn best when taught in large groups.

The Shade's voice grew louder to carry through the surrounding trees. "We've hunted these woods for centuries, and that's not about to change. I understand you're quite comfortable here, Muse, but we don't answer to you."

He growled low in his throat, but the creature showed little concern.

"You are a wasteful bunch, always leaving a trail of destruction behind. It would be wise to bide our time here. See what profit you might turn," she said.

In a blur, he jumped on her and crushed her to the ground. The moment he had an unobstructed shot at her head, he latched on with both hands. The Shade bucked and grunted as Quenton thrust the creature's head into an odd angle and snapped her neck.

Her furious scream cut short. The body dropped face-down on the forest floor. A plume of dark smoke rose around the body's head and condensed to a shapeless cloud that shot into the trees.

****

Marie lost all sense of time with her back wedged against the front door. Her breathing finally settled but her mind remained a rambling mess. Fighting back memories of her youth as wave after wave of fear crashed over her.

Her mind couldn't seem to process what she witnessed. Continually replaying the image of the creature again and again but the face kept changing.

Its features blurred from Heather's haunting frown to Tobin's seductive smile, and worst of all, to that nameless man's sneer from eight years ago. The one that lurked in the shadows of her repressed memories.

Every time she pushed it away, the random carousel of faces bled into view again. She recognized the symptoms but giving a name to the condition only magnified her fear. She was in the middle of a panic attack brought on by post-traumatic stress.

No. No this isn't happening.

"Open up!" Quenton's voice called from the other side of the door.

Her thoughts cooled enough to lumber to her feet and while clutching Anna with one arm, she fumbled with the lock on the door.

The moment it opened, Quenton scooped Anna from her arms and wrapped his coat around her

"Get your keys." He disappeared outside.

With slow and mechanical movements, she collected her keys and cell phone from her nightstand. Against what little judgment she had left, she followed Quenton's lead through the open door.

She found him buckling Anna in the front seat of her SUV. When had he moved the car seat? Her thoughts snagged when he opened the rear car door to an unconscious Claire lying across the back seat. With one shoeless, mud-streaked foot dangling off the edge of the bench and her face partially obscured by a tangled mass of hair and dried blood.

Marie knew she should be scared. Hysterical. Something. But the emotion didn't come.

Everything moved in slow motion, not like the kind of release Quenton wielded on her. No. More like a clotted sludge, sucking her mind down, leaving her dazed and exhausted, and it felt a little too familiar. She clenched her fists. *Not now! I can't do this now. Wake up!*

Quenton appeared oblivious to her internal struggle. He hadn't glanced her way once. A minor relief. The last thing either one of them needed was for her to start coming to pieces. "Keep an eye on Claire, try to keep her comfortable until we reach the hospital," he instructed as he shoved her into the SUV.

Gravel pinged against the undercarriage of the vehicle as they flew down the winding dirt road, bouncing and rocking on the uneven path, and sending Marie crashing into the seat in front of her.

Quenton's eyes never left the road. "Get a seatbelt or find something to hold."

His fingertips caught Anna's chin when she

attempted to look back. "Eyes forward, Princess," he murmured.

Marie couldn't register the instructions. His voice sounded thick and run together as if her ears were full of water. Perched on the edge of the seat, she stared at Claire's battered face.

Purple smudges appeared beneath her eyes, growing deeper by the second. The elegant curve of Claire 's nose grew thick and swollen. A ribbon of blood ran from the edge of one nostril onto the taupe leather seat. The oversized coat fell off her shoulder to expose blue-tinted skin.

Marie tugged the coat back over her and zipped it closed as best she could without moving her.

When they shot onto the main road, they found the asphalt slick with ice. More than once, the SUV lost traction and slid. The vehicle's sudden movement shoved her to one side of the seat then the other, as Quenton corrected the vehicle's path.

"Marie—" he called with a note of caution.

With cold and shaky limbs, she pushed herself off the floorboard to a sitting position in front of Claire.

Crystalline blue eyes flicked to her from the rearview mirror. "Hand me your phone," he said.

Her blank stare wandered the mirror. Blue? She thought his eyes were green. Contacts maybe? Who would want to hide such a beautiful shade of...

"Your phone. Hand me your phone."

She dug through her pockets until she touched the phone's hard plastic casing and handed it to him. He punched in a few numbers and began speaking in a clipped tone. "We're bringing in a female. Age approximately thirty. Hundred-and-twenty pounds with a closed head injury. She fell into a shallow ravine."

The emergency personnel were waiting outside the hospital when they pulled up and ushered Marie out of the vehicle. She stared in horror as they tried to rouse Claire without success, ripped her coat free, and began working to cut off her shirt.

The sound of the zipper ripping open felt disturbing and yanked her back in time to a balmy summer night eight years ago.

****

The acrid smell of urine and garbage hung stagnant in the air, as she crept under a rickety wooden stairway.

The thick smoke from the ongoing protests blotted out the moon, leaving only slivers of light from the apartments above. Shadows licked along the alley, as mobs of people rushed through. She crouched down to avoid being seen.

Yelling and the sound of breaking glass erupted, and then faded off into the distance, only to build up again minutes later. She hoped to find a safer place to hide for the night until she could contact her father, but someone else found her instead.

A thin built man tore her from her hiding place and spun her to face his yellowed sneer. Beady eyes gleamed under a high forehead and slicked greasy hair. When he crushed her to the wall, the back of her head grated against the rough stucco. A grimy hand clamped over her mouth.

The salty taste smeared over her lips when she tried to sink her teeth into his palm but with his other fist held tight to her hair, he beat her head against the wall until lights flashed behind her eyes. She let go a teary sob of defeat.

With the wall behind her, she couldn't escape.

She didn't have to know the language to understand the slur he breathed into her ear. The malice in his voice obliterated all hope she would escape unharmed. The foul smell of his breath combined with body odor and filth made her gag.

****

"*No. No!*"

"Marie, don't do this." The distant echo of Quenton's gravelly voice coaxed her back to the present. She grasped hold of it, hauling herself out of the horrific memory and back to him.

She found him standing behind her with massive arms banded around her like a strait jacket. The stubble on his jaw grazed her cheek as his lips pressed against her temple.

"Shhh. You're okay. We're leaving now." He used a slow shuffle to guide her to the open door of the SUV. Claire was gone, without even a trace of blood left on the seat. Her spine went rigid.

"Claire will be safe here. There's nothing more we can do. We have to go."

His words didn't connect in her brain until he pulled onto the main road. She watched the city limits sign pass her by and felt the bottom drop out of her stomach, and a whole new shroud of anxiety blanketed her.

Leaving? But all her things were back at the house. She couldn't go yet. A crushing panic slithered up her spine and hampered her breathing. It wrapped around her chest and siphoned all the warmth and sensation from her face.

Quenton took one look at her through the rearview mirror and reached over the back of his seat to push her head between her knees. "Marie, breathe!"

Her frantic search for an outlet only added to the anxiety mounting inside her, and before long, her vision grew dim until complete darkness swept over her.

Chapter 17

Marie lay face down on the leather seat when Quenton pulled up to the Weiss Crest Hotel. He squinted against the burn from the mid-afternoon sun, magnified everywhere by a dense layer of snow. Having left the house in such a hurry, he hadn't grabbed his sunglasses.

He released his blistering grip on the steering wheel and stepped out. The cobblestone driveway gritted under his boots.

"Afternoon, sir," called a short, round man standing at attention near the front entrance.

Quenton rounded the vehicle without sparing the man a glance and jerked Anna's door open. Her body slumped to one side with her face angled up, her angelic features suspended in sleep. When he lifted her from the car, she pulled in a deep breath, and went rigid in his arms with a full body stretch.

"Can I give you a hand?" the man asked.

Quenton looked to Anna, then the rear seat where Marie lay. He didn't want the guy touching either one of them, but he couldn't carry them both by himself, and if Marie woke up alone, or worse, in someone else's arms…

He'd already witnessed the fight she put up at the hospital when one of the nurses tried to assess her for shock. He refused to let the hospital security restrain her, being forced to hold her back himself.

She struggled against him. Her broken sobs and pleas for him to release her left a deep gouge in his heart. He wove layer upon layer of his sedative, but it had no effect.

It was like nothing he'd ever witnessed. In desperation, he tried to reach into her subconscious, even without the benefit of sedating her. It was a risky move, but it proved useless. She was locked away behind an iron curtain of fear, and there was no way he could help her.

He never wanted to feel that useless again.

"Take this little one up to my room. I've got one more in the back," he said.

"No problem."

He looked down to Anna. "Is that okay?"

She blinked up at him, released a sigh, and nodded.

Marie flinched when he opened her door, and a cold gust of air brushed at the curls veiling her face. As he lifted her into his arms and angled her out of the vehicle, her head rolled onto his shoulder against his worn leather jacket.

His blood heated when she pressed her face into him and took a savoring breath at the hollow of his neck. But the moment cut short when she grimaced and tipped her face away again.

"Put me down." She groaned.

Not on your life.

"Right this way, sir," the man said.

Quenton turned to the frigid wind. Her eyelids squeezed tight and arms wrapped around her stomach. "I'm serious. You have to let me down."

He ignored her feeble protest and marched into the

hotel lobby with honey oak furniture and camel-colored walls, all centered by a massive stone fireplace. No way could she cover this much distance in her condition, and he needed to get her a place to lie down pronto.

"Marie?" a female voice called out.

Quenton's pace slowed, and he swiveled his head to locate the voice's origin.

With a small whimper, Marie shook her head.

"It is you! Fred, look. Our baby's here."

Marie's eyes flew open wide. Her voice was hushed and frantic. "Put me down. Put me down!"

This time he obeyed, easing her down to sway in front of the woman dressed in a tailored, electric purple suit. A barrel-chested man stood beside her.

"You must be Marie's parents," Quenton said.

The man ignored the statement, turning his good eye on Quenton with guarded calculation, and then using the same gaze on Marie. "You okay, honey?" The tenderness coating his voice seemed incompatible with the imposing scowl.

A distinctive retching sound followed by a slosh of fluid on the tile floor was her only response.

Quenton jumped back a good foot to give her room. He gave her a tentative pat on the shoulder. It was a pathetic attempt to hide his shock. As a Muse, he witnessed the gamut of bizarre art mediums, but puke didn't rank high on that list. *Thank God.*

Fred addressed the woman next to him with his gaze on the toes of his spackled loafers. "Ah, good times. Ruby, see if you can help Marie get cleaned up."

Quenton closed a hand over the curve of her shoulder. "She's staying with me."

Fred waved him away. "She won't go far. We're in

the room next to yours. Let her mother take her. She lives for this shit."

Quenton felt a dull ache swell in his chest as Ruby led her to the elevator. Marie's face in her hands and her mother's arm draped around her shoulders.

In that moment, he realized he hadn't been away from Marie since the day they met. If not holding her, at least watching from a distance.

She started out as a necessity and turned to an obsession. Wanting to consume her soul was far different from knowing he couldn't live without it. He could have let her go before. Not now. He loved her.

After he checked them in, he followed Marie's father into the elevator. Aside from an eye patch and a shaky hand, Fred had a presence that commanded respect from even the strongest of men. *Presence be damned. If this guy wants my respect, he's going to earn it like everyone else.*

When the elevator doors slid together, Fred turned and squared his shoulders at Quenton. "Thanks for the heads up about your arrival. If it were left to Marie, we might have missed her all together."

"She was distracted."

Fred grunted. "I take it you haven't known each other long."

Quenton turned from his reflection in the elevator doors, and fixed him with a cold, penetrating stare. "And why is that?"

"I would have known about you. Marie doesn't keep secrets from me. Besides, this behavior is commonplace for her, and obviously you aren't accustomed to it."

"There's nothing common about the hell she's been

through over the three hours it took to get here." He leaned into the alarm button on the elevator, stopping it cold. "And I want to know why."

Quenton struck without warning, using the heat of his anger to spear into Fred's mind without the benefit of sedation, tearing a small opening in the fabric of his subconscious, and shoving his command inside.

Tell me. Everything.

Fred's posture slackened. He frowned, and shook his head, seeming at odds with himself even as the words tumbled free. "A child should never have to grow up watching their back but that's exactly what I did to her. Always telling her to be aware. To trust no one.

I was part of a rapid response team. Always relocating with little notice. I didn't have to drag my family along, but I did. When our operation went sour in the middle of an uprising on foreign soil, all of that training backfired. I got shot up pretty bad, and we had to evacuate in a hurry. Leaving in the middle of the night was unfortunate but after seventeen years she knew the drill.

"My injuries forced me to stay behind, and I had to send someone else to collect Marie and her mother. Apparently, Marie grew tired of being shuffled around and put up a fight. She ran off, spent the night hiding in the middle of utter chaos.

"Trusted members of my regiment searched all night. They didn't find her until dawn, and by then the damage was done." He pushed his shaky hand through thinning salt and pepper hair. "They say she was assaulted by one of the locals, but the son of a bitch didn't stick around. He left her for dead in a deserted alley. It took months of rehab to heal her outside…and now you've seen the inside."

Quenton's fists blanched white at his sides as pent up rage leaked into his veins.

Fred swallowed hard; his Adam's apple bobbed up and down. "You should know upfront, Marie doesn't lean on others for support. She's determined to fight this on her own."

Quenton released his hold on Fred and pushed the alarm button again. "I'll take that under advisement."

When the elevator opened, Quenton stepped into a whirlwind of activity. A tiny brown and black Yorkshire terrier darted down the hall toward them. Its feet blurred under the current of silky hair, and its collar jerked with every stride, sounding a tinny jingle of victory.

Anna careened around the corner as the dog skidded to a stop at Fred's feet.

"Catch her!" Anna cried.

The dog's nose twitched, then all its attention fell to Fred's defiled loafers. Fred's frown deepened. "Oh great, the rat's out."

Anna lunged at the dog, but it jumped away from her to hide behind Fred. "It's not a rat. It's a dog. The clean lady let him out; and—and—and I try catch her. Can we have her, Dad?"

Quenton's chest constricted. Her first use of that simple name carried more weight than he ever thought imaginable. And when paired with those big pleading sapphires, hell, she could have a whole litter of puppies if she wanted them.

Fred nudged the puppy's butt with the toe of his shoe, urging it closer to Anna. "It's a him. And no. He already has a home."

Quenton's brows lifted. "Yours?"

"No. That's Ruby's mongrel. She doesn't go anywhere without it." Fred tipped his head to Anna. "This one's yours then?"

He nodded.

Fred crouched down, pulled something from his pocket, and pressed it into Anna's hand. "Here, take one of these. See if he'll follow you back inside."

"Okay!"

Anna waved the biscuit under the dog's nose, pulling its attention from the shoes and back down the hall to the open door.

"Cute kid," Fred said.

Quenton nodded.

Fred cleared his throat after the door clicked behind Anna. "I've served my country *and* it's secrets. There isn't much I haven't seen. As far as Marie goes, you're going to need all the help you can get. I'll offer you what I can but if you try that pansy-ass mind control on *me* again, you'll find yourself down looking up."

Quenton grinned. "Yes, sir."

****

Marie woke to the sound of wind heaving against the massive casement window, carrying with it, the occasional tinkle of snow. She rolled over, cocooning herself in the thick bedspread. Every muscle in her body felt tenderized and with the absence of Quenton's scent and body heat, for that matter, she couldn't stay comfortable for long.

She shuffled to the adjoining bathroom and spent the better part on an hour letting the oversized showerhead rain down on her pummeled ego.

Somewhere in between tossing both her cookies and her emotional control, all the confidence in caring for Anna got lost in the mess.

"Why would anyone want a loose cannon taking care of their child?" She wondered aloud.

Quenton would be crazy to keep her around and the thought of his rejection carved the heart out of her chest. Not only did she want to be with Anna, she wanted *him*.

"There. I admit it, all right?" She slapped off the shower. "I want him. Fat lot of good it does me, but I do."

Quenton made his intentions clear. Unfortunately, her naughty thoughts weren't sporting good listening ears. "Too busy doing the bump-and-grind to Barry White's greatest hits."

She swore never to put herself in another short-term relationship, but she couldn't undo the bond between them. Some force inside her acted beyond reason and coaxed the rest of her across that chalk line. Now a new conviction formed.

She hated to admit it, but Claire was right. Better to take this ride as long as she could because life was shorter than she expected. She wasn't ready for her life with Quenton to end. Especially not the way it had for Claire.

It wasn't possible to anticipate the horrific circumstances triggering her breakdown, but she should have muscled through it. Her traumatic past lay dormant for years. It was a sick twist of fate that it all came back to plague her now. Those days were over. No way would she let them control her again.

Anger and determination burned through her body, feeding strength into her muscles and sharpening her mind. Quenton may want to get rid of her but she wasn't going to make it easy for him.

After toweling off, she sampled the arsenal of beauty supplies stocked in the medicine cabinet and found a pair of kelly-green yoga pants and a matching jacket folded over the vanity chair.

She recovered her cell phone from the kitchen, where it lay face down on the black granite countertop. A text message glowed to life when she tapped on the screen.

"We're next door in room 1232. Come join us."

When no one came to the door, she let herself in, stepping into the narrow entryway and the gruff sound of Quenton's voice. Her stomach churned with nervous energy. Tentative steps carried her to the living room.

"Send me your best two. I'm short on time," he said. "We'll be moving soon, and I want this done right."

With his back to her, Quenton moved past the massive atrium doors with a cell phone pressed to his ear. His dark profile looked striking against the bright blue sky and snowcapped mountains.

"No. I only have one but she's a big job," he said.

Was he already talking about a replacement?

When she entered the room, his spine straightened as if sensing her presence. He flicked a quick glance over his shoulder, wearing yet another pair of silver rimmed sunglasses. She couldn't see the message written in his eyes but the tension in his jaw said enough.

"Oh, there she is," Ruby cooed.

Her shoulders jumped in a reflexive wince that always followed her mother's voice. She looked to the nearby seating area. "The one and only."

Ruby sat curled on the couch, the aroma of her traditional spiced chai wafted from the mug in her hands. Anna sat on the floor beside her, playing with what appeared to be a four-legged feather duster.

She crouched down. "And who's this little fuzz bucket?"

"Its name is Flopsey. He's a boy but I put a bow in his hair," Anna said.

She gave her mother a skeptical glance. "Flopsey? Really?"

"You think *that's* bad? Your father wanted to name him Shrinky Dink. Because his…." She cupped a hand around her mouth and lowered her voice. "*Apparatus* is undersized."

Marie ducked her head. "I don't even want to know how you determined that."

"Oh honey, it's not something to be embarrassed about. After spending so much time with Anna's father, I thought you'd loosen up by now."

Ruby nodded and her eyes gleamed in admiration. "Quenton's a good virile name."

Marie looked up in time to see the white flash of his teeth before he paced away again, and then dropped her eyes to one of the pearls segmenting her silver necklace. "So what's the plan today, Anna?"

Ruby made a muffled sound around the rim of her cup before setting it on the glass table. "We've got appointments at the spa, and after lunch, we'll go shopping. Doesn't that sound great?"

Marie's head dropped forward with a defeated

sigh. "Peachy."

"Oh, Anna's going to love the spa, and we won't do anything invasive today," Ruby said.

Marie snorted. After years of going to the spa with her mother, Marie didn't think Ruby owned a body part that hadn't been lasered, sanded, dyed, or fried. Her mother always managed to find some new and disturbing beauty regime she couldn't resist. Her definition of "non-invasive" had more varying shades of gray than she had credit cards.

"Feeling better, are we?" Quenton asked. The warm rumble of his voice came from only inches behind her. She tipped her chin. "I am. And before you make any more appointments, we need to talk."

"We can talk over dinner. I have to meet with some clients in an hour."

With a pleading look, she tried, and failed to infiltrate his reflective lenses. "It won't take long. What are you doing now?"

"Leaving. I'll meet you in the bar at eight."

Marie got to her feet with her newfound determination wallowing somewhere down around her ankles as Quenton's long strides carried him out of the room.

****

Marie pushed through the salon's heavy glass doors, out of the driving snow and into the smell of damp foliage and fragrant shampoo. The spacious atrium with ficus trees stretching overhead and tropical plants spilling over rounded planters looked a world apart from the snowdrifts she plodded through to get there.

Ruby stretched her arms wide in a jazzy *ta-da*

motion. Her voice sang out over the exotic percussion music and trickle of an indoor stream. "Oh, this is so exciting! We're going to leave this place sparkling from head to toe."

On the surface, Marie allowed a congratulatory smile for her mother's effort, but Ruby's peppy attitude didn't touch the clotted tension beneath. Tonight might be her only shot at keeping her job, and her mind felt dead-ended with how to save it.

How could she prove to Quenton that she could keep her mental state intact? To show she wouldn't be a threat to Anna's well-being?

She crossed to the reception area and plopped into the nearest chair. Anna wasted no time jumping into her lap.

"Marie, what those for?"

She glanced to the paisley shaped reception desk where a silver tin was piled high with cheerfully wrapped candies. "Those are treats for little kids getting their hair cut."

"Can I have one?"

Marie shrugged. After a breakfast of maple bars and coffee, or chocolate milk in Anna's case, how much damage could one sucker do?

"Sure, why not," she said.

A few brownie points with Anna couldn't hurt her cause. She was the only one left with pull around here.

Anna skipped up to claim her prize and came back to Marie's lap. A sucker protruded from her smug grin. "This is cool."

"Yeah, they start you on the sweet stuff, and the next thing you know, you'll never want to leave."

While Ruby stood orchestrating their appointments

at the front desk, Marie rummaged through the stack of glossy magazines. She passed one to Anna. "Hey, about yesterday. I'm sorry that I wasn't very helpful. I guess I was just kind of...surprised. You know? Like at a birthday party when everyone jumps up and yells *surprise!*"

Anna stopped crunching down on her sucker and pulled her syrupy lips into a skeptical frown. "I like monsters to my party."

Good point.

Marie flicked through the November issue of *Allure*, barely glancing at the pages. "Well, I'm sorry you had to see that, and I promise I'll try harder not to get scared."

"Girls are 'sposed to get scared 'cause—'cause then boys kill the monsters."

Those seemingly innocent fairytales were beginning to have a negative impact. It wouldn't be a pretty sight when reality finally set in for Anna but that probably wasn't for years to come. Far be it for Marie to derail her false sense of security.

"Good idea, we'll leave the monster slaying to the boys, and we'll spend all our bravery on haircuts and nail polish."

Ruby pranced way from the desk. The maniacal gleam in her eye, and that lively strut made Marie want to wrap her arms and legs around the chair and hold on for dear life.

"Are we ready, girls?" Ruby asked.

Marie studied her mother with a warning look, then pulled the withered stick from Anna's mouth and wrapped it back in its wax paper. "I guess we're as ready as we're going to be."

Anna didn't respond. Her eyes widened, and her face lost all color as Marie guided her to the chrome barber's chair and the stout woman with choppy purple hair.

"Hi, Anna. I'm Dina."

Anna spun away from Dina's toothy grin, and her words rushed out in a desperate sob. "I don't wanna hair cut!" She pointed to Marie. "The sucker. Make her!"

Marie lifted her brows at the withered stick in her hand and promptly tossed it in the trash. "They aren't going to cut your hair. They're just going to style it pretty, like we do at home. Plus she wants to hear all your great stories."

Marie snatched an aluminum squirt bottle from the nearby tool cart. "And here! You can let her have it if she pulls your hair too hard. Sound good?"

The traces of uncertainty fell little by little from Anna's expression. Armed with the squirt bottle, Marie could see the courage build in her tiny frame as her spine straightened. Anna strutted along behind Dina with the nozzle aimed dead center.

"You can squirt me in the *mirror,* okay?" asked Dina.

"Okay." Anna conceded with a crooked smile and a tone that held no intension of signing such a ridiculous treaty.

"You're Marie," a voice crowed from behind her. It was more an accusation than a question.

She turned to face a solid looking older woman with pursed lips and an oversized chest puffed up with self-importance. The woman gestured to a long hallway. "You're with me. We'll start with your Mango

227

salt scrub, then bikini wax—that comes with a free vagazzle."

Vagazzle...What? She scanned the salon to locate her mother, but the evil witch had already disappeared in a puff of essential oils.

The woman's eyes narrowed, magnifying the creases that branched from her eyes, undoing the home-made facelift created from the tension in her severe bun. "Is there a problem?"

She held her hands up. "No, no, I'm fine."

Anna gave her a sympathetic nod. "Have my squirt bottle."

Was she kidding? A fire hose couldn't save her.

The woman's chubby fists planted on her hips. "I have other clients coming. If you've changed your mind, that's fine but your appointment's non-refundable."

She ignored the woman and smiled to veil her hesitation. "Thanks, Anna, but I'm good. I'll be back in a bit, okay?"

"I can call Daddy."

"I'm sure he would jump at the chance to lend a hand, but we'll be fine."

The last thing she needed was to send a Muse into a building full of women with razor sharp scissors, scalding irons, and a desperate need to stay on the bleeding edge of fashion.

With Quenton, there was no telling what kind of monstrosities he could inspire.

She wouldn't mind throwing her mother in as the test subject, but no way would she let him come within a hundred feet of this place while she was stuck in the chair.

No. Right now she needed to suck it up, act like a big girl, and save the inspiration for more important things. Like how to keep her job. Her mother would pay for this later.

The thought of payment gave her pause. Quenton was good at taking what he wanted, and she knew he prided himself on a fair trade. Given the right amount of incentive, he might act first, but he always made sure to even the score later. That might work in her favor this time.

She'd been on the receiving end of his handy work before. She knew he had the power to make her stable again. If that happened, he'd have no reason to let her go.

Could she trade a piece of her soul for a chance at a normal life?

It'd be the most dangerous deal she'd ever agree to, but what other choice did she have?

Chapter 18

That night, Marie shifted on the bar stool and tugged her strappy black dress over her thighs. A great find during her shopping trip that afternoon but with the giant leap of stupidity she was about to take, she felt more appropriately dressed for her own funeral.

After a full day of chasing Anna and her mother from one store to the next, and an incredibly disturbing experience at the spa, she didn't think her pride could withstand much more.

The mango salt scrub was innocent enough she could handle it. It was the glue-on crystals and glitter that sent her on a downward spiral.

Her attention pulled to the gurgling noise in her stomach. It wasn't a good idea for her to have such a serious conversation without food. Hunger always made her irritable, and the last thing she needed was more lapse in self-control.

Where was he?

Picking up her cell phone from the varnished bar, she glanced at the empty call screen.

She saw him approach from across the room in her phone's glossy reflection. He headed straight for her with an intense gleam in his eyes that put her own hunger to shame.

She lowered the phone with a shaking hand. She didn't turn around. Instead she counted the steps it would take him to reach her and forced her breath to come slow and deep against the constriction in her throat.

"Where's Anna?" he asked.

Her body charged with awareness. That look reminded her of the one he gave Claire in the kitchen, only this version seemed three times more potent. It took a moment for her to register the gradual upward tilt of her face. As if some unseen force gripped her jaw and pulled her to attention.

The situation would've felt unnerving if not for the dreamy state of her thought process, overpowered by a sweet numbing elixir that curled around her senses.

He seemed stronger tonight, and yet weak at the same time as if tensing his every muscle to hold back a violent tempest churning beneath his skin. The tempest looked to be gaining the upper hand.

Her voice sounded distant to her own ears. "She's staying with my parents. She and Flopsey have been stuck like glue."

"Good. Let's go to the room," he said.

"But what about dinner?"

He didn't acknowledge her, ripping his eyes away and continuing to the elevator. The space he put between them cleared his spell and her brain founds its gear.

"He better be thinking room service then," she mumbled.

When they entered the elevator, he stood at the far end with his hand manacled on the railing.

She kept her sight fixed on the control panel as the numbers flashed. Her sentences rushed under the beep of incrementing numbers. "About yesterday, I can explain—"

"No need," he said.

"Yes, need. My actions were unprofessional."

His attention worked its way up from her shoes. "I dropped out of finishing school. Tell me, what's considered professional behavior while under zombie attack?"

She fought the urge to squirm under his scalding gaze. "A zombie? That thing that looked like Heather…is that really her?"

"Not anymore."

"Because she's a zombie now?" Were they really having this discussion?

"To you, they're zombies. We use the term 'Shades.' Their origin is in that book you found, about a Muse trading their body to Hades. They're a by-product of our species. Sorry I didn't make a formal introduction. Your bad manners must be rubbing off on me."

With a slow nod she subdued her inward squeal of alarm. "Okay…a Shade. I can handle that." She managed a shaky laugh. "So it's completely understandable that I would act so dim-witted. Given that I've never met up with a Shade before."

He shook his head. "It *wanted* you to do something dim-witted. Slip and fall, get lost, starve to death, die from exposure—anything that might get you killed. They can't kill you outright. not with their own hands. And they can't take your body unless you're dead. So congratulations, you passed the test."

She shifted her weight from one leg to the other when his attention roved from calf to mid-thigh. "But after the test? I came to pieces at the hospital. You saw me…"

"—Your point?"

"We both know that in my current state, it's not safe for me to look after Anna."

His gaze flicked to her eyes with only a hint of irritation and a tiny muscle ticked in his jaw. Clearly he wasn't in the mood to talk.

"But I have a solution for that." she swallowed hard to keep her voice steady. "I know you can cure my nervous attacks."

He folded his arms over his chest. "I'm listening,"

"If you can do that, there won't be any reason to fire me."

He tipped his head to the halogen lights and let go a heavy sigh. "Marie, you're too closed off. I can't reach you."

"I'm just asking you to try just one more time. I'm willing to pay. I'll—I'll give you anything you want—"

The craving that lit his gaze seemed to spring forward from deep inside, like an untamed beast torn free from its chain. He crossed the length of the elevator in two steps. "I want it all. Your body. Your soul. You'd give all that to me?"

She clamped down on the cold railing behind her. "Do I get it back?" She squeaked.

The hard edge of his mouth curved to a slow grin, but his eyes revealed nothing. "Most of it."

Her voice escaped in a timid rasp. "Then yes."

His smile grew in roguish agreement. Cupping the back of her neck, he leaned in until the edge of his nose brushed along hers. "Let's just see about that shall we?"

Determined to pass the test, she welcomed the world around her to thicken and fall out of touch. But it didn't happen.

She lifted her eyes in question. The moment his eyes settled on hers, she felt something sharp pierce through the outer shell of her mind. He touched the far reaches of her subconscious.

Marie gripped his forearms for support. With little effort her mind worked around him, exploring his boundaries. His give and pull. The sensation coaxed warm tingles to flow from the top of her head and spill down her shoulders.

The floor beneath her feet shifted, jarring her balance and her connection to him. The elevator emitted an electronic ping. His presence pulled free.

She blinked.

His hands were still locked on either side of her, his arms quaking from the strain, tendons straining along his neck.

His voice dropped to a low growl. "We do this now, and unless you want it here...room. Now."

She ducked under his arm and rushed out of the elevator, caught somewhere between Oh-God-what-have-I-done and why-didn't-I-do-it-sooner.

The first hasty swipe of her card key didn't take.

Her attention flashed to the empty hallway and back to the door. She swiped again.

The elevator doors began to slide closed, then pinged open.

Her attention ripped from the door to the hallway a second time, where his large hand pressed against the seam of the elevator door, pushing it back. He stepped into the hall with his head lowered, a feral gaze focused on her.

He took one step, and another, rapidly increasing

his pace, lengthening his stride as he closed the distance between them.

With anticipation roaring through her veins, she squeezed through the door and raced across the suite. The heavy, pounding of footsteps behind her fell silent. She spun to face the door and watched him slip inside before it clicked shut, and the light sliced away into darkness.

She heard the metallic scrape of the dead bolt slide into place.

Her eyesight strained to adjust in the dark room. His hazy outline dipped as he toed out of his shoes. She followed his lead, stepping out of her heels.

The heavy shift of leather made her stomach clench as he sloughed off his jacket.

He pursued her across the room one silent step at a time.

His white shirt emitted an ominous glow until it rumpled, bunched, and fell to the floor in a pale heap. The action stripped his image to a dark shadow.

With shaking hands, she unzipped the back of her dress.

"Keep the dress. Everything else goes," he said.

Reaching underneath, she unfastened her bra and pulled it free from one side. She bent to remove her stockings. When she pushed them over the curve of her hips, she felt his hands brush hers.

"Everything else," he said, pulling her panties down to follow the stockings.

She continued a backward motion into the bedroom. The back of her knees hit the mattress. She inched herself up and scooted back until she met the pillows.

Her pulse jumped at the soft grating sound of his zipper.

"You remember what I said," he warned.

She managed an unsteady nod. Not sure if he could detect it from the scant moonlight streaming through the window.

He was offering her a way out, reminding her he wouldn't take anything that wasn't freely given. But this time, she'd make the most of this symbiotic relationship. She would give, but she would be taking much more.

His full weight pressed down on the mattress one knee at a time as he crawled after her. "You'll get what you need first, then I take what I want. I can't afford to sedate you completely this time. It could get…difficult."

Difficult? What the hell did that mean? Panic arced over her nerves. Her hands shook.

He pulled her up to a kneeling position. The warmth of his hands sliding up and down her back caused a rash of goosebumps to race down her limbs.

"Shhh…calm down. Close your eyes," he whispered.

She breathed deep to soak her lungs with as much scent as they could hold. Her knees ached from the amount of time she knelt there but little by little the tension eased.

He caressed the curve of her neck until he found her pulse. His fingertips paused there until her heartbeat came slow and steady.

"Marie?"

She lifted her brows.

"Open your eyes," he said.

The electric blue that lit his eyes shone brilliant in the darkness. A rush of heat poured over her, and the world slowed to a crawl until he was all that remained.

****

Slipping away from his body, his spirit stretched deep into the fluid labyrinth of her subconscious. Her spirit appeared in a gradual accumulation of light and reached out to him.

It took all his concentration to restrain the hunger blazing to life inside him. Every particle of his being urged him closer.

Not yet, he told her spirit. *First show me what you want.*

With a meaningful smile she advanced. Her arms outstretched, as if she knew what he'd really come for and was ready to brush off the formalities and get down to business.

He held up one hand. *Up, up, up, you heard what I said. No tough lovin' till you show me what you need.*

He suppressed a laugh at the sight of those pale lips turning down in a seductive pout.

If only the Marie on the outside were this eager. He would have nailed her a long time ago.

We have to fix this first, he said.

She expressed a slight eye roll before leading him down a serrated passageway. The walls gradually constricted the farther he traveled. The current became notably thicker and warmer, where memories were frequently pulled to the surface carrying a white-hot energy with them. He knew he was getting close.

When they came to an opening, she stopped short. Like a soldier standing at attention, Marie's spirit stopped, made an about face, and refused to move another inch as if guarding the most dangerous predator on Earth.

He looked past her to the jagged crevice. Its walls pulsed with raw emotion, and its passage constricted with angry scars.

Slipping through the entry wasn't easy but watching the memory play out nearly brought him to his knees. She was young, seventeen tops, when that dirtbag cornered her. He recoiled from the helpless anguish that gripped his stomach. The man slammed her head into the wall over and over. Her legs went limp.

He clenched his jaw and pain pulsed through his skull. He wished he could do something, anything to stop it. But he couldn't. The entire memory had to play out before he could obliterate it. Otherwise, bits and pieces could still float to the surface.

The man used his fist, still tangled in her hair, to throw her to the ground. And when she hit, for a few seconds she didn't move.

He held his breath as the man stalked circles around her. *Don't get up. Stay down. Stay. Down.* But dread flooded his chest when she tried to pull herself across the asphalt. She tried to crawl away on hands and knees, but the man circled her with arrogant steps.

He raised his voice, spat foreign phrases she couldn't comprehend, and because this was Marie's memory, he couldn't understand either.

That's when the man stooped down.

He leaned to one side, trying to get a better angle. The man lifted something into his hand and tested its weight.

What was he doing? Robbing her? He couldn't

remember seeing a purse.

It was only when the man lifted the object high in the air that Quenton recognized it for what it was. A brick. He whipped his full body away from the scene but not before the sound of the impact assaulted his ears—a thick, heavy sound that silenced everything else.

Before the scene could replay itself, he wiped out the assailant's face with an abrasive blast of energy. He covered the entire space in her memory ceiling to floor. When he backed himself out, he coated the entry and called to Marie.

She didn't answer. Still standing at attention and refusing to move.

Spending so much of his energy left him without the strength to stay in place. The languid current flowing through her mind started to overpower him. His spirit slid back under the gradual pull that would carry to the fringe of her subconscious.

He knew if he were pushed out now, he wouldn't have the strength to regain consciousness, let alone attempt a second trip.

Marie, please.

Her eyes squeezed shut, blocking him and everything else out. The current stirred the tendrils of light around her, but she didn't budge.

It's gone, sweet thing. It's only me.

One eye peeked open with uncertainty, followed by the second. She followed his backward motion then her eyes grew wide when he slipped beyond arm's reach.

He kept his voice low and calm. "You're safe now. And I need you."

A zap of energy chased up his arm when she

latched on, anchoring him against the current. Her whisper-soft vapors curled and flexed around him, inviting him closer.

He didn't need the invitation. With one swift tug, he melded his soul to hers.

An explosion of energy pushed through both of them. It rushed over the empty cavern in his chest, growing more heated as wave after wave crashed back and forth between them.

On the outside, he heard Marie gasp, but her spirit clutched him tighter. Her breathing escalated into terrified pants.

Afraid the connection would overwhelm her, he tried to ease his grip.

Her spirit wasn't having any of it. Her tendrils of light coiled around him and drew taut to hold him in place.

"I can't. . . I can't stay," he said.

He could feel Marie's heartbeat pounding at a frenzied pace. She wouldn't be able to take much more.

"Stay. You stay." The bonds constricted around him.

O-kay wrong word choice. Again.

As if every bone in her body were suddenly liquefied, her body collapsed against his chest, and he felt true panic race through his mind. He had to get out. Now.

He gave her spirit a brisk shake. "Marie, listen to me. Listen!"

She shook her head.

"I'll come back," he insisted.

She paused, her expression coated with uncertainty, her eyes wide and hopeful. "You'll…."

"I will. Come back."

In the next instant, his restraints disappeared, and her spirit vanished.

He settled back into his own body and closed his arms around her. It wasn't easy to remain upright. His muscles burned with fatigue. But he continued where he left off, stoking her back. Up and down until her breathing slowed, and he could no longer feel her heart pounding against his chest. The open zipper caught his fingertips, and he slipped his hand inside to play along the delicate ridge of her spine. "You all right?"

No response.

Still overcome. He shouldn't be surprised considering what she'd been through. He waited several minutes and asked again.

Nothing.

He counted another fifteen seconds. "Marie?" He held her at arm's length and gave her a gentle shake.

Her numbed features blossomed to life. The soft pink color returned to her cheeks. She blinked. "It's gone. I mean, it's really gone!" She launched herself back into his arms.

He gladly accepted the momentum and let his weight drop onto the bed. His low chuckle cut short when she pressed her lips to his.

He deepened their kiss with greedy enthusiasm rolling the sweet taste of her around on his tongue. His hands moved over her with an urgency he hadn't felt in—well, as long as he could remember.

Desperate to unwrap the payment she'd promised. She'd given her soul, but would she still agree to offer her body?

Thank God she wasn't prone to hesitation,

lowering her head to trail kisses down his neck, following the downward course of her hands. The liquid heat of her mouth made his arousal spiral into a tight pulsing coil.

His penis jumped when her silky thigh brushed against the sensitive tip.

He slid the straps of her dress over her shoulders. The flimsy material dropped to her waist. "Hands on the headboard. Don't move."

He wedged his knee between her thighs, urging her body upward. He closed his mouth over her breast and scored his teeth along the creamy flesh, then gave her nipple a soft tug. She pressed herself closer with a breathy gasp.

His shoulders sank back under the exotic smell of her skin, and his mind toyed with all the ways he could coax more of that scent from her.

He used his thigh to apply pressure to the juncture between her legs and encouraged her into a tormenting rhythm. As she moved against him, the moist heat that pooled there sent his self-control warring against a primal need to claim that heat for himself.

The battle didn't last long.

"My turn." He growled.

He pulled her dress completely off and rolled her to her back. A glint of light flickered on the mound of her vagina, and he couldn't contain his smile.

"What…is that?"

Her hands slapped over her face, and she drew her knees up in a pathetic attempt to conceal it. "Mishap at the salon. I didn't know what I was getting myself into, I swear." She moaned.

"Where was Anna?"

"Getting her hair washed."

He nodded and tried to move her knees for a closer look but met with uncertain resistance.

"Gimme," he insisted, pushing them farther apart to settle his shoulders between them. His thumb traced over the glittery circle, framed by an upturned laurel reef.

"You know what this is?" he asked.

Her voice muffled around the shield of her hands. "Glitter tattoo?"

"It's Greek," he said, using his lower lip to caress the smooth folds of her vagina. "Means praise. Victory." He grinned. "I like victory."

When his mouth descended on her, she seemed to catch her breath in a mixture of awe and surprise. The sound so pure and uncensored, he craved to hear it over and over again.

His tongue flicked over her, lapping up hot nectar, and teasing her urgent cries until they threatened to peak any moment. He watched the rise and fall of her chest, the arch of her spine. Her face turned away. Her eyes sealed off the inward climb to ecstasy. Only her voice let him in.

Why wouldn't she open her eyes? Let him see everything he did to her?

"Please," she begged.

"More?"

"More of you. All of you!"

He positioned himself between her silken thighs and slowly rocked forward. He stretched and filled her until she took him in completely.

The promise of release swelled inside of him, and he strained to hold it back.

His name came out husky and urgent from her lips, but he quickly stifled it with his hand.

He couldn't have her cry out. Not now. That sound commanded an answer, and he wasn't willing to let this moment end. He had to draw it out. Taste it. Feel her softness under him for as long as he could.

She rolled her hips against him, urging him to move.

"Eyes on me," he said.

Gratification fueled him on, rocking forward and back in smooth, easy stokes with his eyes fixed on her. Every motion playing back to him through those lust-drunk emeralds.

Their actions became rougher and more demanding as they both raced toward climax. When she found her orgasm, her wild moans caused his control to snap, and his release quickly followed with a prolonged groan of fulfillment.

Entwined in the slick weight of each other's arms, he found it difficult to discern where he ended, and she began. She unknowingly gifted him with the mortality he'd been seeking for centuries. In the beginning, he'd planned to cut her loose the moment she quenched his soul. That wasn't going to happen. Not ever. His soul might feel full but his need for her would never be sated. Her warmth. Her laugh. Hell, even her tears. He relished them all.

His only unfinished business lay with the Shades at this point. His future with Marie was certain. The battle with her ended now.

Victory is mine.

****

Marie shifted against Quenton into that familiar

position, where her head nestled into the crook of his elbow, and her backside cradled in the warmth of his body.

Fatigue pulled every inch of her as though the Sandman himself frowned down on her, like someone stole his job. She mumbled in dreamy nonsense. Pauses between her thoughts lengthened as the wall clock officially chimed into the next day.

"So that's what it's like for people like you?" she asked.

His lips were soft on the back of her neck. "Mmm."

"I can see why you do it so often."

His breath stilled. "Out of necessity Marie, not always desire."

She struggled to stay alert under the weight of her eyelids. "Just a necessity?"

"Well not with you. You're…." He slid his hand from her waist to cup her breast. "My business mixed with pleasure."

Sure, like he'd never thrown that line out before. She stifled a yawn to cover the smile lurking underneath. "So what…else can you do?"

"I could erase tonight from your memory. Every time could be like the first."

"I like the memory better. It'll keep me warm when you aren't around," she said.

He brushed away the damp curls sticking to her forehead. "I'm not going anywhere."

If she were lucid, irritation would be prickling up her spine. Using people for sex was his thing, not hers. And she couldn't in good conscious agree to do that, but she knew there weren't any wedding bells in the future either. It didn't seem his style.

But wouldn't it be a nice change to hand the job of party-pooper to someone else? Let her naughty thoughts toast each other and enjoy their vacation? There wasn't any harm in ignoring the fact that someday she'd say good-bye and move on with her life.

Not for a little while anyway. It could satisfy her lust and pacifying her heart at the same time. Everybody's happy.

On the flip side, she couldn't allow him to play into her fantasy. That would stir up more excitement in the piece of her heart she was trying to anesthetize, then everything would fall apart.

She toyed with the corner of the pillow. "You have work. You have to travel. I can't always be with you."

"You can. And you will."

Back to that again? She twisted in his arms to send him a drowsy look over her shoulder. As she shifted, her bottom brushed against him and his arms clamped down tighter around her.

"I still haven't forgiven you for dragging me here in the first place," she said.

He arched a dark brow. "Where else would you go?"

"I don't know, but not all over the country. In case you haven't figured it out, I don't like traveling. My condo has been perfectly safe for years. Maybe if we were closer to town—"

"Sterling Springs is no longer an option. We're not going back. From here on out, the only place you'll be, is with me."

****

Breakfast was long overdue when Marie shuffled

down the hallway to her parent's room. She gave a tight rap on the door before breezing inside, heading for the kitchen.

Ruby folded her arms over the table and wiggled her painted brows. "So how'd it go?"

She ignored her mother's eager grin and scanned the hotel room. "It went great, Mom. Where's Anna?"

"Still sleeping. I took Flopsey out a couple times. I can't keep him out of there." Ruby looked down into her oversized mug of chai and stirred lazy circles with her spoon. "So how great is great? I could have sworn I heard someone running down the hall last night. When I put my ear to the wall, I couldn't hear anything from your room."

Mmmm, guess she lost her stethoscope. She didn't know why she felt surprised but there it was. Her mouth gaped open, a silent "*MOM!*" hanging off her tongue.

"Oh, don't give me that look, Marie. We're all adults here."

"Yes. And we're all entitled to our privacy. Excuse me." She marched toward the spare bedroom.

Ruby stretched up in her chair and called after her, "I hope you don't mind but I've signed us all up for snowboarding lessons today."

"I've suffered enough bodily harm thanks."

She pushed the door open; Flopsey stood guard next to Anna. His tiny black lip curled to bare needle-like teeth.

"Hey, Mom, has Spike here had his shots?" she asked. She didn't wait for a response and edged around the bed.

"Come on, sleepy head. You should've been up hours ago. It's time to rise, sunshine."

She jostled Anna's foot, but the little girl gave no response. Flopsey bounded over Anna's legs and snapped at Marie's hand.

"Hey!"

Marie eyed Flopsey as she backed away and opened the heavy curtains. "That's some guard dog you've got."

When sunlight fell on Anna, she whimpered and covered her face with her hands. "No! It hurts my eyes." Her voice sounded croaky.

Flopsey erupted in a fit of bouncy yips when Marie perched on the edge of the bed.

"Oh, be quiet!" Marie shooed him to the floor.

He gave an indignant huff before trotting out of the room.

"What's the matter, Princess? Not feeling well?"

Anna shook her head and large tears tumbled from her sealed eyes.

Heat radiated from Anna's flushed cheeks as Marie dabbed the falling tears. "Oh Princess, you're really sick."

Anna's bottom lip jutted, and she let go a timid sob.

She shifted Anna into her lap, cradled her head to her chest, and rocked until the tears slowed. The fever intensified with each passing minute, and by the time Anna fell asleep again, sweat beaded on Marie's brow.

She slid Anna back onto her pillow and returned to the kitchen where Ruby sat hunched over her chai, chattering in hushed excitement.

"I think with the right teacher, she could be a wild woman. It's in her blood." Ruby said.

Quenton raised his eyes to greet her as he pulled a

large jug of orange juice from the fridge.

Color rushed into Marie's cheeks. "Mom, isn't it time for your snowboarding lesson? Maybe you could plow down some unsuspecting teenagers?"

"You're really not going?" Ruby asked.

"Anna's sick. We're staying here. Maybe we'll see if the hotel has an in-house physician."

Quenton's shoulders stiffened. "I'll look at her."

She directed him to the spare bedroom before turning her frown on Ruby. "I'm going to the lobby to get something for her fever. Try to stay out of trouble until I get back."

Ruby's brows shot up. "I'm only trying to help."

She lifted both palms in exasperation. "I can handle him on my own. I don't need help."

Ruby canted her head. "You can handle him, but can you keep him?"

"What the hell's that supposed to mean?"

"Well, given your history—"

Her spine drew taut. Her knuckles blanched white on the back of the chair. "*What* history? I have no history! You guys moved me around so much, I'm surprised I can remember what continent I'm on."

Ruby smacked her cup down on the table. "So we moved around a lot. You can't keep using that excuse for all your failed relationships. How much time do you think you need? A month? A year? You had that long. If a relationship isn't solid by then, it isn't going to be."

Ruby's gaze dropped to the table. "I just don't want to see you lose this one."

Marie's posture didn't ease but the emotion dropped from her voice. "Curb your desperation, Mother. He's not mine to lose."

Quenton marched into the room with tension in his step, and his lips pressed in a grim line. "Do you have anything in the other room, Marie?"

"A few things, yeah."

"Get them. We're leaving."

A sickening weight sagged into her stomach, with an almost audible thud. "Where?"

"Back to Sterling Springs."

Chapter 19

Whap. Whap. Whap. Marie pulled her clothing down one after another, setting the hangers to swinging. She stuffed each article into her glossy new shopping bags. "But you said we weren't going back. What changed your mind?"

"Unforeseen circumstances," he said.

"Are you sure that's a good idea? It's a long drive for a sick girl. I don't know about you, but I've seen enough puke to last me a lifetime."

Quenton took the heaping bags from Marie's hands, and started for the door. "She'll be unconscious most the way."

She chased after him through the suite and down the hallway. "Did you? You didn't! You didn't put her out... Quenton, she isn't just some inconvenience you can find a quick solution for."

She nearly stumbled into his chest when he made a quick pivot and stopped cold. He lifted the bags above her head she wouldn't crash into them. "You think I don't know that? I'm not the one who put her out, she put herself out."

Understanding lit her brain like a pinball machine. She took a step back. "She's like you?"

The line of his jaw hardened. "We have to take her back to Sterling Springs before people take notice."

"What about the Shades?" she asked.

He lowered the bags to his side. "We're in the middle of the Shade migration. I hoped that coming here would give us a break, but we aren't far enough north. Ideally, they would've moved on by now instead they're converging on a central location, and we're in the middle of it. Staying here won't help us. She's safer in Sterling Springs where more than one of us can protect her."

"Okay, it's back home we go then." She swiped at the bags, and he lifted them out of her reach, missing her fingertips.

"You need to know what you're signing up for."

She watched the slow descent of his arm. "I've already seen them. I know what they're about." She lunged at the bags again. His hand flattened against her chest as the other held them out of reach.

"They're going to come after her," he said.

The desperation in his voice hooked her heart, stunning her with potent fear and disbelief. She stopped the useless windmill of her arms and swallowed hard to relieve the enormous lump forming in her throat.

"The Shades hunt nearly anything with a body. But a muse is the ultimate prize. Can you imagine if they caught someone like us? Anna's weak in physical strength but her skills may one day surpass both Tobin's and mine. She is an irresistible temptation," he said.

"All this time, they've been after her?"

He gave a lopsided nod. "They hunt like wolves roaming through their territory until they find someone and quietly close in. Preying on the weak and using their kill to lure stronger prey into their grasp. Like a demonic game of leapfrog. They're hunting Anna and the easiest way to get her…is through you. They'll hunt you down first, and count on your voice to intrigue Anna long enough to get her."

He leaned into her, his face sober as granite. "Once the Shades take down their prey, they use the body like a temporary shell. Giving them all of the senses the original body had but it wasn't meant to fit them. The muscles, tendons, and ligaments stretch beyond their normal capacity. The entire body becomes distorted and unrecognizable. Except for the voice, it remains fairly intact."

She closed her eyes. "This is my fault. If I hadn't pitched such a fit, we'd be half-way around the world by now."

"I wouldn't leave Tobin to fight off an entire pack by himself."

She narrowed her eyes on him. "Why do you do that?"

He started to pull away, but she latched onto him. Using her own hand to sandwich the one pressed to her chest. "Why do you always stick up for him? I know he's your brother, but blood only goes so far," she said.

"I owe him more than blood."

****

Seasons changed fast in Colorado. With one brutal drop in temperature and a well-placed storm front, the entire state could sleep for the winter.

But not this time.

She found it frightening; the way Sterling Springs lost itself in the deepest part of fall when the land turned brown and barren of life, waiting for the thick cover of snow to lull it into hibernation.

The part that scared her most was although the

outside remained stationary, nothing felt the same.

She dreaded going back. She felt like Goldilocks after being chased away by the three bears. Only this Goldie must have her ringlets on too tight because why on Earth would she want to stroll back into that den after nearly being eaten alive?

Quenton lifted a hand from the steering wheel to rest on her shoulder. "We won't be here long. Just a few days until Anna's recovery."

His words did little to ease the weight of impending doom that hung over the car. She knew deep down he wanted to ensure Tobin's safety too.

What kind of factor did Tobin play in all this? Whatever guilt he held over Quenton's head, was the dark and selfish kind. Like a spoiled child hell-bent on getting his way.

The low rumble of Quenton's voice cut into her thoughts. "Not so happy to be home?"

She forced a tight smile. "I'm already planning my second going away party."

Her mouth went dry when they turned onto the path leading to the family estate. The charcoal stone house stood as a lone fortress in the middle of a ghostly clearing. She almost expected a screeching bat to come darting out of the woods and perch on the rooftop then transform into Tobin's sulking silhouette.

Black SUVs walled off the perimeter of the yard, crammed bumper-to-bumper, and forced them to park at the bottom of the slope.

"Looks like our reinforcements are here," he said.

When he shut off the engine, her ears perked to greet the settling clicks of the vehicle and the frantic pace of her heartbeat.

He turned to the spindly tree line. She followed his lead, training her eyes on the forest edge.

"You stay here while I get the bags." He unloaded the car and headed for the front door. Not one minute after he disappeared from view, the hairs on the back of her neck stood on end. Her mind whirred through the possibility of a Shade creeping toward the car while they were left unattended.

The lock. Reaching for the button, her hand couldn't move fast enough. She slapped it down, locking all the car doors with a dull thud.

She turned her attention to the back seat where Anna lay curled in a tight ball with her fists clenched, and her eyes pinched shut. Her only movement was the slow rise and fall of her chest.

Why did Anna have to fight through yet another struggle of this magnitude and without anyone to help her? If this illness was as severe as Quenton let on, why would he want to keep her hidden? Why not take her to the hospital?

She understood now that Anna had put herself in a coma after Christie's car accident. No wonder she had Dr. Scott so baffled. But how far under would Anna burrow this time? If she stopped eating and drinking, she'd wither away to nothing.

She needed to be in a hospital where better people than she could pretend to know what they were doing.

She knew enough to recognize a fever, but her nursing skills ended there. Working at the childcare center didn't lend much more expertise beyond a quick draw with the phone and access to one of the dozen parent phone numbers branded in her memory.

When she turned back around in her seat, a flicker

of movement caught the corner of her eye. She jumped, smacking her head on the rearview mirror.

It took a full agonizing second and a huge gasp of air before she recognized Quenton standing outside her door. The view from the neck down appeared calm, rocking back on heels with his arms crossed as if he had all the time in the world for her to contemplate the universe while staring at his comatose daughter.

He tapped lightly on her window.

Her gaze rose to his face where calm ended, and apprehension began. His eyes were bright and watchful as he panned the tree line with inhuman speed. His lips pressed to a sober frown. He motioned her outside the car with a tilt of his head.

Trying to swallow the heart suddenly lodged in her throat, she suppressed the instinctive *nuh-uh* head shake and forced her hand to the door handle. She stepped out into the encroaching cold, thankful for the numbing distraction to her nervous system.

"Tobin's in the study," he said. More a warning that a casual statement.

So stay out of the study. No argument here. She had some unfinished business with Tobin but that would have to wait. Anna's safety came first.

She watched Quenton slide his hands under Anna, lifting her from the car as if he were cradling an unfurled rose, whose petals were stretched to near collapse. A sludge of icy guilt poured over her.

Of course her safety came first, not only for Marie, but for Quenton as well. At what point did she forget he was only trying to protect his daughter?

He gestured for her to go first with a tilt of his head. She entered the house and flipped on the entryway light. Down the hall to the darkened study, Tobin's silhouette lounged in one of the chairs. A slender bottle glinted as he moved it to his lips. The distinct scent of booze wafted to her nostrils.

She expected him to bust from the chair and breeze by, announcing that he and his tool were off to right the wrongs of sexual frustration for the morally weak and oppressed. Or some other lame innuendo that fed his purpose. But he didn't move.

Never in the time she knew Tobin had she seen him this quiet. The soundless tip of the bottle and the calculating tilt of his head told her there was something stewing just below the surface. Her every fiber charged with hesitation, whispering to the rest of her not to go within a hundred yards of that surface tonight.

The clatter of dishes and rumble of male laughter pulled her attention to the kitchen.

"When you get settled, I'll introduce you to the guys," Quenton said.

Settled? Not likely. She left her luggage near the door as reassurance they'd leave the place soon. Not soon enough but soon.

A soft nudge between her shoulder blades urged her down the hallway to her room. She moaned inwardly and dug her heels into the floor until Quenton gave her a second not so gentle nudge. "He's not going to bother you tonight," he whispered. "He'll be lucky if he can even get up from the chair."

"In that case, do you think we can keep him like this until we move?" she asked.

Quenton flashed a quick smile. He reached for Anna's door, and with a flick of his wrist, opened it without making a sound. She stared at his hand, still perched on the knob.

"What's wrong?" he asked.

She shook herself and pushed the door wide open, allowing him to pass through. "These doors. They're always so loud when I open them."

He shifted Anna onto the bed and covered her with a pink chenille blanket. "There isn't a door in the place I can't sneak in or out of."

Marie shifted her weight to one hip. "Then I better keep my door locked tonight. Keep you out of trouble."

"As if that would stop me." He pulled her to his chest and brushed his lips against hers in a tender caress.

"We have company tonight. A few guys to help keep things secure around here. With limited space, we'll share a room." He murmured against her. "I'm sure you won't mind."

Her stomach bubbled with nervous energy. She tipped her head back to meet his gaze and wrapped her arms around his neck. "That depends. Are you going to snore?"

He nipped at her lower lip. "Like a bear. I talk, too. Say all kinds of dirty things. And I'm terrible at staying on my own side of the bed."

"Mmm...how could a girl refuse?"

"We'll be heading out for a look around. May not be back until late. Try to get some sleep. You're going to need it."

She inched back and her chin took a skeptical tilt. "So you weren't just being charitable when you cured my insomnia? You just wanted to be sure I had the energy to keep up with you?"

His lips twitched. "Already told you, sweet thing. I

need something. You need something. We both get what we want."

"I think I got the bigger portion. All that I want, and half of yours, too."

His eyes lit with seductive intent. "We'll compare portions in the morning, because tonight, you're all mine."

****

Quenton could see the deep scowl etched in Tobin's face as he directed his men to the study. There were eight in all, divided equally between his two most trusted officers, Artino and Barros. He still hadn't replaced Tobin's position as the third, and the reunion wasn't going to be pretty.

A cheesy grin grew on Artino's face, and he splayed his arms wide to Tobin. "Pee-wee! I've missed you. How long has it been since I kicked your ass?"

The trailing laughter filtered into the study. Tobin's expression twisted like that of a cornered rattlesnake. His eyes were dark and watchful and his shoulders tense. "'Bout time I returned the favor."

Barros interrupted by stepping between them. "This isn't a play date." He jerked his head to Quenton. "What've you got for us, boss?"

"Suck up." Tobin muttered, then took another pull on the bottle.

Quenton powered up his touch pad. A satellite image appeared, smattered with orange dots. "Leaving the house isn't an option. We've got precious cargo that won't be moved for several days, and Shades crawling all over the place."

"How many we talking?" asked Barros.

"Fifty or more. With or without bodies."

The five to one odds sent a collective hum of approval through the room. "Sounds like a party. You got bait?" Barros asked.

"No bait."

Artino clicked his tongue. "You work us too hard, Blake. I don't know about the rest of us, but ever since I heard the word 'Colorado,' I've had a hankering for a snow bunny somethin' awful. Now there's no snow, no girlies, and no—" His speech halted when the men shuffled to reveal Marie standing in the hall.

Artino's voice dropped a full octave. "Hellllo."

"Um…hi," she said.

Artino captured both her hands and pulled her into the room. "Well, don't just stand there, sweetheart, come in. Let's have a look at you."

He cast a smile over his shoulder to Quenton. "So this is why we haven't seen you since Beirut." Artino's gaze drank her in from head to toe. "She causes a distraction just say the word. I'll throw her over my shoulder and carry her out for you. Nooo problem."

"Not her. It's the baby, asshole." Tobin muttered.

Barros' gaze flew from the touch pad to Quenton. "You have a baby? Since when?"

"Since about two-and-a-half years ago," he said.

Barros made no comment, just lifted his brows, and returned his attention to the touch pad.

"So you're the mommy?" Artino asked.

"Nanny," she replied, extracting her hands.

He turned to Tobin. "So that makes *you* the mommy. This new insta-family just keeps getting better and better."

Quenton shot him a lethal glare, before facing the touch pad again. He opened his mouth to speak but

Artino piped up again.

"I gotta see this baby. No, no, no, wait! Let me guess. It's a Chihuahua, right?"

Barros punched Artino in the shoulder hard enough to knock him off balance. "Pay attention."

With Artino frowning over his sore limb, Quenton continued. "More Shades are heading in from the north. We've only got one shot to take out the leader before their numbers increase. She's a wily bitch and won't be easy to catch.

"Artino, I want your team in position on this northeast ridge. Barros, you're coming in from the west. With any luck, we'll corral them before they descend on the house. Get warm and get out. We're finishing this tonight."

Chapter 20

Marie sank another three-point shot into the giant moving box and reached for the next stuffed animal on Anna's shelf. A one-eared bunny with matted fur and a droopy smile sailed through the air and bounced off the corner of the box.

She sighed and moved to retrieve it.

"You don't really need this one do you?" She faced the toy to Anna then dropped it in the box. "You have three of them. And what about your dress-up clothes? They're too small for you now." She lifted a fat toffee-colored puppy and lobbed at the box, missing again.

"You can have the dresses in my room instead. Except the red one. I'm keeping that until you're thirty. Or forty."

She crossed the room to the next shelf, drawing the curtain over the window as she passed. Fear trickled down her spine when for a moment, one frilly pink drape and a thin pane of glass became the only thing standing between her and the outside world.

And Quenton was out there somewhere.

When he left the office, his step oozed with cool determination, and she knew there would be no stopping him. If only she could harness a little of that confidence for herself. Maybe she wouldn't be pinging all over the house just hoping that with one wrong move she'd crack her head on a drawer or cabinet, knocking herself out cold until it was over.

So far, she managed to push Heather's grotesque figure deeper into her imagination by loading everything she could for their trip to Alaska. Or Canada. Even the North Pole sounded good.

She held up what appeared to be a decapitated goose. Its neck hung like a wet noodle, bouncing as she presented it to Anna. "Okay, this is where I draw the line."

A faint moan passed through Anna's lips, and her head lulled to the side.

"What are you going to do with it? *It doesn't have a head.*" She frowned turning the goose at odd angles. She tilted her head. "Elephant maybe?"

Anna's brows wrinkled.

She paused. "Princess? You awake?"

With her eyes sealed shut, Anna tried to lift off the pillow. Her head lagged behind as if she lacked the strength to support it. She stretched her arms out to Marie in the universal "hold me" sign.

Marie reigned in the helpless turmoil bubbling in her chest and pulled Anna onto her lap. "Hey, I'm glad you're up. Just wait till your dad gets back. He'll be so happy to see you."

When Anna pulled her face from the crook of Marie's arm, a clear jelly-like substance oozed from beneath her lashes.

Marie furrowed her brows and peered closer. "Princess let me have a look at you. Can you open your eyes?"

Anna forced her sticky lashes apart to reveal two colorless orbs. Once a vibrant shade of blue, her eyes were now clouded over to milky white. Her pupils fixed and contracted. Like staring into the face of a marble statue.

Shock and panic hit simultaneously, and her arms went limp. Anna's head rolled back, before she caught it again, and cradled her to her chest. This was unlike anything she ever witnessed, and far beyond comprehension.

She pulled in a quivering breath. "Okay...okay, you just stay right here while I go get your daddy."

She exploded from Anna's bedroom and rushed down the hall. Her voice broke as she choked back the tears. "Tobin? Quenton? I need your help!"

Anna's cries echoed through her open door as Marie entered the study and slapped on the light.

"Be right there, Princess. Just hold on," she called back.

She scanned through the empty study and ran to Quenton's room, knowing that he wouldn't be there, but too far gone not to hunt for him anyway. She cast a brief glance at the room before heading for Tobin's.

She flicked on the light but no Tobin.

Suck!

Her gaze coursed over the rumpled sheets, and the toys strewn across the floor until she found his cell phone amid an impressive collection of lubricants. He didn't have his phone with him, but maybe Quenton did.

Crossing the room, her foot caught on the bed sheet, and she tumbled over the trunk lying at the foot of his bed.

"Ow-ha-ow." She held her throbbing shin and bounced up and down until she snagged the phone.

Damn thing's password protected.

Marie tossed the phone back to the dresser top and glared at the oversized steamer trunk. Near the hinge, a sliver of plastic protruded from the seam. Marie knelt down and worked it back and forth until it slid free. She studied the plastic card. "Roxanne's driver's license."

Marie looked to the doorway then back to the trunk. Anna's cries were becoming weak and drawn out as exhaustion overtook her.

With a pop can and a pair of scissors she could shim the lock but didn't have time for arts and crafts. She needed something quicker.

"There." She rushed forward to claim a thin, curved, metal wand. She tried not to contemplate its use as she jammed it through the latch on the padlock and stomped down on it. The rod slipped out, and her shin scraped down the edge of the trunk.

She clenched her fists and stifled a whimper and wedged the rod in a second time. Stomped again. This time, the lock popped free.

She threw open the lid and gaped in horror at the countless laminated faces looking back at her. She swiped through the collection of IDs until she came upon Heather's then Claire's.

She gathered as many as she could stuff into her pockets and tried to arrange the leftovers the way she found them. She paused when her motions uncovered a small syringe, the needle still sheathed in plastic. She tossed it back into the pile, slammed the trunk closed, and charged back to Anna's room.

"Come on, baby. We're getting some help."

****

Glass doors whooshed open and welcomed Marie with the scent of antiseptic and adhesive tape. She marched to the front desk with Anna shrouded in a dark blanket.

"How can I help you?" the woman asked.

"I need to see Dr. Scott. He's her neurologist. There's something wrong with her eyes."

The clerk's tight smile masked over, and she shifted her attention to the monitor. "Name."

"Anna Blake."

"Address."

Marie adjusted Anna on her hip. "I'm not sure. She just moved and—"

The clerk leaned around the monitor. "Are you the parent?"

Marie's head scooped forward in a here's-my-neck-please-cut-along-the-dotted-line motion. "No. I'm her nanny."

"We'll need to contact her parent or guardian to finish her paperwork. Go ahead and take a seat. The nurse will be right with you."

When the thin blonde wearing *Cat in the Hat* scrubs called them back into a small exam room, Anna's body tensed in her arm.

"So, Anna, what's shakin'?" the nurse prompted. She leaned forward to uncover Anna's face. Marie blocked her. "The light bothers her eyes. We'll wait until Dr. Scott gets here."

A mosaic of different emotions tugged at her conscience. Anna needed help but she wasn't an average child. What if her illness masked some medical anomaly that drew attention on a grand scale and exposed her family's secret? She couldn't let that happen.

The nurse pursed her lips. "O—kay. Let's start

with the easy stuff then. Anna, can I see your arm, sweetie?"

Anna thrust her arm out from the blanket with her hand balled into a fist. The nurse jumped back before it connected with her chin.

Marie bit back a smile.

The nurse wrapped a blood pressure cuff around Anna's arm. "She's pretty warm. How high has her temperature been?"

Marie's voice escalated over the hum of the machine. "103?"

The machine released Anna's arm with a hiss, and the nurse tore the cuff free then burrowed under Anna's blanket to swipe the thermometer across her forehead. "Well, let's have one of our guys take a look at her before we page Dr. Scott."

"Sorry. It's Scott or no one."

The thermometer sent out a rhythmic chirp. The nurse frowned. "Her fever is too high. We can't keep her covered up like this." She pulled at the blanket's corner, but Marie snatched it back, even as the panic swelled into her throat. "Then you better get Scott here now."

"Look, I know you like Dr. Scott but there are others here that can help her."

Marie got to her feet. "No. There aren't. And if you don't call him, I'm going to find him, myself."

The nurse held up her hands and pushed out a frustrated breath. "Fine. Just…stay here and I'll page him but it's gonna take a while. How about we find you a bed where we can turn off the lights. We'll give Anna something for her fever."

"Sounds peachy."

Marie stole frequent glances at the gurney and paced to sound of beeping monitors and the drone of machinery. Neighboring patients came and went. Her ears trained on the shuffling feet and frequent passing chatter from the hospital staff. She felt more forgotten every minute.

She could only imagine what must be going through Quenton's head right now, returning to find Anna missing. In her rush, she neglected to pick up her phone from wherever it landed the night before. Hopefully the hospital managed to reach him.

The clomp of hard-soled shoes entering the room stirred her attention.

"Ms. Durrant?" asked the uniformed man standing next to the nurse.

"Yes."

The nurse opened her mouth to speak but snapped it closed again with a wave from the Uniform. "I understand you've brought this girl here for treatment and now you're refusing care."

She moved to stand in front of Anna. "I'm not refusing care, I'm waiting for Dr. Scott. Where is he?"

The Uniform hooked his thumbs in his belt loop and puffed up his chest. "He's in surgery. In the meantime, we need to take Anna's best interests into consideration."

She took a step back and reached for Anna's shoulder. "Her fever came down. She's not in any danger. We can wait for Scott."

"Look, the physicians here only want what's best for her. Let them do their job."

She turned her glacial stare on the nurse. "You're not putting one hand on her."

The Uniform shook his head and smug delight gleamed in his eyes. "All right. If you want to play hard ball…."

Marie tore away from his grasp and stumbled into the bedrail before he caught her a second time. Her whisper turned fierce. "Let. Me. Go."

He slammed her against the wall face first, crushing her nose, and forcing her hands behind her back. Pain shot through her sinuses. Her eyes watered.

"Don't make me restrain you—"

She jerked her head back, slamming into his left eye.

With a grunt he forced all his weight against her, squeezing the breath from her lungs. He slapped the cuffs on and locked them down until the cold metal cut into her wrists. A sickening weight fell into her stomach when she felt him run his hands down her sides. He found her back pocket.

"What's this?" He held one of the ID cards under her nose. "Is this you?"

"No it's—"

He shuffled to the second one in the stack and tapped it on her nose. "How 'bout this one? Is this you?"

She closed her eyes. *What are the odds? What are the freaking odds? I try to nail Tobin, and I get screwed instead.*

The Uniform continued to shuffle through the cards, his grin broadened. "You know what this looks like, *Marie*. Looks like a whole lot of trouble for you." He pressed the talk button on his radio and angled his face into it. His voice broadened with enough self-entitlement, the whole emergency room could have heard it. "We need an officer to the ER for possible ID theft."

"All right, what's this all about?" Dr. Scott asked.

Her ears perked at the boom of Dr. Scott's voice and relief poured over her.

He shuffled to a stop and flashed Marie a beaming smile. "Oh look, there's trouble. What have you done now? "

The Uniform started to explain but Dr. Scott held up both hands. "Wait! Wait, hold on." He fished into his coat pocket and pulled out his phone. "Just hold it right there…."

He snapped Marie's picture, then held the phone up as if admiring his handiwork. "Beautiful. Revenge is just beautiful."

"Very funny." she sneered.

He sighed and dropped the phone back in his pocket. "Okay, let her go, Mitch. She's harmless."

Mitch handed the stack of identification cards to Dr. Scott. "Sorry, doc, Can't. Found these on her."

"Where'd you get these?" he asked.

Marie let the thud of her forehead against the wall answer for her.

"Everybody clear the room. Marie isn't going anywhere, and we've got a little girl to worry about," he said.

"I already called her in. Cops should be here any minute," Mitch said.

"Have them wait outside."

Mitch left her hands cuffed and gave Marie a parting nudge into the wall.

Dr. Scott shelved his hip on the edge of Anna's gurney. "All right, Princess, let's have a look-see.

Where are those pretty blue peepers, huh?" He looked once, blinked, and leaned in for closer inspection.

"Hmm." He sat back and tapped the end of his pen onto his lower lip.

"You know I hate it when you make that sound," Marie said.

A heavy silence weighed down on the room before Dr. Scott looked to the wall-mounted computer. His hand glided over his mouse, darting and clicking like a mad scientist.

"The IDs are from Tobin, aren't they?" he asked without looking up from the screen.

She blew a puff of air at the loose curls obstructing her vision. "I found them in his room. I don't know if it's enough to get him convicted but I think if it gets the detectives' attention, maybe we can keep them on the trail."

Scott lowered his eyes to the keyboard and shook his head. "They seem to be scaling back the search. Looking at other options. They found a dirty needle in her purse, and it came back with her blood type on it. Still waiting on the DNA. Three vials of Propofol went missing from the pharmacy the day she disappeared. They figure she was abusing and left before she could get caught."

Marie's mouth dropped open. "She wouldn't do that."

The stool made a metallic squeak as Dr. Scott turned his full attention on her. "You're right. If she was trying to get away with it, she wouldn't have taken so much at one time. It's too noticeable. Three vials are enough to kill a horse."

"I found a needle in Tobin's room. It sounds like

he's trying to cover his tracks."

Dr. Scott turned back to his computer with a snort. "Doesn't surprise me."

He pushed out a sigh. "Okay…for Anna, we'll have to contact the on-call eye specialist in the meantime, I'd like to run a few tests."

She gave a slow nod, but her mind wasn't in it. The commotion from outside became too big of a distraction. Panicked male voices and pounding footsteps intensified as they neared their room. She and Scott looked to the door.

"Sir, you can't go in there!" one man shouted.

"Stop!" called another.

The third voice came in a fearsome growl that snapped her nerve endings to attention. "Get out of my way."

Oh brilliant! Her face flushed with anticipation for the fury she was about to have unleashed on her.

Quenton stormed into the room with Tobin in tow, both of their expressions fierce with rage.

Dr. Scott jumped to his feet. The force sent his stool skittering to the wall behind him. "You're not taking them."

Quenton advanced in a blur, catching Scott by the throat and lifting him to his toes.

"The hell I'm not," he seethed.

Before the last word escaped his lips, Scott's eyes glazed over, and his shoulders fell limp. Quenton released his grip. Scott crashed to the floor with his eyes wide and unblinking.

Marie drew in a painful gasp.

Quenton didn't spare her a single glance as he scooped Anna into his arms and stormed out. He passed

Tobin on his way out the door. "Get her."

Tobin moved slow to collect the stack of IDs from the desk where Dr. Scott had placed them. He craned his neck in Quenton's direction, seeming to wait until his brother was out of earshot.

When Quenton disappeared, Marie's head snapped to one side, and sharp numbness chased a sharp pain across her cheek. Tobin struck so fast, she didn't have time to flinch. Tears stung the back of her eyes as she narrowed in on him.

He looked to the vacant doorway where Quenton had stood. "Hey, you never told me she liked the rough stuff." He latched on to Marie's arm with a punishing grip. "All the fun I've been missing out on."

They moved through the emergency room. Quenton took the lead up ahead, cradling Anna in his arms and shielding her from the light.

****

The sun's rapid descent left the house grayed and dismal, smudging out details as the forest grew inky around the edges.

Marie's freak-o-meter buzzed when their convoy rolled to a stop at the bottom of the gravel drive. Tobin slammed the door of his own vehicle and marched to the house. Quenton unfolded himself from behind Marie's steering wheel and carried Anna out. He nudged the door closed with his elbow and left Marie in the back seat.

Between the cuffs and the car's child lock, Marie became effectively imprisoned in her own car. Yes, operation make-Marie-look-like-a-moron was now a complete success.

Feeling helpless and enraged all at the same time.

She sat back against the seat but flinched forward again as the cuffs cut into her wrists.

She should have spoken up and fought harder to convince them Anna needed help. Instead, she lost Quenton's trust and any hope for getting Anna medical attention.

Quenton emerged from the house again and jerked the car door open. "Time to talk."

Willing herself not to look directly at him, Marie scooted to the open door and angled herself out. "Do I need a lawyer first?"

He stepped behind her to examine the cuffs. After a few clicks, her right wrist swung free, then her left.

"Thanks."

The grunt under his breath sounded an awful lot like, *Sure, no problem, and the next time you get cuffed I'll leave them on.*

She looked down at her chafed wrists. "Where'd you like to go for this all-important discussion? We've got the mighty ogre planning his next orgy down the hall, a sleeping princess in limbo, and a bunch of hungry zombie-thingies prowling around out here."

"*Gourmet* zombie-thingies?"

"Whatever! Where we going?"

"Your room," he replied evenly.

"Ah, the *Room with a View*. An excellent choice," she mocked.

She spun away from Quenton's openmouthed expression, effectively hiding the guilt that warmed her cheeks. Her annoying habit of running her mouth was really going to get her in trouble someday.

His voice sounded too causal for comfort. "What's that supposed to mean?"

"I was being sarcastic," she mumbled.

Marie took a seat on the edge of the bed. Quenton wasn't far behind, putting his feet up, and propping his upper body with three large pillows at his back.

This was gonna be a long night. She tried to settle the escalating pace of her heart. She frequently entertained the idea of having Quenton in the seclusion of her room again but not under these circumstances.

His voice was cool and calculated. "I haven't been very forthcoming with you, and for that I'd like to apologize. Can't imagine it's been easy to accept all the demands placed on you here."

She tipped her head and offered a smile. "I'm sorry. Have we met? I'm Marie, the nanny, part-time pasta-whatever, Oh, and don't forget, I moonlight as a doormat."

"Contrary to your opinion of me, I don't like leading you on."

"Then don't," she challenged. Her voice grew serious. "Don't tell me I'm safe when I have a pack of monsters outside my door. Don't tell me everything's going to be okay when I have a small child in torment. And don't *tell me* you aren't going anywhere when you disappear the moment I need you."

"There's nothing wrong with Anna. You were safe here."

Her voice quivered with anger, and hot tears ran down her cheeks. She grasped the comforter with both hands. "That little girl's in pain, and you're not a doctor. Not that they had any idea what's going on anyway. But you could at least let them try."

His jaw hardened. "You don't think I can care for her, do you?"

275

She brushed the tears away with an angry flick of her hand. "Please. I don't know any more about parenting than you do. This isn't a science."

"I know enough to recognize the symptoms. Anna's going through a metamorphosis."

She was about to speak up in protest but Quenton held up a finger to silence her.

One of these days, that boy's gonna lose that finger.

"Kids perfect their speech patterns, learn to socialize, lose their first tooth. The process Anna's going through is nothing more than a growing pain. More severe than most but the worst is over for her. Her vision will be restored ten-fold in a matter of days. If I could take away her suffering, I would. But unfortunately, it's a waiting game until she finds her new strength."

She couldn't hide her smirk. "So the next time Anna blows me a kiss, I have to duck? Is that what you're saying?"

His chest bounced in a silent snort. "Her ability to numb human senses won't come till her teenage years. I hope. Of course, she'll have to be taught how to use it."

"Well, there better not be any tutoring sessions from ole Uncle Tobin."

He shook his head. "Tobin has no taste. And I mean that in a literal sense. He has no inner compass for what souls are accommodating."

"Accommodating?"

Quenton paused. "Think of it like food. He can't tell the difference between an orange and rancid steak. It's physically repulsing for someone like me to influence a soul that isn't right. Tobin doesn't have that and refuses to accept guidance from anyone else. He chooses unwisely. Sometimes deliberately."

He crooked his finger for her to join him in the nest of pillows. She pulled in a shaky breath and complied. She stretched onto her stomach and used her elbows to brace her upper body. A rush chased across her skin when his sparkling gaze dipped to her cleavage.

His voice continued at an even pace, although a little husky around the edges. "Some souls can't handle our influence. Their impression of the world becomes unnatural. They start making mistakes."

When his fingertip traced the curve of her collarbone, the delighted chant of her naughty thoughts shattered her trail of logic.

Lower. Lower, they chanted like spectators at a beachfront limbo contest.

She shoved them aside with a seemingly casual toss of her head. She couldn't afford to get distracted. She needed answers.

"By mistakes you mean getting themselves killed?"

He didn't respond. His attention followed the path of his fingertips. The sultry curve of his smile promised that the limbo was far from over.

She closed her eyes and savored the warm tingles spiraling out from his calloused touch. She pushed her words out in a single breath, hoping to satisfy her mind so her body could take it from here. "If he didn't kill them, what's with the IDs?"

"They're a reminder for a debt he caused. He owes them for the condition he left them in."

"Why does he deliberately choose the wrong ones if he knows it will end in a debt?" she asked.

Her frisky thoughts released a collective grumble

when he dropped his hand.

He sighed. "Tobin is scorned. He fell in love with a woman he wasn't compatible with, and she strayed. Then he found out she was pregnant."

Marie's eyes grew wide. "Christie?"

He gave a sober nod. "I didn't know Christie was playing both of us, but it didn't take long to figure out. She had a certain appeal. She could accept what I gave her without demanding more. That's because she was taking twice her fill.

"Tobin thought she was the one—and I took that from him. By the time he and I found out, it was too late. She professed her love for Tobin, and I let her go. But despite Tobin's love for Christy, he couldn't excuse the infidelity. He refused her."

Marie dipped her head. "I can't believe it. She never let on."

"Her attraction to Tobin came from an addiction to his influence. It fled from her the moment Tobin stopped giving her what she wanted, but she was still family," he said.

Her attention fell to where her hands stroked the segmenting pearls of her necklace.

"So the feelings that I have for you? Just another addiction?"

"You tell me."

She nodded. Her fleeting courage too weak to drag her gaze back up. "I'm afraid this addiction is the hopeless kind. It won't be going away when you do."

His hand slipped under the hem of her shirt. "I already told you. I'm not going anywhere."

Her lips pursed in mock skepticism, even as heat skittered from the upward path of his hand. "I thought staying in one place made you stir-crazy."

"There's no difference between here and the other side of the world. I still find all my favorite places." He leaned in to nuzzle the curve of her neck. "Mmmm…like this place."

His hand moved to palm the curve of her breast, dragging his thumb over her hardened nipple. "Or this one."

Warmth rushed over her body to pool between her thighs, and her lips parted. The tip of his tongue coaxed her lips farther apart and taunted hers into a wild dance.

He brushed the obstructing curls from her face, tucking them behind her ear.

Pain lanced through her bruised cheekbone when the heel of his hand made contact.

With her instinctive flinch, his hand froze.

His brows lowered in confusion and angled her chin up to inspect the swollen flesh. Hot breath pushed past his teeth in a quiet growl, making her head swim.

"Stay here." He vaulted from the bed. "Tobin!"

Marie swung her legs off to follow him. "Quenton. Don't—"

He jabbed a finger at her on the way out the door. "Stay put."

A command like that begged to be disobeyed. She chased after him. "Like hell! I'm not just going to sit here while you two duke it out over—" The door slammed mere inches from her face. With a huff, she flung it back open again.

"Quenton! You're all out of trees to tie me to, so stop acting like a thug and listen."

She latched on to his upper arm, but his forward momentum proved no match for her. She felt herself being tugged down the hall along with him like a cat on a leash.

"Tobin's trying to provoke you. He's up to something. I know it." She raced around in front of him and put her hands out to block his path. "If you go after him, I'll…I'll have to track down your guys to separate you. It would spoil your whole mission, running outside like a raving lunatic."

His expression revealed nothing as he placed his hand to the small of her back and guided her to the room. His haste left her feeling less than confident but when he slapped one end of the cuffs onto the bed post, she knew she'd been had.

Her stomach clenched, and all her words rushed together. "What are you doing?"

"No trees, huh?"

Suck!

She lifted her wrists in self-defense. Showing him the scarlet chafe marks. "Look at this. You can't cuff me again. That's cruel and unusual punishment."

He tossed her onto the bed and as she was about to jump up again, snatched her ankle and dragged it to the bedpost. He slapped on the cuff.

She narrowed her eyes on him. "Oh, you are *so* going to regret this."

He gave her a little pat on the head. "I bet. Now keep quiet. I don't want to have to knock you out."

"Not if you get knocked out first," she called as the door swung closed behind him.

Wait. Knocked out?

Shrill panic rang through her head when her snappy comeback bridged the crack in Tobin's motive.

Her thoughts spun back to the syringe in Tobin's

steamer trunk and the missing Propofol from the hospital. Tobin wasn't trying to cover his tracks with Heather; he was going to use it on the only person he couldn't knock out with his own powers.

Chapter 21

For a minute, Tobin thought that pretty pink love tap might go unnoticed, but the big boy pulled through just like he'd hoped.

He'd even gone the extra effort to restrain Marie. That was a delightful surprise. From the other side of the glass, her voice sounded more panicked by the minute. The look on her face and frantic struggle with the cuff made it clear she'd figured him out.

Hitting her was an act of desperation and clearly she saw right through it. But not soon enough to stop Quenton.

Good thing too because other options were in short supply.

Regret weighed heavy on Tobin's shoulders as he looked over the missing person flyer. His thumb trailed over the monochromatic photo of a young woman posing on a white-washed front porch, her head tipped, and her smile beaming.

Evlin. So that's her name.

Five-foot tall with blonde hair and blue eyes. Wearing a bright blue flower behind her ear. Last seen driving a red Jeep.

Quenton wouldn't allow Marie as a pawn but the only way to find his mate was to give the Shade what it wanted.

The bang of the exterior door caused Marie to

jump, and Tobin turned to the sound of Quenton pounding up the stone steps. He kept his eyes on the flyer as he rolled it up, using the precious seconds to steel himself for what he was about to do.

"You son of a bitch!" Quenton roared.

"Hey, she's your bitch too—" Tobin's head snapped back, and pain shot through his cheekbone when Quenton's fist slammed into him. Tobin took several steps back to reclaim his posture.

"I told you keep your hands off!"

"Hmmm. Guess you're right. My bad. Must have got a little carried away when I found out she ran off with your daughter, nearly exposed us, and tried to have me arrested. But I guess none of that matters to you now?" Tobin asked.

"You know it matters."

"If that were true, she wouldn't still be hanging around, would she? You would have ditched her by now." Tobin pointed to the glass with the funneled paper. "Not spilled all our family secrets and tucked her away for safe keeping and make-up sex."

"What the hell's your problem?"

He shoved the paper at Quenton. "This. This is my problem. My only chance for mortality hinges on you. Again."

"You need to make good on your plan to use Marie. It's the only thing they want."

Quenton let the paper curl up and handed it back, shaking his head. "Can't do that."

He swiped it from Quenton's hand. "You *can* do that. You owe me that much."

"My men have their orders. I'm not calling them back in. This has gone on long enough."

"Yeah, about that…the fact that you're mortal makes you a liability to the Muse guild. You'll have to step down. That leaves your position open to the next highest officer. Me."

"You're not fit to take the position."

His gaze followed his brother as he moved across the room. "You seem to think that because I'm not picky, I can't command this operation, but your delicate taste failed you this time. You've fallen for our only acceptable decoy and put your own daughter and our men at unnecessary risk."

Quenton stared through the glass to Marie. "A decoy isn't necessary. They already know where we are. I'm not sending Marie out into harm's way on the maniacal hunch that this girl belongs to you."

Anger bubbled through his veins and heated his face "You think Marie's special because she gave you mortality? She's no different from the rest of them. This can only end in one of two ways. Either she becomes an addict, or she already is one." Tobin let the syringe slide out from the inside of his sleeve and caught the thin plastic device in his palm. "Looks like there's only one way to find out."

Before the needle's plastic casing hit the ground, Tobin jammed the syringe into Quenton's shoulder blade. The needle ground against bone as he pushed the plunger down. The thick milky substance seeped into his flesh.

Only a portion of the fluid went in before Quenton threw his elbow back and smashed Tobin square in the face.

His vision flashed to fuzzy white. Blood spurted from his nose and rained on the cobble floor in inky splatters.

Quenton crossed an arm over his chest and twisted to reach the protruding syringe. He pulled it free, staring down at the crooked needle before facing Tobin with fury in his eyes. After two steps, his knees buckled, and he hit the ground.

He threw a right cross into Quenton's jaw. Quenton's whole body twisted under the force of the blow, and he fell down sideways like a massive tree.

He looked down on Quenton's still form. He wiped the blood from his nose with the back of his hand. "You'll thank me for this later. Once you see how common she is, you'll let her go."

He licked his lips. "Bet she tastes good, doesn't she, Quentie? Like cream and sugar. And I'll bet she's got plenty to go around. I'll just leave you here to enjoy the show. And don't bother with the lock, I've had it changed."

****

Marie's ears picked up the distant plod of heavy footsteps on the tiled hallway. She squeezed the hair pin in her palm and willed her heart to maintain a steady rhythm. The sound became crisper with every step.

A scuff sounded outside her door. Her spine went stiff with panic when the doorknob clicked.

She watched in horror with her mouth hinged open. Tobin slipped inside and locked the door, then braced the moving boxes under the knob.

He faced her with nostrils flared and red-rimmed eyes fierce with pent-up rage. He used back of his hand to wipe away the blood glistening on his upper lip.

"Oh, my God. What did you do? Where's Quenton?"

He gave her a mischievous grin and stalked a tight circle around the bed. "I have to admit you've come to surprise me, Marie. So standoffish, so feisty, and yet you jump into bed with my brother the minute he takes interest in you. What gives?"

He shook his head. "You were supposed to take care of *Anna's* needs. Not Quenton's. Did I not explain that in our verbal contract?"

"Where is he?" she demanded.

With viper strike speed, he snatched her hand.

She yelped in surprise and dug her nails into her palm, desperate to keep hold of the pin, but he pried her fingers away one at a time until he could retract it.

He showed her both palms before approaching her ankle and spoke in a slow drawl as he picked at the cuffs. "Okay, let me rephrase. Taking care of Anna includes feeding her, bathing her, and gushing over her artwork."

With a flick of his wrist the cuffs fell free. "This does not include going down on, bathing with, or gushing all over her father—if you catch my drift."

He closed a hand over her ankle where the cuff had been. Marie tried to yank her foot away, but he tightened his grip and gave her a brisk tug.

Desperation knotted in her muscles, urging her to move—to get away from him.

His voice sounded unfazed. "We need to work on the reputation you've built for yourself. Don't get me wrong, I'm immensely pleased you're willing to go above and beyond your job description but Quenton needs to know you're a professional. Your position here doesn't come with preferential treatment. It's time to even the score—give me my fair share."

Alarm bells screeched in her head as she forced her attention to his feet. He would easily detect her panic, and who knew what kind of power he'd inflict if she met him eye-to-eye.

She tried to smooth over the fear in her voice. "I know it's probably been…." She checked her watch. "…a few hours since you've had any action but now is not the time for drastic measures. You don't share, remember? And you don't do leftovers."

He stuck out his lower lip, and his voice took on a patronizing lilt. "Oh, usually that's true but once the value is diminished, we seem to lose interest in fighting over things. And I've never tasted you, so technically you're not *my* leftover.

"I've always wondered what it would be like to taste a coupled soul. One strong enough to grant mortality."

He rested one hip on the edge of the bed and closed the space between them.

She leaned away but her posture remained insolent, and her gaze locked on the bedspread. "You're drunk, and you've clearly lost it."

He rocked back, and his dark brows lifted. "No, no, I'm serious. Didn't Quentie tell you? Your soul is potent enough to make him mortal. You see what I mean? Talk about playing favorites."

His fingertip spiraled up her leg in lazy circles, and she kicked his hand away with her other foot.

Tobin *tsked*. "I think those years at the nunnery have done you a disservice with all that suppressed enthusiasm. Not to worry, we'll get you out of your shell. It just so happens, I have a very special key, and it fits…" He tapped her temple. "…right about here. I can bring forth every fantasy in that pretty little head of yours. And I can make them all happen."

He lifted his palms in casual disclosure. "It's what I do. And the best part? No matter how hard you try, you can't deny it."

Adrenaline shot through her veins spurring her urge to escape. She scrambled to get off the bed, but he caught her and tossed her like a rag doll onto the pillows. He closed his hand around her neck and pushed her into the mattress.

Hot breath met her cheek when he hissed into her ear. "I see the way you look at him, but he won't ever look at you that way. He doesn't have it in him. He'll always keep you at a distance no matter how close you think he is.

"He's using you like he does everyone else. You deserve to know the truth. To understand the gravity of what you've both done."

He brushed a tendril of hair away, and his thumb slid along the edge of her jaw.

She turned her head, recoiling from his touch. Her eyes squeezed shut to shield her fear. Tobin's scent had her head spinning and pounding like a marching band.

She overlaid her shaky voice with thick sarcasm. "Please, good sir, spare me your nobility. You of all people should understand that nothing lasts forever. When Quenton and I are over, we're over. I don't need your help to understand that."

He gave a low growl. His soft touch turned to steel when his hand clamped down on her jaw, forcing her face to meet his. "Is that really what you want? To be used and tossed away? Look at me, Marie. Look me in the eye and tell me he can take everything from you without giving back. Tell me how forgettable you are."

Her eyes burst open, and she nailed him with a glare.

An arrogant grin stretched across his face. "Ah, so there you are." He purred.

The energy around her snapped when she met the anger and revenge in Tobin's eyes. They were an endless shade of blue and deep as the ocean itself with irises that churned and darkened with every passing second.

The air tainted with a sticky-sweet musk that caught in her lungs. Her breath came in sharp wheezes. A scream bubbled in her throat, but she couldn't push it out.

"I guess I finally found a way to shut you up," he said.

She drowned into unconsciousness. Her vision fell out of focus into fuzzy blobs of color.

To her surprise, he cut the sedative he wove over her and lifted her back to consciousness. His voice sounded clouded and distant as her vision sharpened again. "Marie. Wake up, cutie. We don't want you sleeping through the show."

She came to and pulled in a heavy gasp at the sight of Tobin looming over her. A mix of air and lingering sedative poured into her lungs. Her eyes rolled back of their own accord, and she slipped away again.

She could hear his chuckle as he dragged her back to the surface again. He patted her cheek. "Easy. Easy. Slow breaths this time...you girls get so excited."

She forced her breath to come shallow and steady to buoy her against the sedating current. The bed jostled as he shifted his weight. With one fluid motion he was on top of her, pinning her legs. She tried to push him away, but her arms felt so numb she wasn't convinced they were her own.

He held both her arms high above her head with one hand. "That's it. Good girl. Now this might sting just a little."

An icy claw of pain ripped through her head, rendering her completely immobile.

****

Tobin tore through the fringe of her subconscious with inhuman brutality and charged deep into her mind. He flew down narrow fissures and around sharp turns. He hunted the subtle pulse of energy that trailed on the languid current until he found her cowering in a narrow crevice.

He lunging after her spirit, seizing her in a vise-like grip, biting back the pain as her energy soaked into him.

Like a helpless insect caught in a web, the more she struggled, the more subdued she became. Panic flared the energy around her, and Tobin leached onto it with voracious enthusiasm.

Careful not to take too much of her energy, he let go of her as soon as she stopped resisting. She slid free without a sound, and her motionless spirit floated away like a leaf carried down a lazy stream.

It wouldn't take long for her to recover. He had to work quickly, Retrace his steps to the fringe of her subconscious. He caught sight of a thick white casing of scars, ones that branched out in an unnatural pattern, a clear indication of a Muse hard at work.

A secret? He loved secrets, wasn't very good at keeping them, but they sure were fun to play with.

He'd bluffed about tapping into her fantasies but

couldn't resist taking a peek at such a tightly wrapped package. With no time to waste, he sliced through the raw barrier until he found the vile face of Marie's assailant.

His stomach twisted with disgust at the scene playing out before him, but he couldn't look away. He stood transfixed until the scene ended and started to replay from the beginning. The hollow ache constricting his chest persisted even as his soul settled into his own body.

His voice deflated. "Why do you ladies always have to be so damn complicated? Where are all these dumb, easy blondes I keep hearing about?"

He tilted her head toward the large mirror that reflecting the entire room.

"Mirror, mirror on the wall." He chanted soft in her ear. The wicked amusement disappeared from his tone. Nothing in that reflection could save her now.

****

A wave of fear washed over her. Her eyes pinched closed against the searing pain in her head. She tried to will the image away, tell herself it would all be over soon. Eventually he'd have to let her go.

Tobin, however, seemed to have no intentions of a swift encounter. He moved slow, methodical, and with an alarming confidence. His free hand trailed down the inner portion of her raised arm, along the curve of her body. His gaze traced that same path, and then raked back up her trembling torso to rest on her mouth.

His stare lingered on her swollen lips for an agonizing amount of time. He fed off her tiny whimpers of distress, nipping and lapping up the fear that baited her breath.

"I don't want to do this. I really don't. But you've caused too much damage here. You've stolen Quenton's immortality and taken Anna's father away from her.

"Her life will go on long after you and Quenton are pushing up daises. She'll be left alone. The only one powerful enough to protect her now is me."

His lips brushed the edge of her chin. "How does that feel knowing you've taken his long life away from her?"

He paused momentarily at her throat when she swallowed hard against his lips.

"Hey, listen. I'm not going to hurt you."

He continued his meandering path from her throat to her collarbone. She forced out a cry of frustration.

He paused. "Your angel in waiting's a little hard of hearing. Try again."

The next instant, she was wrenched from Tobin's spell by the ear-splitting sound of breaking glass.

Quenton stood quaking in the center of the room, surrounded by a million shards of glass.

"Get away from her!" he roared.

Without the least bit of surprise clouding his expression, Tobin rolled to his side and casually propped himself on one elbow. "Thank heaven. It's about time you got here, sleepy head. Little Marie Poppins was about to have her way with me."

The pounding in her head quieted. She blinked at Quenton then the floor. There were no remnants of splintered wood or powder debris from the sheet rock, only glass. Her eyes shifted to the dark chasm lying beyond the gaping hole in the mirror.

It was a hidden room of some sort, separated from

hers by only a single pane of glass.

A two-way mirror?

His nightly excursions to the exterior door of the house must have led him to the very room that stood behind hers.

With her body still numb, she struggled to prop herself up before her muscles gave way. She opened her mouth, but the words still wouldn't come.

She expected Quenton to rush to her, but he remained frozen, didn't even turn his head. "Don't speak," he said. "You're still overcome. It takes time to wear off."

"Oh, Quentie." Tobin laughed as he jumped from the bed. "I knew all that carnal rage would catch up with you some day."

Tobin moved around the bed and blocked her from view. "She's figured it out now. You were watching her, studying her, and playing her like a fiddle for your own cheap entertainment."

Tobin grinned over his shoulder to Marie. "And you've been so accommodating, too. Since you can't keep your comments even inside your own head, he led you into a custom-made illusion.

"And using her as a decoy to hunt down Shades was ingenious. Not even I have the balls for that one. It's kinda like…" He tipped his head up in a thoughtful pose. "Feeding a goldfish to a cat."

Shock slammed into Marie. Her memory spun back to Anna's discussion in the salon.

"Girls are `sposed to get scared cause-cause then the boys kill the monsters."

My God, she was a decoy!

Large tears rolled down her face. The muffled sob

that erupted from her paralyzed vocal cords sounded more like a hiccup.

Tobin clicked his tongue at her. "Ah, now you've gone and made her cry. And we were having such a great time."

Quenton's expression softened. "This isn't what it seems."

"Of course it is!" Tobin said. "And he played the whole thing out beautifully."

He widened his stance to a crouch. "That's enough."

"It isn't any wonder she came to me. A woman like Marie has a simple need, and she hungers for an honest man who isn't afraid to give it to her."

Marie forced a guttural sound from her throat. "Nnno!"

Tobin raised his voice to drown her out. "She'd rather experience a fleeting moment of pure and honest lust, than a lifetime of calculated deception."

Quenton lunged at Tobin in a blind rage. They collided mid-air and crashed to the floor. His momentum gave him the upper hand, and he landed a solid punch to Tobin's jaw. The force knocked Tobin backwards. Quenton jumped to his feet. He turned his attention to Marie.

"Get outta here!" he yelled as Tobin plowed into him, knocking him to the floor.

"Quenton!" She tried to scream but the harder she tried the more her voice evaded her.

His head crashed into the bedpost.

She watched his shoulder muscles bunch and ripple as he tried to push himself off the floor, but his arms wavered, and his body fell limp.

Tobin's attention snapped to Marie. The determination hardening his jaw said he planned to finish what he started. She dropped on wobbly legs and darted across broken shards of glass to the gaping hole in the wall.

He caught her by the upper arm and pulled her back into the room. Shards of glass scraped across the cobblestone floor. Sharp pain needled at her bare feet as she dug in her heels. She clawed at his hand as he pulled her back through the serrated mirror frame.

Her footprints painted the snowy white carpet in crimson splotches, and the glass imbedded in her feet sent pain lancing up her legs.

Her mouth fell open in a silent gasp, and she stumbled onto her hands and knees.

Tobin shoved the obstructing boxes away from the bedroom door then gripped her by the torso and hauled her out of the room.

She let out a muffled scream which he covered with his hand. "Mustn't do that. Wouldn't want to wake the princess."

Chapter 22

A cold blast of air hit Marie's face. What little breath she pulled in, caught in her throat. Her heart plummeted to her feet when the front door slammed shut behind them. Feeling exposed and defenseless, she stiffened against Tobin's arms. Her ears strained to detect any approaching sound.

No humming insects.

No tree limbs thrashing in the wind.

Only the rhythm of gravel crunching beneath Tobin's feet as he carried her into the woods.

The cloud cover shifted apart, cascading moonlight across the clearing. The inky shadows filtering through the trees swayed and danced as though floating on the wind.

But there wasn't any wind.

Her view of the lawn's perimeter shifted and changed as lurking shadows materialized from the tree line to reveal lanky silhouettes.

Tobin continued to advance as the creatures closed in to greet them. Long angular limbs seemed to teeter and pivot like stretched and broken marionettes. Their hair hung in matted clumps, framing grimy faces.

A smell of thick perfume and rot hung in the air.

She scanned the crowd of about twenty-five bodies until she found Roxanne.

Tobin dipped his head and whispered. "Don't.

Don't look it in the eye. Even the slightest hint of interest will prompt an attack."

Her captor continued past them and into the dense cover of trees. The zombies crept alongside, like curious children, whispering their excitement to one another.

He lowered her to the frozen ground. She wasn't sure which felt worse, the slivers of glass piercing her feet or the bitter cold soaking into her skin.

Tobin spoke to the encircling crowd as he knelt down to inspect her feet. "I want your leader here. Now."

"She's been detained," one said.

"Now!"

A handful of bodies scampered off, and the remaining circle of Shades fell silent, their large black eyes devoid of emotion.

Tobin's fingertips slicked across the bloodied pad of her foot. She jerked when another pain jabbed up her leg.

He smirked. "Ticklish?"

She narrowed her eyes on him.

She sucked in a cold breath of air when Tobin dug his fingers into her flesh to pick out a shard of glass. He held up the fragment in his palm, but her surroundings were too dark to see anything. His thumb coursed over her foot again without complaint. He switched to the other one.

"Ahh." she gasped. She tried to jerk away from the pain, but Tobin held fast.

"You're such a girl," he muttered.

He pinched at the bottom of her foot. "You're getting your voice back."

She stared at him. She couldn't reach someone five feet away, let alone the house. Her vocal cords were completely useless. But maybe that was the point.

He lifted his phone from his pocket and snapped her picture, then tapped in a few keys and slid the phone back into his pocket. "Souvenir."

"Why are you repairing her?" The voice sounded raspy and sweet and distinctly familiar.

His face darkened. "We had a deal. You wanted the girl. Now you've got her."

"A deal, yes. But we can do nothing with this one. She's still alive. If you want what's yours, you'll have to kill her to get it."

Her blood turned to slush and drew the warmth from her face.

"Do your own dirty work. I have more than fulfilled my obligation. Now where's Evlin?"

"Your one mate?"

"Don't play stupid. Where is she?"

"She is unharmed. She is safe."

His mouth turned down in a scowl. "You don't have her. You don't even know where she is, do you?"

It straightened to its full height as more Shades filtered through the trees. The crowd of Shades grew twice its size. "True. You've been played," she said. "We have no intention of bringing your bride. We like you just as you are, a merciless womanizer serving up wasted flesh on a silver platter."

When he took a menacing step forward, the Shade slid into Marie's view. The sight of its lanky blonde female body made Marie gasp.

"Christie." The name tumbled free in a soft croak before she could stop it. The Shade leaned around

Tobin. "What's wrong with her voice?"

Tobin held his hand out to stop her from making another sound. His eyes grew dark and fearsome. The muscles in his back and shoulders rose. He crouched down into a poised position, then did something Marie never expected.

He lied.

"Her vocal cords are destroyed." He gestured to her bloodied feet. "And she's unable to walk. Now who's been played?"

He unleashed a deafening battle cry and attacked. He barreled into the Shade who met him at full force. Its hands contorted into spindly claws that swatted and tore at his flesh.

He landed a hard punch to the Shade's face, and she snarled, shook her head, and lunged forward again.

They both hit the ground and wrestled for control.

He crushed the Shade to the ground with his knees on either side of her head. He grabbed with both hands and snapped her neck with a quick twist.

The Shade's withered body collapsed, and it unleashed a high-pitched gurgle. A serpent-like plum of black smoke rose out of its mouth and condensed to form an inky apparition that streaked off into the darkness.

With a collective shriek, the crowd charged forward in an overpowering mass.

She shrank away. The rhythm of her heart went into hyperdrive, and her breath came in quick pants to fuel her rushing adrenaline. She braced herself for impact, but nothing came. All the attention fell on Tobin, allowing her a brief opportunity for escape.

Could she leave him to die here?

She tried to make out his shape through the picket of thrashing bodies, but they were too dense.

She couldn't defend him. Not against this. The only people who could help now were Quenton's men. Gritting her teeth, she lumbered to her feet and started running for the house. If she could only reach her phone.

Her labored gallop picked up speed as she ripped through the tangle of underbrush. She willed herself to ignore her lacerated feet.

The home's perimeter crept into view when an iron grip caught her from behind and slammed her to the ground. She put her hands out, but they did little to absorb the impact. Her head crashed into the rock-hard surface. White light blinked behind her eyes.

Something flipped her onto her back with a vicious kick. Pain exploded through her abdomen. Her arms and legs coiled to guard against a second blow as she looked into the face of her attacker. A pale, angular face with an obsidian gaze seemed to reflect everything and reveal nothing.

Its icy hand closed around her throat and lifted her off the ground.

She gagged and struggled for air. She clawed and pushed to free herself, but the grip was too strong. Her lungs burned. The hazy edges of her vision expanded.

The zombie lowered her to eye level as if watching for the last glimmer of light fade from her eyes.

A small amount of air squeaked past her throat when the creature's grip loosened. As if some unexplainable force took ownership of its hand. It cocked its head in confusion, snarled, and squeezed again.

Then loosened.

In that moment, she caught sight of the awkward teetering motion of the creature's arm. The lack of oxygen seemed to smooth over her panic, and thoughts swam through her mind in slow motion.

She remembered the self-defense course about chokeholds, and what she had to do to get out of them. Just one strike and she could break free, but she only had one shot.

She gathered all her strength and slammed the heel of her hand into the creature's elbow, forcing the joint to bend opposite its normal rotation. She heard a thick pop, and the creature dropped her to the ground.

It howled in rage as the useless arm dangled at its side.

She took advantage of the creature's distraction and shoved it backward, knocking it off kilter and into the rough vegetation. As she sprinted for the house again, she heard the injured creature scramble to its feet behind her—closing in fast.

The golden rule of cardio may work when trying to survive a normal attack, but it didn't apply here. She broke through the clearing and launched forward when a force from behind knocked her to the ground again. Pain seared the back of her head as a large section of hair tore free from her scalp.

She heard a furious scream and flipped over.

Quenton stood heaving over the spent remains of the Shade. Its claw-like hand still clutched wavy strands of Marie's hair, and to her surprise, the pearl necklace.

A rivulet of blood ran down from Quenton's temple, and his shirt hung in tatters. Every muscle seemed engorged with wraith-like power, and his eyes were crystal blue flames of rage.

As he stalked to Marie, his torn shirt billowed around him. His head and shoulders were caressed with streams of milky blue moonlight. He stretched his hand out to her. After a moment's hesitation, she took it.

"You all right?" he asked, his voice a fierce growl.

She nodded but the rest of her body betrayed that acknowledgement when she turned her head away. A sob wrenched from her chest.

She wanted him to take her in his arms and make the world disappear like before, but the man she knew didn't exist. Only the fear was real, and he couldn't protect her from it.

****

Quenton didn't have much time. He couldn't have Marie come apart on him. He grasped her shoulders and gave her a shake. "Where's Tobin?"

She nodded in his direction.

"Stay behind me." Quenton grabbed her hand, ignoring her initial resistance, and pulled her along behind him. He rushed through the vegetation, forcing her to duck to avoid the backlash of branches. His stomach tightened with the image of her arms and legs covered in razor thin scratches.

She stumbled over rocks and fallen trees littering the ground, but he continued to pull her onward. Flesh wounds could heal. Their lives were at stake.

Rapidly approaching their destination, she pulled back at the horrific screams of war. He spurred her on faster, whipping head-on in the sound's direction.

The small clearing exposed a battlefield of twisted bodies scattered in every direction, and the acrid smell of sulfur made his eyes water.

Tobin must have fought off over half a dozen Shades and stood cornered with little strength left.

Tobin lashed out wildly, but his punches failed to connect. He staggered and fell to his knees.

Quenton dropped Marie's hand and raced into the group.

He tore his enemies away with alarming speed. In the darkness, the blur of stick-like bodies became the only discernable target. He tossed and kicked at the constant flood of bodies until his muscles locked with fatigue.

Shouts rang out across the clearing and narrow beams of light jumped and danced through the trees. His guild thundered over the hillside, closing in around the battle.

The men raced past Marie without faltering into the thick of the fight. The zombies reared up in panic when the team struck from behind. They ducked and scrambled like fleeing insects but Quenton's men made short work of them, pouncing before they could escape into the woods.

The last several of them were snapped apart in quick succession.

The war ended quickly, and the clearing fell quiet.

He staggered through the clearing, riding out the lingering effects of adrenaline and tried to calm the beat that pounded in his head. His voice rumbled through the clearing. "Artino, need a hand over here."

"Look around. You've got spare parts everywhere. How many you need?"

He glanced to where his officer sat, wrapping Marie's feet in gauze.

His ragged breathing stilled when he saw the

blood. He'd hoped the blood trail was Tobin's, not hers.

Artino helped her up and lifted her into his arms when she was unable to bear weight. He picked his way through the uneven ground and mangled corpses. He couldn't suppress his initial shock at the sight of her.

Welts and shallow scrapes feathered every inch of exposed skin. Her face looked mottled and tearstained, and a splotchy purple bruise rose up from her forehead.

He did this to her…. He did this. Not only had he failed to protect her, he dragged her through a battlefield like a gunnysack.

"Boss?" Artino asked.

Quenton failed to cut the thickness of emotion from his voice. "Find Tobin."

He pulled Marie out of Artino's arms and cradled her to his chest. He pressed his lips to her forehead, careful to avoid the bruise. "God. I'm so sorry."

Marie's shoulders shook. He could feel her warm tears sliding down his chest, but he couldn't look her in the eye. He pulled her tighter, letting the commotion around him go unnoticed as his guild searched through the aftermath.

"Boss…."

"Boss."

"What?" he growled.

"Found Tobin."

He turned toward the sound of Artino's voice where a gathering of soldiers knelt around Tobin's body.

He moved closer and stared down with Marie still clutched to his chest.

Artino applied pressure to a huge gash at Tobin's temple. The cloth eclipsed the entire upper portion of his face. "Hold this," he barked.

Barros took over for him as Artino inspected Tobin for more injuries. When Artino flexed the right leg, Tobin screamed.

Artino looked at Quenton. "Broken. We may as well splint it here, get it over with."

Quenton gave a brisk nod.

A third man, with a large first-aid kit, cut long strips of cloth and pulled out two wooden splints.

Tobin groaned and rolled his head from side to side.

"He's coming around," Barros warned.

Artino didn't waver from his task. "Pity. This'll hurt then."

With arms and legs held down, Tobin howled in pain. His back jumped off the ground as Artino set his broken leg.

Quenton felt a dull ache in his stomach. "Talk to him. Keep him calm," he ordered.

"Tobin, we're trying to help you. Hold still," Barros said.

"I can't see," he cried.

Barros tried to ease the cloth away from his eyes and maintain pressure on the wound, but his eyes were the major target for the zombie's wrath. Tobin's head, neck, and shoulders were covered in gouges. His eye sockets were tattooed with deep purple bruises. Lids so swollen and caked with blood, it would be impossible to open them.

Quenton swallowed hard.

"You're gonna be okay. We're getting you out of here," Barros said.

Tobin's voice shook. "I'm sorry. Quenton, you

don't understand…I know you don't understand but I had to try."

"No. You didn't," Quenton spat.

"They had my mate!"

Artino tied the splint with a quick downward jerk on the cloth.

Tobin gritted his teeth.

Quenton tried not to look at his tortured face and instead kept his eyes on Artino's hands.

"You're lucky you sent that text image when you did. Otherwise you'd both be zombie kibble," Artino remarked.

Tears seeped in blood and dirt streamed down Tobin's face in dark rivulets.

"I would have given anything…."

"Your mate wouldn't want you this way," Quenton whispered.

****

The trip back to the house went slow and silent. Skulking by way of bright moonlight and the eerie glow it cast upon the ice-dusted landscape. Quenton and a handful of his men stayed on the lookout while the rest held back to bury the bodies.

Quenton set Marie down in a chair and ransacked the kitchen's medicine cabinet. The soft rattle of plastic bottles filled the room. Then he snapped the cabinet shut.

Marie's attention fixed on the table, and her thoughts wound through erratic twists and turns. She flashed back to late night conversations with herself: flaunting in the mirror, the red dress, and the dancing-*the dancing*! He saw it all. Every conversation, every interaction tainted.

She felt nothing like the priceless artifact he made her out to be. That title was meant for Anna alone. No, she was more like the bubble wrap that protected it; cheap, useful, and you can't help squeezing until it pops.

Quenton pressed a glass of water into her hand. "Take these."

Two large pills ticked onto the polished wood table.

She shook her head.

"Marie, please. I know you don't like them—"

She frowned. "You shouldn't know that. You shouldn't know anything about me." He stood silent. His arms hung limp at his sides.

Artino's voice came from behind her. "Can I finish patching her up, boss?"

"Go ahead," he said.

Quenton's hand brushed down her cheek. "But when he's through, we'll talk."

The plod of his footsteps left the room, then Artino's chair scraped against the wood floor.

"All right, pretty lady. Let's have a look at you," Artino said.

She didn't protest when he tilted her chin to the left and right.

He gave a low whistle. "Hoo-wee. Let this be a lesson to you. Never pick a fight with a cheese grater. I hope I have enough to cover all this."

"What I really need is a hot shower but my room's…. compromised." Her shoulders dropped in her sockets. "Can you take me home?"

An apologetic smile stretched across his face. "I'm all for defying authority but didn't Quenton say he wanted to talk to you?"

"He knows where to find me."

Chapter 23

A potpourri of familiar scents greeted Marie when she hobbled through her condo. She didn't bother flipping on the lights, having memorized the layout long ago.

The dressers and bookshelves aided her navigation, but she didn't want to see more of the lifeless room than necessary. She shrugged out of her wool coat on the way to the bathroom, leaving it in a rumpled heap on the floor.

This was home, yet oddly enough, she still felt displaced. Her stomach roiled with unease. She dropped her suitcase to the ground. She may as well pack her stuff into a shopping cart and move under the viaduct since she couldn't even feel at home here.

Sitting down on the tiled shower floor, she drew up her knees. Her tears lost in the scalding liquid that rained down over her head. The initial sting of her wounds faded under a lobster red stain, but she still couldn't get warm. Nothing soothed the bitterness that hollowed her insides. Nothing could take that away.

Somehow her heart broke the treaty it formed with her logic. She left knowing he wouldn't come after her, and yet her heart hung on.

She crawled out of the shower and made her way to bed. "Get over it already. He isn't who you think he is. He's not…he's not safe."

But why couldn't he be? Why couldn't he be honest, instead of leading her on as everyone else did?

"Why couldn't he be different?" She collapsed face down on her bed.

The instant she landed, her body tensed. Something else, much heavier than she was, caused the bed to weigh down on one side, and her whole body tipped into it.

"I am different," he said.

She shrieked as she shifted backwards. She tipped over the edge of the bed. Arms and legs flew out in front, and her backside met the hard wood floor. Her startled cry cut off with a dense thud.

Quenton peered over the edge. "You okay?"

She ignored his question and scooted back another foot. "Wha—why are you here?"

"I should be asking you the same question."

She gestured to the bed. "Well, I couldn't stay there. Not after…."

He lowered his head. "I'm sorry I couldn't protect you tonight, that I couldn't keep you safe."

She frowned. "When I said you weren't safe, I didn't mean physically. You were knocked out. It's a little difficult to play bodyguard while you're laid out on the floor. You did save me, and for that I'm grateful. But—" She shook her head. "No. No, I don't want to talk about this. You should be with Anna right now…why are you grinning like that?"

"Anna has an entire army watching her sleep. She's good. Besides, you're in no condition to pack all this stuff on your own." He gave her a look. "You mean to tell me I busted my ass trying to play the white knight when all you needed is for me to come home to you every evening?"

She brushed impatiently at her tears. "I've no idea what you're talking about. But as far as packing goes, that's awfully presumptuous don't you think?"

"Extremely. But you're a smart girl. You make wise choices."

She raised a speculative brow. "Really? You think a lifetime of misguided affection is a wise choice?"

He swung his legs over the edge of the bed. "Misguided isn't exactly the term I'd use."

She cocked her head. "Oh, okay. How about deceitful?"

His lips curved into a thoughtful grin. "No, not that either."

"Dishonest."

"Not even close."

She threw her hands up. "Quenton, what do you want from me?"

He rounded the bed and knelt down in front of her. "For starters, it's time we had a little chat."

Having managed to back herself into the wall, she crossed her arms and compacted the anguish that threatened to unravel her. "I can't talk to you."

"Yes. You can."

A heavy silence weighed down on her, but she locked her teeth together.

He lowered his head and dealt her a stern look from beneath his lashes. "You can't ignore me because I'm not going anywhere. You're not just leaving me in your past because from here on out, I'm your present. Whether you like it or not. And let's be honest here. You know you like it. And so do I." He pulled her into his lap. "Talk to me, sweet thing."

His scent lured her into the safety of an iron grip and awakened a startling hunger that sprang from deep inside her chest, one that urged all her logic to step aside.

Her fists shook. She clenched his shirt, and the tears poured down again. "I can't talk to you. I wouldn't even know where to start! You're not the person I thought you were. Everything about you is different."

"I'm exactly the person you thought I was," he said.

"You spied on me! You invaded my most private thoughts and feelings. Can you imagine how that makes me feel?"

"I can." He brushed a stray curl from her forehead, and her skin came alive on contact. She curled both hands around his arm and turned her face to the pulse point of his wrist where his scent seemed more potent.

He held his breath when her nose grazed along the warmth of his inner arm.

"Marie—"

She knew deep down she didn't want to fight him. She wanted to believe him. At this point he could sell her a barrel to sail down Niagara Falls as long as he would go with her. Because she loved him.

When she turned to the crook of his neck, Quenton leaned away. He cupped her chin with his palm and forced her to keep her distance. "Marie, we have a problem."

Irritation grated her. She jerked away from his hand, but his fingers pressed into her jawbone, holding tight.

"You've become too attached."

"Isn't that the point?" she sputtered.

"You're too attached to my influence." He didn't look her in the eye when he slid her from his lap and stood. "You're addicted."

She stared in disbelief, unable to find words to support her denial.

Hurt and disappointment played across his face as he searched the matted carpet at her feet. "For every person there's a threshold. You've reached yours." He lowered his head. "I have to go."

"You're leaving me? Like this is my fault?"

"This isn't your fault. And I'm not leaving. Not completely. I just…I can't stay with you unless you can kick the addiction."

"Oh, so you're just going to cut a peephole in my bathroom wall and play the creepy stalker thug again? Is that it?"

Hurt flashed in his eyes, and he met her unyielding stare only for a moment before locking his gaze on the floor. "You've invaded my every thought from the moment we met. I knew who you were. What you meant to me. After centuries of misery, I couldn't stand another minute away. It's not a good excuse but there it is. I had to find a way to stay close."

Her shoulders dropped. "Centuries?"

His hand slid over the back of his neck, kneading at taught cables of muscle. "I spent immortality searching for the one person who would make me whole. Knowing that I could spend my last lifetime with you? Every moment became precious. I couldn't sleep if you weren't sleeping. My every thought and feeling linked to yours. But I had to remain at a distance until you could accept me. To love me. Till I knew your threshold." He looked with bare honesty. "So I watched you."

"And then you sacrificed your daughter to get what you wanted. And I played a part in that!"

"Please don't think I'm not carrying a shitload of guilt for that. I love that little girl. And I love you. Anna hasn't changed. She's no better or worse for my decision. Who's to say that in twenty—no, thirty years from now, she won't find her own mate?"

"Forty," Marie mumbled.

"Forty then. But when the time comes, I can hardly stop her. I can't even stop her from eating potato chips for breakfast."

"So you're leaving. For how long?" she asked. She couldn't stand the thought of Anna growing up without her.

"A month, maybe more. But, Marie? I will wait for you."

"Just go."

The stubborn ridge in her spine loosened. Her shoulder muscles eased their tension. She managed to find Quenton in the predictable pattern she came to know and despise: Boy meets girl, boy makes his move, boy gets rejected, girl leaves.

But the story doesn't end there. Boy comes back to even the score and give her a taste of her own medicine.

He grasped her shoulders, soothing over her humiliation with the soft stroke of his thumbs. "I want you to know, you will be safe with me." He dipped his head to fasten his gaze on hers. "Do you believe me?"

She nodded. Fresh tears welled up in her eyes.

He closed his lips over hers in an urgent bid to seal his commitment. She answered back with equal enthusiasm. But the moment ended too abruptly, when he tore himself free and marched to the door without another word.

Chapter 24

Marie couldn't zip away the uneasy flurry in her stomach. It crept up the moment her sock-clad feet slid into her running shoes. She hooked her fingers around the laces and pulled tight, the friction burning her skin.

It took several days of arguing with herself to get this far, and she wouldn't let her stomach's protest unseat her victory. These shoes wouldn't come off until her skin was slicked with either sweat or blood.

She pushed the earbuds in place in an effort to shore more courage and pulsed the volume until her head swam in a heavy urban beat.

One step at a time her pace quickened. Feet pounded the damp road, keeping time with the music. The pain in her scarred feet were forgotten. Her mind too busy relishing the feel of crisp air and open space.

Being outside seemed a shocking contrast from the constrictive walls of her condo. The place still felt like home, and yet it didn't. More like a burden now than a refuge.

But after three months of all condo all the time, anyone would feel tempted to start counting down to freedom.

Funny thing, she realized, the only person keeping her under house arrest was herself. The moment it dawned on her, she stopped mentally carving tally marks and hit the jogging trail.

Passing through her quaint neighborhood, the distance she put behind her felt invigorating. she pushed beyond the constriction in her muscles from months without exercise.

The park's rough landscape panned into view where evergreen trees towered overhead, spackled with bits of unmelted snow. The path meandered through the grassy lot where the warming sun bore holes into the white crust, revealing the raw withered grass. As she gained more ground through the park, her steps faltered, and her joints ached with fatigue. She clenched her teeth. Stopping was not an option today.

She wove around ominous shadows, cast down from the trees, and thoughts of an unseen stalker crawled out from somewhere in her brain. A shiver raced up her spine. Her instinct to stay alert began to win over her battle for distraction.

The assault on her ears felt too overwhelming, and she ripped the buds out, clutching them in her fist as she pumped her legs faster. The foliage on either side whizzed by as she tunneled her vision to the park exit. Adrenaline flooded her veins.

Almost there.

She rounded her last bend through the park and gave everything she had in that final sprint. Her shoulders sagged with relief when she finally crossed the exit and headed for home.

Twice the burn at the same distance in half the time! Maybe the Crypt keeper could market her new exercise plan. But on the plus side, she hadn't thought about Quenton for nearly thirty minutes.

Speak of the devil. Her pace slowed when she spotted him climbing out of his vehicle then crossing the length of her parking lot. A cringe of nervous excitement pulled at the corners of her mouth.

She hadn't been out of the house the entire time he had her under surveillance, not that she'd actually caught him, until now.

Strolling toward his back, she folded her arms and added an extra twitch to her hips. Her eyes fixed on the dark outline of his shoulders. He rapped on the door to her condo, and then stooped to lay his customary bouquet of flowers on the mat.

For the first several weeks they had collected in a wilting pile until her neighbors complained, and she threw them all out. But the next day, she had found another bunch in their place. Her bunker of stubbornness wore away knowing that he wasn't giving up.

With tremors that rattled her teeth, cold sweats, and the return of her raging insomnia, she looked forward to those flowers every week. She breathed them in on occasion without subconsciously trying to lift any lingering particles of Quenton's scent.

She started forward but hesitated.

What if it's too soon? What if she hadn't kicked the habit yet? What if she approached him now and had to start all over because she wasn't ready?

She expanded her lungs until they couldn't stretch any farther, then blew out. What the hell. At least this way she was guaranteed a conjugal visit.

She knew Quenton wouldn't bother waiting for a response from the other side of the door. After this many visits, he knew better. Instead, he spun back to the direction of his car.

"I like the daises this time. Nice touch." She huffed

with more giddiness than she cared to reveal.

His voice flowed smooth and effortless, but the sound started a hormonal uprising in her blood.

"Hello, Marie."

"Hi." She tried to ignore the charge flowing over her skin, as she brushed past to unlock the door.

"We need to talk."

Her heart withered painfully at the sound of those words.

"I'm sorry." She lied. "I have an appointment I've got to get to. Maybe some other time?"

He shoved his hands in his pockets as she walked into her condo. She left the front door open behind her.

She tried to toss back the overflowing happiness at seeing him. She schooled herself not to mold her body to him just yet. It would hurt twice as bad if he peeled her off a second time.

"How's Tobin," she ventured.

"Still recovering. I've been trying to call you," he said.

"Yeah, about that. I accidently flushed my phone down the toilet."

"You accidently—"

She managed to flick a glance over her shoulder as she bent down to remove her shoes. "People do it all the time. I don't really need to get into semantics, but it slipped out of my pocket and got flushed away before I could stop it. Are you coming in? Don't worry; I'm not going to shackle you to my bed post or anything."

His eyes glittered. "I can see that. You look better."

Her fingers paused. "You're surprised?"

He let his body weight press against the door until it clicked shut. "Well, yeah, that's never happened before."

"Never?"

He looked to the long fluffy towel she tugged from a basket nestled in the corner of the couch. "It all depends on how much sedative accumulates in your system, but you've managed to withstand more than most. An exposure like that should make kicking the addiction impossible."

She flung the towel over her shoulder and anchored her hands on her hips. "Well then, what have you been coming here for? Just to watch me wither away with no hope of recovery?"

He looked to the bathroom door, then back to her. "No, I grew tired of waiting. I came to have you fitted for your cage."

"*What*?"

"I figure a sex-crazed nanny that can't get enough of me, could be a *good* thing. I even had it custom made with enough room for dancing, should you choose to tempt me with another show."

She could almost see the blatant lie growing with every inch of the smile spreading across his face.

How about that. She could finally read him. And it only took a near death experience, the sacrifice of her soul, and an afternoon of salon torture with her mother. Piece of cake.

"Besides, Anna misses you," he said.

Marie's heart swarmed with emotion. "She does?"

He nodded. "She wants you back. *We* want you back."

He used both ends of the towel to rein her into his chest and dipped his head to brush a tender kiss over her lips. "I'm glad you're better."

"Me too," she whispered.

Her naughty thoughts twittered with delight when he angled his head to the bathroom. "Shower?"

She gave him an impish grin. "I'd invite you in, but—"

"I'd accept."

She tossed her head back in a laugh. "But you haven't worked up a sweat yet."

"Do you really expect me to wait for a twenty-five-and-a-half-minute shower?"

"And-a-half? You timed it?" She headed for the bathroom with him following close behind.

"Cut me some slack, Marie. That's a long time for a man to wonder what you're doing in there."

She pulled off the towel and slung it over the glass door. "How about this? I'll call your name in ten after I take care of all the necessities."

"I'll have you calling in one."

She shot him a grin. "Really?"

He nodded and turned on the shower with a twist of his wrist.

"And should I be trembling?"

"You better be."

Her lips twitched. "I think I can manage that."

A word about the author...

Kacey Mark is a voracious reader and paranormal romance author who makes her home near the Wasatch Mountain range of northern Utah.

She loves writing eccentric characters and unpredictable plot turns.

She enjoys a good book that pulls her into its world and holds her captive until the very last page. But then again, who doesn't love that?

She's often caught laughing at a book in the middle of a crowded room and loves it when people wonder what she's up to.

Visit her at:

www.kaceymark.com

Thank you for purchasing
this publication of The Wild Rose Press, Inc.

For questions or more information
contact us at
info@thewildrosepress.com.

The Wild Rose Press, Inc.
www.thewildrosepress.com

www.ingramcontent.com/pod-product-compliance
Lightning Source LLC
Chambersburg PA
CBHW070045030726
47506CB00002B/359